The Bartender's Guide To Murder

DEATH FROM BEYOND

ALSO BY
SHARON LINNÉA

FICTION

Death in Tranquility (Bartender's Guide to Murder 1)

Death By Gravity (Bartender's Guide to Murder 2)

Death Among the Stars (Bartender's Guide to Murder 3)

WITH B.K. SHERER

Chasing Eden

Beyond Eden

Treasure of Eden

Plagues of Eden

YOUNG ADULT, WITH AXEL AVIAN

Colt Shore: Domino 29

NONFICTION

Princess Ka'iulani: Hope of a Nation, Heart of a People

Raoul Wallenberg: The Man Who Stopped Death

Chicken Soup from the Soul of Hawai'i

Lost Civilizations

America's Famous and Historic Trees with Jeff Meyer

The Bartender's Guide to Murder

DEATH FROM BEYOND

SHARON LINNÉA

COCKTAIL RECIPES BY JAMIELYNN BRYDALSKI

BARTENDER'S GUIDE TO MURDER

Book 4 DEATH FROM BEYOND

ISBN 978-1-933608-38-9 (Paperback)
ISBN 978-1-933608-39-6 (ebook)

First Edition September 2023

Cover Art and Cover Design by David Colón

Interior Design by Phillip Gessert

For Crystal Paul Watson
and Linnéa Juliet Scott
who daily demonstrate how to live with compassion
while seeking justice

1

ALL HALLOWS' EVE EVE

S HE SAT DOWN at the bar at 9:14 PM on the last Friday in October, a tall woman, with large hazel eyes, a long nose, a chiseled chin, paperwhite skin, and thick black hair. She wore an ecru shirt topped by an olive green jacket.

"I need some liquid courage," she said.

"You've come to the right place." I plunked down our Scary October Cocktail menu.

"The problem is, I can't drink alcohol. Doesn't mix with my meds."

"Got you covered." I turned over the cocktail menu to the mocktail side. The list was equally as long. "I'm afraid you'll have to provide the courage yourself."

"I'll try the Fall Fiesta," she said, choosing a cider-based libation.

"Coming up."

It was Halloween weekend and the Battened Hatch was crazy busy. The Adirondack town of Tranquility went all-out for the holiday; in fact, it had been named Best Halloween Town by an upscale travel magazine. Folks flooded in. The Visitors Bureau concentrated on events for kids—parades, daytime trick or treating on Main Street, scavenger hunts. If you wanted witchy doings, you still had to head for Salem, Massachusetts. Or parties here to which I was not invited.

"Visiting for the holiday?" I asked, setting down the drink. "Would you like to see a food menu?"

"No, thanks. And I'm only kind of visiting. I grew up here. There's a mini high school reunion tomorrow. My class was always weird. Instead of meeting up on Labor Day or some other three-day weekend, we did stuff on Halloween."

"Oh, wow. I'm always of two minds about reunions. Is your family still in town?"

"Yes. Hence my need for alcohol."

"Which you were smart enough not to drink." I smiled and offered my hand, which was engulfed in her own. "Avalon."

"Sandy."

As we shook, I recognized the scent she wore: lily of the valley. It was one of my two signature scents. "Diorissimo?" I asked.

She stared at me, then a small smile crept onto her face. "How did you know?"

Certainly no one would accuse me of knowing my designer perfumes. But I did recognize this one. "Lily of the valley. Hardly anyone uses the fragrance in perfume anymore."

"It was in our backyard, growing up. In the spring we had a volleyball net up. My friends and I spent many happy hours there."

"It was in the garden behind my mormor's brownstone in Brooklyn. They were planted closest to the house, in the shade. Every year, my grandmother spoke of how it grew outside the family homesteads in Tennessee and Småland, Sweden. She's gone now—that whole generation is—but it makes me feel close to her, even for a while."

"It reminds me of the happy parts of growing up," Sandy said.

We took a second to smile.

It was then I noticed a pin she was wearing, a small pink flower with a scroll that said *Sensitive Badass*.

"Doubleclicks," I said, nodding at it.

"You know the band?"

"Yeah. That's a good song. Who these days doesn't feel like a badass—albeit a sensitive one?"

"You got that right."

"Let me know if you need anything else," I said, pulling myself back to work.

Drink orders were stacking up. Halloween is a big creative cocktail holiday, unlike, say, Easter, when mimosas are your best bet. Tonight, the large carved bar behind me was glowing with an array of two hundred bottles; those in the center were being used almost as frequently as those in the well. I remembered the first time I saw it. While the rest of the Scottish pub is paneled with cherry wood, the bar itself is mahogany. It must have cost a fortune. Mahogany darkens over time. The carved wood wore its age and care impressively.

Marta, my assistant manager and co-bartender, swung back through the kitchen with a green plastic rack filled with glasses from the dishwasher. Marta used to think of herself as Goth. Now she wore the same clothing, which had miraculously morphed into bartender black. She's eighteen, just graduated from high school, and taking a gap year to save money before going to art school. I honestly didn't know what the Battened Hatch would do without her next year.

She stowed the glasses and we both got to work.

"Hey, Marta," said Sandy.

"Hey..."

"Sandy."

"Sandy," said Marta.

"You work here?"

"Yes," Marta smiled, holding up a martini glass.

"Cool," said Sandy.

As the evening wore on, I watched Sandy out of the corner of my eye. Like virtually everyone who sat alone at the bar, she was checking her phone. She was naturally charismatic, with a twinkle in her eye, but there was something on her mind. She exuded an odd mixture of confidence and hesitation. She'd be perfectly cast in a Neil Gaiman series: ruler of some fascinating realm, who could tell plenty of interesting stories to a therapist. Or to a bartender. Maybe, if she was from here, she'd return when I had time to chat.

It's funny how when you meet someone who will impact your

life, you seldom know it. But sometimes, as happened that night, there is a connection, a silent buzzer that goes off, and you aren't surprised when your lives become somehow intertwined.

Meanwhile, three ghosts and a woman dressed like Princess Leia in the Jabba the Hutt scene pressed in towards the bar for orders. This far north in New York State, nights were already dipping down into the thirties. Even inside, Princess Leia had to be freezing. She tossed her head haughtily towards any male person who smiled her way.

Around 9:45, a young man, maybe five-eight with a long-sleeved pullover and short hair, sidled up to the end of the bar. He held the hand of a wafer-thin woman of the same age, who followed behind. They both looked too young to drink.

"Hey. Marta," he beckoned. She looked up, finished the potion she was mixing, and went over.

"Hey, Toby."

"You're coming Sunday, right?"

"I don't know."

"Come on. This is the last year we're all going to be around, probably."

"I'm still thinking. But maybe."

"Get Colin to come. He's always the best."

"I'll see."

Toby did a two-fingered salute and headed back out of the Hatch. Which is what we call the Battened Hatch when we're busy. The actual name, still on the pub sign outside, is That Ship Has Sailed. It's inside MacTavish's Seaside Cottage, a Scottish hotel that has never had cottages or been seaside. Whoever named the inn, I've long been a fan. I've managed the bar since I arrived in town in May and found the last bartender murdered, then stayed to find out why.

"Who was that?" I murmured to Marta.

"That was Toby and his girlfriend. He wants me and my friend Colin to go with them to investigate Appleton Lodge on Monday."

She used the soda gun to finish a Collins. She looked straight ahead as she said, "It's supposed to be haunted."

"Okay," I said.

"They go every year."

"And you don't?"

"Why would I go looking for ghosts?"

I chuckled. Marta was a sensitive, meaning dead people found her. She was learning to control her gift, but I could see why she didn't want to go into overload.

"Why don't they go on Halloween?" It seemed like a natural time for exploring haunted venues.

"The other two lodges attached to Appleton burned down mysteriously, so the cops always watch it super carefully on times like Halloween. Then, the day after, they don't."

"Got it." I could see how Marta would be hesitant to go. The large, rambling Adirondack-style inn had been empty for years. Probably everyone in town wondered if it was haunted. I could see how visiting it could entice local explorers.

Halloween was on a Saturday this year, which was tomorrow. Tonight was crazy enough that Marta and I fell into a time warp. The only time I looked up was when Sandy paid with cash and I had to make change. "Hey, listen," she said, seeming nervous. "Is there a chance…I could leave my suitcase here…and pick it up in an hour?"

"In an hour?"

"My folks live on Ivy Circle, just off Maple. It's close enough I can walk, but I don't think I can drag a suitcase all the way up. I'll get my dad to drive down and pick it up." When I paused, she said, "I asked the lobby bellman. He said the hotel is so full, if I'm not a guest, no can do."

"Sure. Stick it in the back hall there, past the bathrooms. It should be safe enough."

"Thank you very much," said Sandy. She got up and dragged the brown suitcase I hadn't realized was at her feet towards the bathrooms.

I turned back to work.

Oddly, our clients didn't voice objection to us closing at eleven, our regular time. Maybe they had other places to go, or perhaps they were saving their Halloween energy for the next day. They all paid up, we closed out quickly, and my crew headed out happily enough that I knew they were going to continue celebrating. I never cared how they celebrated—as long as they were back in working form the next day.

I stood alone looking at the streamers of black and orange along the walls, mentally counting the hours until I could rip them down. Not a fan of streamers, crepe, or orange and black.

As I turned out the lights in the back hall, I saw that the brown suitcase was still there. It was well past an hour since Sandy left. Likely she and her family had been distracted and she'd come back for it tomorrow.

I put on my coat, hat, and gloves and locked the inside door—although Hugo, the night janitor, was heading over to start cleaning.

An expectant buzz tinged the frigid air even though the streets were emptying. I walked down Tranquility's homey Main Street and turned up Maple, the same street Sandy would have turned up earlier. It climbed at a steep angle. Three cul-de-sacs branched off to the right. The first was Forest, the second, Orchard, the last, Ivy Circle. As I climbed that hill, north winds picked up, warning empty tree boughs of a hard night to come. I was glad to turn right onto Forest. It sat quiet and dark, interior lights glowing discreetly behind windows of well-built older homes, each surrounded by an acre or more of woodland. I walked the road to one especially solid residence at the end of the dead-end street. It was one story, Craftsman-style, its painted wooden porch empty. Dark windows on either side of the front door seemed to signal no one was home.

I knew someone was.

I didn't go up the driveway but walked past it and started through the dead leaves on the left side of the house. It was the more level side of the property. Still, I knew enough to step carefully and go from tree to tree, steadying myself by holding onto trunks in the murky darkness, swirling leaves crackling like cellophane beneath my feet.

Finally rounding the back of the house, I came upon a profusion of illumination spilling from tall windows. Escaping strains of Rachmaninoff's "Symphonic Dances" filtered, nearly muted, into the woods from inside the panes.

Before me sat an artist's studio, attached to a back hallway of the dwelling. It was like another country. Intensive warm light, huge canvases with dancing colors, careful strokes, slashes, blues, green, browns, yellows, in shades of colors only artists know: cadmium chartreuse, India yellow, alizarin crimson, cerulean, phthalo emerald.

And a tall young man, wearing thick painter's pants and no shirt, focused like a laser, like a train through Siberia, or Smaug guarding treasure. The strokes of his brush were purposeful, masterful, almost violent. The muscles of his back and his arms were firm and tensed in service to the work, gingerbread skin glistening with perspiration. His thick black hair was a tousled mess.

I stood and watched Philip work until the wind's constant assault shook me. I realized how irritated he'd be if I froze to death and my body was found in his yard and he had to stop work to deal with it.

I made my way back, again from tree to tree. Gray flakes of early snow zipped past but nothing stuck. Thankful to be back on the road, I walk-jogged down to Main Street, then up to the employee parking lot, where I turned on my Subaru and cleared the frosted windows while waiting for the heater and my seat to warm up. I drove back down Main Street, now devoid of traffic but bursting with toy witches and cauldrons and promises of the next day's treats.

The dirt lane from the main road up into my little glade was frozen firm. I parked in a makeshift spot down below just in case it got slick overnight.

The living room lamp I'd left on in my cottage served as a beacon. I walked up the path easily, past my landlady's lodge, then grasped the railing tightly as I crossed the footbridge. The back patio was somewhat sheltered. My arrival cued the motion-activated light, which helped as I punched in the code to unlock the back door.

"Hi, Whistle," I said to the little Pomeranian at my feet. I let her out to relieve herself, and we both happily returned to the warmth of the house.

"Yeah, I saw him," I said. I made a cup of tea, and the small dog and I went into the living room, where I turned on the gas logs in the fireplace and pulled a soft white throw over my lap. My watch declared midnight. "Happy Halloween," I said, as the little dog settled in. I knew it was going to be another lonely night.

That is what I knew. Here is what I did not know until much later:

That Sandy shivered the half block down Main Street, then turned to trudge up the hill through the biting wind, until she came to the top, to Ivy Circle. That her parents were having a party and though it was late, the street was lined with cars. That the house in which she grew up, a lovely three-story dwelling, had light pouring from each window, golden light, like in the fairy tales. The pine tree in the front yard had a string of golden twinkle lights and the outline of a horn of plenty sat at each window. Her parents did not celebrate Halloween. There were no witches or ghosts. It was a harvest gathering.

As she climbed the front steps, the door opened and a middle-aged couple in heavy coats and carrying a tin of cookies took their leave. "Goodbye! Goodbye! Thanks for the lovely time!"

Sandy waited until they'd departed before she started up the steps.

I did not know that her father saw her first and started to ask,

"What are you doing here?" when her mother saw clearly who it was, then said, "I need you GONE," and slammed the door.

I didn't know Sandy stood behind the garage, shivering, watching old family friends depart the house, get into their cars, and leave.

When her fingers stabbed with cold even through her gloves, she wandered back to the main road, walked down to Main Street, and retraced her steps to MacTavish's Seaside Cottage. The bar was locked, but the lights were on. She sat unobtrusively in the lobby and watched a couple, late arrivals, check in at reception, others stopping to ask what around this town was still open—didn't they know this was Friday night?

When Hugo, a sturdy, balding man who did the cleaning, opened the door from the pub dragging his floor polisher, she told him she needed to grab her suitcase. Hugo knew there was a suitcase in the back hall because he'd cleaned around it. He let her in and dragged the shiny steel contraption across to the janitor's closet and prepared for his next room. He remembered letting someone into the pub, so he went back, opened the door, and called out to see if she was still there. No one answered. Convinced she'd gotten her bag and left, he locked the door.

I didn't know that Sandy shrunk into the back hallway, hoping he wouldn't come in. He didn't. She heard the door lock.

Grateful for the warmth, and exhausted, she took off her coat and made herself a bed. She opened her suitcase, found a shirt, and used it as a pillow. She did her best to pull the coat up around her as a blanket as well as a mattress. She found it worked best if she rolled onto her side.

She didn't want to give in to tears, but they streaked her face as she finally let her body relax and passed out into sleep. I also didn't know that she was awakened the next morning by the noisy sound of the adjoining kitchen preparing to serve hungry, impatient tourists the breakfast that came with their expensive winter stay packages, in Pepper's, the restaurant overlooking the lake.

She got up and changed into a pink sweater and ecru pants—her best outfit—and went into the pub's bathroom, injecting her meds, doing her makeup, and getting ready for the day. When she was done, she closed up the suitcase and left it like a sentinel in the back hallway. She put on her coat, hat, and gloves.

She looked through the window from the pub into the kitchen, by now controlled chaos, and chose her path. Then she pushed through and walked quickly out the back door into the bright Halloween morning. She went around to the hotel's front door. She smiled and talked to Rusty, the doorman, who welcomed her as a newly arriving guest. She crossed the lobby and got herself a cup of coffee and a hot cookie. Then she wandered down a hall towards the meeting rooms where there were plenty of benches to sit and wait until it was time to meet her classmates up the street at the high school for the first welcome event for their reunion.

I did not know that no one would admit seeing her alive after the reunion—that no one would ever pick up that brown suitcase.

ALL HALLOWS' EVE EVE

Fall Fiesta

Ingredients

2 oz apple cider
½ oz pomegranate liqueur
1 oz Bourbon
Sprinkle of fresh ground cinnamon
Ginger beer
Cinnamon stick
Fresh pomegranate seeds
Ice
Mule mug

Method

Fill mule mug with ice.
In cocktail shaker, add ice, apple cider, pomegranate liqueur, Bourbon, and ground cinnamon. Shake all ingredients together.
Strain contents of cocktail shaker into mule mug. Top with ginger beer.
Add fresh pomegranate seeds and cinnamon stick for garnish.

2

SINS OF OMISSION

THAT HALLOWEEN WAS, for me, a day when everything went wrong.

It started when Mike Spaulding came in for a drink. Mike is an investigator with the local highway patrol. We worked together once to figure out who'd committed a murder. We were inching towards mutual respect and, dare I say, friendship. Then came a case he was working when I didn't tell him everything I knew.

In fairness, it was a fairly egregious sin of omission. I didn't lie, exactly, but the person he was looking for was staying at my house and I didn't mention it.

There were reasons. Good reasons.

Mike arrived on Halloween wearing a crisp collared shirt and chinos, much the same outfit he wore whether he was on duty or off. The shirt had one extra button unbuttoned, laying white against his dark brown skin, showing off a flat, braided gold chain.

Off duty.

His face was oval, with a tall forehead, accentuated by his close-cropped black hair. An alarming intelligence hid behind his dark eyes. His eyes weren't piercing—that would give too much away. I'd learned the hard way that he was paying attention even when he didn't seem to be—a perfect trait for an investigator.

In the olden days (a month ago), when he came in, he'd lean casually on the bar and we'd check in with each other. Now he came and sat at a table and picked up the menu without even glancing my way.

The Battened Hatch was not a cop bar, which was why I suspected Mike felt comfortable coming in. There was only one other

Black officer working out of the local highway patrol barracks, and I'd witnessed multiple microaggressions Mike couldn't mention if he wanted to continue doing his job.

I let Davros, our lanky thirty-something waiter, take Mike's order, as I turned to mix together a pitcher of the Fall Fiesta cider drink, which could be served either with or without alcohol.

Mike did not look my way.

Even once.

It hurt as much as any words could have.

"Morning," said Marta, arriving two minutes before noon. Marta was always on time and usually cheered me up. She's a couple of inches shorter than I am, nicely filled out, and her shoulder-length jet-black hair has had a teal stripe running through it since I've known her. I sometimes wonder if she might change colors one year for Halloween or her birthday or Fourth of July or something. So far, no go.

Marta hung her coat in the storeroom and returned. She was dressed like a pirate: black pants, white shirt, blue vest, red bandana as a belt. Davros, with thick curly black hair, pretended to be Greeker than he was. He was dressed like a pirate, too, only his vest was red. It is completely likely a study somewhere proved wearing a costume improved your tips.

Me? Well, I was dressed like a bartender on Halloween.

"Same drink specials?" Marta asked.

"Yes, we'll finish up the spooky ones and swap drinks tomorrow." The only part of the holiday I actually enjoyed were the drinks with activated charcoal, which turned them pitch black. Okay, and the raspberry blood pouring down the sides of the glass.

"What have you decided about the Lodge?" I asked, to make conversation. "Are you going tomorrow?"

"Don't know," she said. She stopped and looked straight at me. "You wanna come?" she asked.

"Where? You mean to the Lodge? Why?" I asked. "I'm not exactly in the age range of your friends."

"It's not like you're old," she said. "And, well, I trust you."

Exploring the old Lodge was tempting. It was built a hundred years ago in the classic Adirondack style, and grew to be a sprawling set of buildings, the size of the Grand Hotel on Mackinac Island or the del Coronado in California. A private club, it was set on hundreds of acres in the hills above Lake Serenity, the centerpiece of our town. (Yes, I know the town is named Tranquility, and Lake Tranquility is located in the next town over. I've got no explanation.) I am irresistibly drawn to old architecture that acts as a time machine to take you back to another era. I'm not interested in ghosts as much as I'd love to wander back and find everyone and everything as they were a hundred years gone by.

Also, at twenty-seven, it was good to hear I'm not considered old. I hoped I still had a few good years ahead of me.

"What would your friends think of you inviting me?" I asked. "And what if we're caught? The last thing we need is for the bartenders from the Battened Hatch to be arrested for breaking and entering."

"Toby and Colin wouldn't care if you came," she said. "And we wouldn't be caught. Even if we are, Toby's brother Dwayne is a policeman a couple of towns over. All the cops here know Toby. We'd be okay." At my hesitation, she said, "We could meet here tomorrow morning and walk over."

"It's tempting," I said. "Are there any stories? I mean, ghost stories?"

Marta rolled her eyes. "The most often repeated story is that Alfred Whisk, the founder of the Lodge, was quite the ladies' man. His wife Adelaide had no idea. When he was eventually confronted by various husbands about his egregious behavior, he couldn't or didn't stop. When Adelaide realized everything they'd built would be destroyed, she threw herself off the cupola. People say they've seen her ghost fall, screaming."

"That seems dramatic but unlikely," I said.

"Agreed."

She swung through the dishwasher side of the kitchen behind us and returned with clean cocktail glasses, which she proceeded to disperse and hang, ready for the day.

A trip to the Lodge felt more intriguing by the minute.

As lunch hour revved up, an unexpected patron made her way in through the lobby door and swung onto a seat in front of the bar. It was Rachel Hunt, my former nemesis-turned-friend. Maybe that would even out the bad vibes I was still feeling from Mike.

"Hey, Rachel," I said.

"Hey, Avalon."

She was one of those women who is svelte and mighty. Curves in all the right places, chestnut skin, hair that manages to be ethnic yet appears to do exactly what she asks of it. She was wearing a black shirt and trousers under a red jacket. Her slacks were unwrinkled.

When I met Philip, Rachel was his girlfriend. His ending things with her and starting things with me got a little...messy. Then Philip left for France and an old friend of mine came to town and Rachel moved to Saratoga Springs and I got her catering company a great gig, and well, now, here we were, glad to see each other on a Halloween Saturday.

"What brings you back to town?" I asked. "Catering a Halloween event?"

"How did you guess? It's the fundraiser up at the Sally Allison/Pepper Porter Theater and Arts Complex later this afternoon. Things seem to be under control, and I have twenty minutes to spare. I don't want to arrive too early to look overeager or anxious."

"Of course not. Food, or beverage?"

"I'll take the date and nut salad, with just the tiniest pour of Chenin Blanc."

"Coming up."

I put in the order and served her the wine. "How are things in Saratoga?" I asked.

"Actually, going well," she said, then looked down, color rising in her cheeks.

"Um, new man?" I asked. She'd have to get better at hiding it if she didn't want the question.

"Maybe," she said. "I hope so."

"Not ready to discuss?"

"Not yet." She tipped her glass as if for a toast.

"Cheers," I said.

"So, how's Philip?" she asked.

Now there was a loaded question. Philip Young and I had tentatively found our way back to each other after our summer apart. Things had seemed normal and well, wonderful.

Then he disappeared. He disappeared to the point where, when I offered to take care of his beloved dog, he let me remove her from his place of residence.

How truthful should a person be when discussing one's current beau with his old flame, to put it in Hollywood terms?

"I'm not...seeing him much?"

"Oh. I thought you were together."

"I mean, he's not seeing anyone. He even let me take Whistle to my place."

She circled the wine inside her glass. "Oh," she said. "That. It happens."

I leaned in. "What do you mean?"

"The first time it happened, it really threw me. I thought it was something I'd done. He wouldn't talk, wouldn't answer texts or the phone. Was up all night painting and slept all day.

"The second time it happened, I thought maybe he was bipolar or something. Except his gran had a small heart episode, and when he heard, he snapped right out of it. That proved to me he can snap out of it. He chooses to let himself be 'gone.'"

"How did you deal with it?" I asked.

"Obviously not well," she said.

"Is it why you broke up?"

"One reason. I need someone I can count on."

"Got it. Thanks."

I remembered the first time I saw her and Philip together. He had his arm casually flung around her shoulder, and as they walked, he bent his head in to listen to what she said. I was envious of that kind of relationship. All right, I had been envious of her. At the time, Philip seemed sexy and caring in equal measure, the perfect man.

Then, when we were together, those things proved to be true. He also expressed ways in which he saw the best parts of me. That was the most dangerous kind of relationship, one in which your self-perception and self-esteem get wrapped up with the person's opinion of you.

I guess I should be grateful. Someone like Philip—for whom I'd fallen, hard—couldn't be perfect. In fact, he had to have some pretty big defect to balance his wonderfulness.

Found it.

Rachel had decided she couldn't live with it.

Well, damn.

It wasn't until after she ate her salad, paid, and left that the other shoe dropped.

Marta was working behind me, refilling the ice, checking the well bottles. It took me a second to realize she wasn't doing it with her normal precision. Some serious slinging and clanking was happening. I turned to find her fairly snorting.

"Hey," I said. "What's up? Did something happen?"

"Are you fucking kidding me?" she asked. "When were you going to say something?"

"About...?"

She stood holding a bottle of Stoli, glaring at me.

"What?" I asked, honestly confused. I played back everything that had recently happened in the bar. And landed on...

Philip.

Marta was a talented artist in her own right. She took lessons from Philip and had for more than a year. He was helping her find and get into the right art school. I'd known since the first time I'd seen them together that she was a goner.

I couldn't fault her for that. I was, too.

Since Philip's return from Paris and our happy but hesitant reunion, we hadn't hidden our relationship, but we hadn't broadcast it, either. I'm guessing that with Rachel out of the picture, Marta thought Philip was finally free and this was her chance. She hadn't known he and I were together until my discussion with Rachel.

Shit.

Marta was the closest I'd ever come to having a little sister. Obviously, I'd never steal her boyfriend.

But boyfriends aren't something you can give away, like an ugly holiday sweater. Philip had a say in whom he was with. Of course, just then he was choosing painting over me and over Whistle.

Who knew what was going to happen?

"How long?" she demanded.

I didn't think I needed to explain the whole Rachel-messy-ending thing. "A month?"

Marta was trembling when she stomped off. She actually exited the pub. I let her go.

I looked over at the now empty table where Mike had eaten. I didn't have that many close friends, and I was losing them right and left.

Who did I have to talk to about it?

Apparently not Philip.

Shit.

The night couldn't end fast enough for me. Did I mention I hate Halloween? It's not Halloween itself, it's all holidays that give the wrong people a free pass to misbehave. Davros had come to me earlier, suggesting we have a local DJ run a trivia as well as a costume contest. I said no, absolutely no way would I pay for that. He said fine, he'd run the contests.

I paid the DJ. The place was crowded and I was a bit on edge, just wanting everyone to leave with all the glasses and chairs and other people's body parts intact.

Marta returned and worked as diligently as ever, even during closing, which she managed without speaking a word to me. Everyone was hauling in good tips.

By midnight, the place was empty. The furniture seemed fine. I didn't believe anyone had been roofied. I turned out the lights and locked the door from inside. Then I walked the room, tugging down crepe streamers. They crumpled in my hands and left streaks of orange and black where my hands were wet from the last wipe-down of the bar. I crumpled them into a ball and threw them into the trash.

Heading into the back hall to get my coat, I tripped over the suitcase Sandy left the night before, promising to pick up within an hour.

Hunh.

I flicked on the hall light and looked at it more carefully. It was an old-fashioned, hard-sided Samsonite suitcase in tan with dark brown leather trim. Boy, this had seen an age.

It had a matching luggage tag. I opened the flap and read: *Frank Wilcox, 12 Ivy Circle, Tranquility, NY*. Wow. This had to be her father's suitcase—if not grandfather's, or even great-grandfather's. I wasn't sure what was up with Sandy, how she'd gotten so distracted, but I decided to throw the suitcase into my car and drop it off on my way in to work the next day.

Twelve Ivy Circle still existed in Tranquility, and according to my phone, was still inhabited by the Wilcox family.

Carrying the suitcase out to my car, I tested the feel of the handle, the sturdiness of the case. It could be a ticket to the past. The feeling made me sorry Marta was furious and I was undoubtedly uninvited from visiting the old hotel.

SINS OF OMISSION

Ingredients

Simple Syrup

    1 ½ pints fresh raspberries
    2 cups sugar
    2 cups of water

Raspberry Foam

    Whipped cream dispenser
    3 oz raspberry simple syrup
    3 oz sour mix
    4 egg whites
    2 whipped cream chargers (N2O - nitrous oxide chargers)

Cocktail

    1 oz tequila blanco
    ½ oz raspberry liqueur
    1 ½ oz sour mix
    1 oz raspberry simple syrup
    ½ activated charcoal capsule
    A few fresh raspberries
    Ice
    Collins glass

Method

Raspberry Simple Syrup

In medium sauce pan, add water, sugar and fresh raspberries. Bring to a low boil over medium heat, stirring occasionally. Let reduce until mixture has thickened. Take off heat. When mixture is at room temperature, put in blender with raspberries and blend until silky and smooth.

Raspberry Foam

In whipped cream dispenser add egg whites, raspberry simple syrup, and sour mix. Place lid on tight and shake all ingredients together. Add the N_2O charges to dispenser to make a nice raspberry foam.

Cocktail

Dip Collins glass into raspberry simple syrup and let drip down the sides of the glass.
Fill Collins glass with ice.
In cocktail shaker, add ice, tequila, raspberry liqueur, sour mix, raspberry simple syrup, and activated charcoal.
Shake all ingredients together.
Strain contents of cocktail shaker into glass, add raspberry foam on top.
Add fresh raspberries for garnish.

3

SECRETS OF THE SUITCASE

I WOKE UP crazy early on Sunday morning—7:30 AM, which is middle-of-the-night, bartender time. Since I was up, I decided to run to the grocery store while it was still mostly empty. Although Hannah Bricksford had somehow become my best friend and she was rector of the local Episcopal Church, she hadn't roped me into church attendance.

I had my reasons. She didn't seem to mind. At least she'd taught me not to paint all religious people with the same brush.

As I loaded my groceries into the backseat, I saw Sandy's suitcase and decided to drop it off.

I turned onto Ivy Circle around 8:45. As I approached number twelve, I could see the flat part of the yard where young Sandy had played volleyball through leafless trees. Farther back, the property sloped down, following the shape of the hill.

I pulled up in front of the three-story house in time to see a middle-aged couple exit and make the short walk to the garage. Its door was manual, and the man stooped to grab the handle and raise it. They wore expensive cloth coats. His was black, hers forest green. My guess was they were headed for church.

Coming to a halt by the curb, I killed the engine. They turned to me in surprise. "Hello," I said as I opened the back door of my Subaru and pulled out the suitcase. "Is this where Sandy Wilcox is staying? I have her suitcase."

Both of them stopped dead.

"She left it down at MacTavish's. Thought I'd bring it up."

They stood staring. Maybe I had the wrong house somehow. "Is Sandy your daughter?"

"No," the man finally said. "We have no daughter."

"We have no daughter," the woman echoed.

They got into their white Volvo SUV, the man in the driver's seat. He turned it on, backed into the driveway, got out, pulled down the garage door, got back in, exited the driveway, and drove past me without further acknowledgement.

Well, alrighty then.

Had I read the address incorrectly?

Nope. It said 12 Ivy Circle, and this was number twelve.

Not knowing what else to do, I stashed the suitcase back in the car and turned around.

On my way down Main Street, I happened to look up at the church pastored by Marta's father. It was a large Gothic affair made of dark local stone that rose from the hillside like a warning. Congregants were gathering, greeting each other. Somehow I wasn't surprised to see the couple from Ivy Circle pulling into the parking lot halfway up the hill.

Back home in my private glen, I brought in the bags of groceries and put them away. Then, out of pure curiosity, I went and got the suitcase.

I put it down on my living room sofa and stared at it for a moment. Even though I was trying to return it to its rightful owner, was it wrong to open it? Not if all I was doing was looking for information about how to find her. Right?

The lock was to the right. It had an old-fashioned tiny keyhole. Next to it was a small button you pressed to release the bar that held it closed. Fortunately, it wasn't locked. I squeezed the button and the brass top of both clasps flew up.

I took a breath and opened the case.

It was mostly clothes. Two pairs of pants and three long-sleeved tops undoubtedly for chilly weather. Then, on the bottom to one side, I found a plastic toiletries bag that said *Well Hello Sunshine.* It unzipped easily.

I remembered her saying she couldn't mix alcohol with drugs.

There were drugs.

The one on top, the one I picked up, was oxycodone.

Well, damn. I hadn't taken her for an addict.

I took a breath and looked at the label. It had her name, Sandy Wilcox, and an address in Brooklyn, New York. It was prescribed by a doctor.

As I sat there, wondering about the street value of what I held, or, more likely, the trouble I'd be in were I caught with it, my cell phone buzzed with a text.

It was from Marta.

So, are you coming? it said.

To what? Where are you?

At the Hatch. For our excursion.

Really? She still wanted me to come? Did I want to? If I let myself think about it, the cautious/lazy gene would win out.

There in 5.

I put the pill bottle back into the toiletries bag, which I laid back into the suitcase. I closed the clasps.

I made sure all my cold grocery items were in the fridge and gave Whistle an extra outing. Then I put on my darkest, flattest winter coat, picked up the suitcase, and headed for the car.

Marta followed me into the Battened Hatch. I unlocked the storeroom and slid the suitcase inside, then relocked the door. I'd deal with it later.

As we headed for the car, I remembered that Sandy had greeted Marta by name.

"You know Sandy?" I asked.

"Who?"

"Sandy Wilcox. The woman sitting at the bar on Friday night. She left the suitcase."

"Oh, yeah. His—sorry, her—family goes to our church."

"I think I saw Sandy's parents there this morning. But when I took the suitcase up to their house, they said they didn't have a daughter."

Marta stared at me. "You don't know?"

"I guess not."

"Sandy Wilcox used to be Frank Wilcox. Tranquility High football player and everything. I mean, not a big, burly quarterback, but played every game. He was a popular guy. Not snooty popular but the 'everyone liked being around him' kind. He was nice, even to us little kids at church. Not all the older kids were."

"So, she's transgender."

"Yes. I hadn't really seen...her...since she transitioned. She left Tranquility after high school, and who wouldn't? I don't know if you've seen the sign in Oscar's Garage that says *We can fix your trans but not your TRANS.* Or the one under it that says *We will service your trans but not your TRANS.*"

I stared at her, shocked by such open hate. "Isn't it illegal to refuse service to someone due to prejudice?"

"I'd have left Tranquility, too," was all she said.

"I'm guessing him transitioning didn't go over well at church."

She simply shook her head.

"What time are we meeting at the Lodge?" I asked.

"Like in five minutes. I was thinking we'd leave the car here and walk, but it's pretty cold. Now I'm thinking we could park on a side street."

I concurred. We drove to the other side of Lake Serenity and parked my car on Poplar, a residential lane. A Jeep Cherokee pulled up behind us, and Marta's friend Colin Keene got out. Marta had obviously sent him our parking location.

In light of Marta and my earlier discussion, I wondered for a moment how Colin found living in Tranquility. If it occurred to me he might be gay, I'm sure I wasn't the only one who thought so. Especially since he didn't seem to mask it. He was tall, curly-haired, wasn't easily annoyed, and seemed a little goofy. In other words, the perfect friend for Marta.

Marta was texting and announced, "Toby says to meet them by the back door to the lobby." To my surprise, she started up the hill.

"Wouldn't it be easier to go down?" I asked.

"We can't just march up the street and into the front door," she answered. "We've got to get there the back way."

Colin said, somewhat cheerfully, "So, we're really going to do this?"

"Why wouldn't we?" I asked.

"This is the anniversary of when she jumped," he said.

"Ghosts aren't good with anniversaries," said Marta brusquely. And she headed for the Lodge.

SECRETS OF THE SUITCASE

Ingredients

Rosemary Simple Syrup

    8 sprigs fresh rosemary
    2 cups sugar
    2 cups water

Drink

    1 egg white
    1 ½ oz Fernet Branca
    1 ½ oz Carpano Antica Formula vermouth
    3-5 dashes Angostura bitters
    ½ oz rosemary simple syrup
    Sprig of rosemary
    Ice
    Nick and Nora Glass

Method

Rosemary Simple Syrup

Chop rosemary into small pieces.
In medium sauce pan, add sugar, water, and rosemary.
Bring to a slow boil. Remove from heat when sugar is
dissolved. Bring to room temperature.
Strain rosemary from mixture and discard. Store in fridge.

Cocktail

Chill Nick and Nora glass by adding ice and a small
amount of water.
In cocktail shaker, add ice, Fernet Branca, vermouth,
rosemary simple syrup, egg white, and Angostura bitters.
Shake all ingredients together.
Discard ice and water from Nick and Nora glass.
Strain contents of cocktail shaker into glass.
Add rosemary sprig for garnish.

4

E FOR ELIMINATE

COLIN AND I followed Marta up Poplar, then across on Birch Street. There, we left the road and walked through pine-scented woods. I assumed at this point we were on Lodge lands. Within a few minutes, we emerged into daylight. The hill swept down below us with a stunning view of Lake Serenity, the town of Tranquility behind it, with a backdrop of majestic mountains.

Okay, I'd consider joining this club.

Two small cabins sat to the side of the forest, and as we came around them, we could see the remains of the main Lodge. It was huge, even without the footprints of the burned and demolished buildings on either side.

The front of the property, as you drove past, still showcased the building, magnificent even in its abandoned state. To approach the front entrance, cars would leave the road and drive up to the porte cochere, a covered driveway where members could unload without getting wet in the rain or snow. The top of the porte cochere was large enough that it had an entrance from the second floor and still held rusted iron outdoor furniture where members could sit and take in the view.

What was especially notable, both from the front and from the side of the building, were the different levels from which porches and view windows extended, and how they emerged at all angles. No straight box for this Lodge.

The lobby, up front, rose two-and-a-half stories tall. Hallways behind it ran up the side of the hill, leading to a large octagonal structure, a smaller octagon on the top, with rectangular windows gracing each side.

Above the octagon rose a belvedere, a wide three-story cupola whose top level was open to feature the impressive view. If Adelaide Whisk had really thrown herself to her demise, she'd been lucky to do so successfully from such a low height. I think I'd want a surer thing.

"Come on!" Marta spied Toby at a back door into the front lobby. We all ducked down and ran across the open field as if we were in the French Underground.

Toby held the door open as we filed past. His willowy girlfriend stood inside, herding us through.

"I'm Lily," she said. She had straight brown hair, pulled into a long, thin pony tail. She wore jeans and a white puffer coat. "Have you been here before?"

"Nope," replied Colin.

"Well, I guess we start with the lobby. If you were staying here, you'd start with the lobby."

We continued through a short hallway on thick carpeting with black scrolling that was in surprisingly good shape.

As we entered the lobby, I admit I was disappointed. Instead of tall, sweeping ceilings and polished wood everywhere, it had a boxy design.

"It isn't an Adirondack décor?" I asked.

"Nah, this part was built around the turn of the last century, the aughts, as they say, nineteen-aught-six or something. These buildings were the first on the property to be year-round. The lower ceilings kept the heat down here where members needed it," Lily continued as guide.

Admittedly there were different levels, but the descriptor "sweeping" had no place here. This was built to be functional. Morning sun hadn't crested the mountain behind us, and shadows ran deep. The place felt truly abandoned.

Six steps led from the back hall to the lobby floor. Farther front, on the side of the lobby, four more steps took you down to the service area, where the bellhops waited. On the other side, the same number of steps took you down to—I walked across—the barbershop, the hair salon, and a doctor and dentist. A red and white barber's pole was still mounted near the door.

Colin slid behind the long, low check-in counter to a desk on the right. "Western Union! Anyone need to send a telegram?" he called. A large sign told patrons they could indeed accomplish that task.

I couldn't help but slide behind the long front desk, too. As I walked down the long low counter, for the first time I felt the tug of yesteryear. One station was marked *Reservations*, and another *Cashier*. On either side were large wooden shelves with hundreds of small, flat compartments—and pieces of paper still peeking out of some of them.

Curious, I grabbed the nearest one. "Stone, Dr. Richard, wife Amanda, children Debbie and Kurt." It had a check-in and check-out date, and the room assigned to them.

Holding the card in my hand, I could almost see the Stones arriving, as they likely did every year, the kids in starchy travel clothes, dying to run off and play.

There was an *A* on the top of the card. I put it back and pulled out a card from further down. *Parker, Gerald, and Thelma*, it said. No offspring. There was a *C* on the top.

Toby had come up behind me. "Do you know what the letters signify?" I asked.

He sighed. "I do. Even if you were allowed to join, and stay here, you were constantly observed and rated. *A* meant preferred; *B* meant general; *C* meant 'do not cultivate, they're common; *D*, doubtful and *E*, eliminate."

"Yikes." I put the card back, as if someone might start to assess me.

"Bellhop, oh, bellhop!" Lily cooed, acting as a guest.

"Can we see the rest of the place?" Colin asked Toby.

"What? Oh, yeah, sure."

As we turned to leave the lobby, Marta walked past me. "See any-body?" I asked quietly.

"Only one. Old guy behind the registration counter. Balding. Narrowest head I've ever seen."

"You mean where I was standing just now?" I tried to keep my voice low.

I must have given a little jump, because she said, "He isn't responding to me, to any of us, so it might just be a residual. Some-one whose presence was so strong here, it keeps repeating. Not inter-active at all."

That was good, I guessed. Even though Marta was in contact with another older sensitive who gave her reassuring advice, she was not comfortable with the fact that she could see formerly living peo-ple.

The three of us followed Toby and Lily up the few stairs to the landing. We exited through a center door to find ourselves in a large square room dotted with small wooden tables and wicker chairs, awaiting people having tea, perhaps? "This doesn't look like a full-service restaurant," I said. It seemed a place that would have used lots of doilies.

"Oh, it's not one of the restaurants," said Lily. "They were huge affairs with windows, windows, windows. They were in the build-ings that burned down."

"This was tea service? Or a bar?"

"The tearoom. Not a bar! To join this club, you had to swear not to drink or smoke or dress up too stylishly. But stylishly. Just stylish enough."

"You had to be a White Protestant Christian," added Toby, con-tinuing through double doors into a long hallway. White wood and glass display cases lined either side, their shelves empty. Whatever had been exhibited there was long gone.

With their explanations of membership requirements, the fun factor had diminished exponentially. "That can't be right," I said, without thinking. "For one thing, for most clubs, a large part of the profit comes from serving alcohol. How could they stay open?"

"Well, they did," said Lily. "Until they didn't."

"How do you know so much about the club?" I asked her.

"My dad worked here in high school. As a bellhop."

"Everyone's parents worked here," said Toby.

"Or grandparents," agreed Colin.

"At its zenith, it employed just about the whole town," said Lily. The wide hallway brought us to a T-turn. Either way you looked, the hallways rounded and continued out of sight.

"I assume you weren't allowed to dance?" I added.

In response, Lily shoved open the double doors ahead of us. "You certainly were allowed," she said. "In fact, on Saturday nights, you had to."

And we entered an enormous wood-paneled room with a stage at the front. Did I say enormous? I meant cavernous.

"Voila! Welcome to the Agora," said Lily.

"Big enough stage to perform Broadway plays," said Colin. "That, I would have liked to see."

I walked into the center of the room and slowly spun around. The back and sides held a mezzanine and boxes, like you'd have in a Broadway house. There was room for an orchestra on the floor in front of the stage.

"Holy smokes," I said. "Where are the seats?"

"They could be set out and removed," said Lily. "Remember the dances. The kids were taught dancing and manners in a cotillion all season. On Saturdays, at 7:00 PM, they danced. At eight, they went to bed. At nine, the grownups took the floor."

In my mind, I heard the *tap-tap-tapping* of a conductor's baton, then the start of Benny Goodman playing "Let's Dance." I also spent a minute happily contemplating how I would have tried my hardest as a youngster to turn my cotillion into a train wreck.

It was hard these days to be in a big ballroom and not picture it full of folks from the past, a la *The Shining*. I admit the air was thicker here, almost as if it was flecked with swirling glitter.

"In the corner," said Marta before I could ask. She nodded her head. "She's just standing there. "Calf-length dress. Blue-gray sequins."

"Residual?" I asked, like I knew what I was talking about.

"I don't think so. I'm getting a strong feeling of longing. But she has no interest in us."

"Works for me."

I couldn't help but stare into the seemingly empty corner.

"Let's dance," Lily said to Toby, her arms extended.

He shook his head. Colin stepped up and took Lily's hands. He hummed "Paper Moon" and they twirled through the empty space. In my imagination, I heard the rustles of women's fancy dresses, the squeak of men's hard-soled shoes on the wooden floor. Colin gave Lily a final spin and a deep bow. She couldn't help but smile.

"Is there more to see?" asked Marta as we joined the others. She didn't seem enthusiastic as much as she sounded like she was ready to go.

"Yeah, the chapel. It's this way." Lily led us forward to the front of the theater, then out a side door. "They built it—and this was clever—so that the Agora stage could open up to the back of the church." We walked out into the wide hallway that surrounded the theater, then around and through arched carved doors into the back of the chapel.

Finally, we'd wandered into something that felt old. And spooky. It might have been because there were no lights on, and no sun shining through the three stained-glass windows at the front. The chapel was made from local stone, with curved inner arches. A brass cross still sat on the altar up front. The pews were made of light-colored wood. The floor was stone. And there was...a feeling there.

"This is the Adelaide Whisk Chapel," Lily said. "She always wanted one, and Mr. Whisk finally built one after she died."

"A fine way for him to behave," said Toby.

Marta and I chose not to fully enter the chapel. We stood by the open doorway as the others moved inside to explore. They were quiet, hushed, really inside the sacred space.

"Marta."

I looked at her, then around her to see which of our friends had spoken. It had been a male voice.

Marta looked at me, confused. She'd heard it, too.

"Guys," I said to the others, walking up the aisle. Toby and Lily were examining the cross, testing its weight. It must have been Colin who called Marta.

In the chantry, on the side wall, hung a photo of a hefty matron. "In memory of Adelaide Whisk," was penned below in flowing script.

"Look at this!" Colin popped up from behind the altar, holding a rectangular piece of stained glass. It had a picture of the same stalwart woman in her sixties, clutching her breast and looking heavenward. *Adelaide Whisk*, it said. *God, have mercy.*

God have mercy, indeed.

"Interesting," I said. "Did one of you call Marta?"

Each shook their head.

"Why?" It was Toby.

"Someone called her name. Very clearly. I heard it, and Marta did, too."

I turned toward the narthex of the chapel for Marta's agreement.

But Marta was gone.

E FOR ELIMINATE

Ingredients

½ oz fresh lemon juice
2 oz cranberry juice
Fresh ground turmeric
Fresh ground cayenne pepper
Sparkling water
Fresh cranberries
Ice
Collins glass

Method

Fill Collins glass with ice.
In cocktail shaker, add ice, lemon juice, cranberry juice,
and a tiny pinch of both turmeric and cayenne. Shake all
ingredients together and strain into Collins glass. Top off
of with sparking water.
Add fresh cranberries for garnish.

5

BENEATH THE BELVEDERE

W E ALL STOOD, silent.

Then we hurried back down the aisle and out of the chapel.

No one.

"Marta?" I asked.

No response.

The hallway was wider here, where attendees could mill about before and after services.

I expected to find a door to the outside, but there wasn't one.

Yet there was a door.

Lily gestured flippantly towards it. "That's the staircase up to the belvedere."

I grabbed the handle and yanked it, roughly, pulling it towards me, trying to force it to open to reveal my friend. It was locked. Not only locked, it seemed as though it hadn't been opened for decades. The wood had breathed and stretched, attempting to take up more of the doorway than the frame allowed.

"Locked," Lily said. "Cemented shut, even, I think, after Adelaide, you know."

"Marta?" I asked through the door. No response. Of course.

"Maybe she went on ahead," said Lily, going for nonchalant but not quite hitting it. She turned down the hallway, sliding deeper into the old building.

The last place remaining turned out to be a music room. It was dim and musty, reminiscent of an unused church basement. There were even brown metal folding chairs, the slim pads on the seats fraying.

"This was the first music room," said Lily. "But then they built a better one in another building and stopped using this one."

I didn't listen to her continued explanation, because there, seated on the front row of metal chairs and facing the small, raised platform, was Marta. She did not acknowledge our arrival. I walked towards her, carefully. Even as I stood beside her, she was focused elsewhere.

Behind me, Toby flopped onto another chair. Lily sat on his lap.

"So," Toby addressed Marta, "this place is supposed to be full of ghosts. How many have you seen?"

She didn't answer.

He continued, oblivious.

"This is the anniversary of Adelaide's death. There has to be something."

"Marta!" Lily called, demanding her attention.

Marta looked up, confused, as if awakening. "What?"

"How many ghosts? We brought you here to see if there are any ghosts. How many are there?"

"One," said Marta, diffidently. "She was in the dance hall. She was longing for something."

"That isn't very dramatic."

"Most aren't."

"Oh, come on!" said Lily, hopping up, her ponytail bouncing behind her as she addressed the room. "Ghosts! You've got to be here! Adelaide, you died only feet from here! Surely you were mad! Surely you have something to say!"

The shadows in the music room stretched dark and portentous.

We sat in silence. "I want to go," said Toby.

"Maybe we should come back with a Ouija board instead of a lame psychic," his girlfriend said. Then, "Adelaide, it's Lily. I want to talk to you. Are you there? If you're there, knock twice."

We sat in silence. Nothing.

"Let's go," Toby repeated, standing. We followed suit.

He went back out to the hall, past the locked door to the belvedere steps.

No one spoke. As we passed in single file, there was suddenly a knock.

And then another.

"She knocked twice!" trumpeted Lily.

I couldn't help myself. I stepped back over to the door, grabbed the handle, and flung myself against it.

Nothing.

"Nooo," Lily chastised me. "That's no way to show respect!"

All right, I'd show respect. "Adelaide," I said. "Marta's here, if you want to talk to her. Come, talk."

We all stood, Lily still miffed that I was making demands of a ghost.

And then we heard footsteps, going up stairs, the sound becoming muffled as the person climbed.

"This is the anniversary!" said Colin. He ran.

We all ran. Ran, as if all the doors would suddenly be bolted, as if something otherworldly was at our back.

We ran past the Agora and made it into the Tea Room, when we were stopped by a booming voice. "Tobias!"

We skidded to a halt and turned around. There stood a police officer in uniform. He'd been wearing his sunglasses—completely unnecessary in this darkened atmosphere. His blond hair was in a buzz cut, his face long and slightly reddened. His chin had a slight stubble.

I had the same thought as everyone else. Oh, crap.

"Toby, I wasn't expecting to see you here, let alone running tours," he said.

Toby choked.

"I saw your car down the road. What the hell?"

"It's the anniversary," Lily said, meekly. "Come on, Dwayne, who wouldn't come here on the anniversary?"

"Anniversary of…"

"Adelaide's death."

"We were leaving," said Toby. "Let's just go."

Toby's older brother Dwayne looked each of us over. Finally, his gaze settled back on Toby. "You should know better," he said.

"I do."

We walked in a line to the unlocked door behind the lobby. Dwayne held the door open as we each passed in front of him into the cool air. He smelled of aftershave. One I didn't know and wouldn't purchase for a friend. I noticed the patch on his shirt was for the North Pass Police Department, in a town about forty-five minutes southeast of Tranquility.

"I've got to get to work," he said, exasperated.

"I know," said Toby.

We all started down the hill together. No point in explaining to a law officer that we'd snuck in from the other direction.

We were nearly to the front driveway when a scream cut through the late morning stillness. The six of us turned, in unison, just in time to see the person fall, flailing, against the steel gray clouds, from the top of the belvedere.

We all heard the thud when the body landed.

BENEATH THE BELVEDERE

Ingredients

A few slices of seedless cucumber
Fresh basil
1 oz fresh lemon juice
Sparkling water
Ice
Collins glass

Method

In cocktail shaker, add a few fresh basil leaves, cucumber,
and lemon juice. Muddle all ingredients together. Add ice
and shake ingredients together.
Add contents of cocktail shaker to Collins glass and top
off with sparking water.
Add fresh cucumber to rim of glass and a sprig of fresh
basil leaf for garnish.

6

BACK ON EARTH

"SHIT!" SAID DWAYNE and, to Toby, "Did you see anyone, anything, when you were in there?"

"No!" said Toby.

"Then go! If you're not involved, if you don't know who that was, just go! All of you. Get out of here."

Dwayne turned and ran up the hill, toward the person now on the ground on the other side of the Agora.

We made it to the road and turned our different ways on the sidewalks. Marta, Colin, and I turned up Poplar before the first sirens grew loud and emergency vehicles swung up the Appleton's front drive.

We reached our cars. "Come, sit," I said to Colin.

The three of us got into my Subaru, Marta up front, Colin in the back.

We sat, shaking, trying to breathe normally.

"Fuck," said Marta.

"Yep," said Colin.

We listened to "I Made You Look" on the car radio.

"I guess we should go," I said. "You good to drive?" I asked Colin. He nodded, albeit shakily. He got out of the car and back into his Jeep.

As Marta and I drove back, I kept asking myself if this was right—if I had witnessed a death, crime or not, should I have left? Granted, it was in the hands of the police from the get-go, and we hadn't seen anyone. We heard knocking and footsteps but had no idea whose they were. We'd been dismissed by the authorities. Well, by one authority.

Back in the parking lot of MacTavish's, I left the car idling and turned to Marta. "Okay," I said, "Spill. What did you see in the music room? More to the point, who?"

She looked at her hands. "A woman. A Black woman in her twenties or thirties. She was wearing a fancy dress, with beading, maybe?"

"Did she want anything? Could you communicate?"

"She was holding a medal of some kind. It was rectangular and painted. It might have been made from a precious metal. In the center was a green gem. Around it were painted mountains and farmland, with corn growing. It was beautiful. Across the top, in letters that formed a little arch, it said *Beulah*."

"*Beulah*? What does that mean?"

"I don't know."

"She wanted you to do something?"

"To find Beulah, maybe? Or the medal?"

"It would be helpful if these spirits could talk. Or do charades, or something."

Marta gave me the side-eye.

"Sorry. I don't mean to be disrespectful."

She sighed. "It would be helpful if they could. But I'm really bad at charades."

I turned off the car and asked Marta, "Are you okay to work? You want the day off?"

"No," she said. "I need to be here, with something to do."

"Me, too," I agreed. "And I hope that person who jumped..."

"Isn't dead."

"Exactly."

We headed for the pub. "You're saying that besides the apparitions you mentioned, Appleton Lodge isn't especially haunted?"

"Not that I could tell. Something was off, though, something with Toby."

"Oh?"

"It was weird how Lily took over the whole thing. Usually, Toby is much more in charge."

"Lily seemed disappointed not to talk to any ghosts directly."

Marta shrugged and we got to work.

The day was busy enough to give our hands something to do. Every now and then Marta and I locked eyes, communicating something along the lines of, "That really happened?"

After the lunch rush, Glenn MacTavish, the inn's proprietor, came in and sat at his usual spot at far end of the bar and ordered a whiskey. Today, he wasn't wearing his plaid, but jeans and a button-up navy blue shirt.

"Did you hear anything about someone jumping off the tower over at the Lodge?" I asked him. "I don't mean Adelaide, I mean today."

"Aye," he said. "It was a fellow named Jarrett Banks. Damn fool. Jumped off the belvedere. Broke both his legs and his collarbone. Concussion. Collapsed lungs. Damn fool."

What did I say about needing to jump from higher up?

"He'll be all right?" I asked. "He's, what, in the hospital?"

"Yes, it sounds like he'll survive, although he'll never again do pole-vaulting in the Olympics."

"He pole-vaulted in…"

Glenn's eyebrows gave away the ruse.

"Oh. Never mind."

"So, the Appleton Lodge," I said. "It seems it was a big part of Tranquility for a long time."

"That's an understatement, lassie."

"How did it fit in with MacTavish's? Was there business enough for both?"

He took a breath. "Not everyone in the world is a White Protestant Christian who doesn't drink or smoke or who wants to be judged and rated for membership. You might have heard they got into trouble for their refusal to allow Jews and Black people in in the 1970s, but they were already in hot water for it in 1903.

"And then, there was Alfred Whisk himself. Revolutionized library science. Started a school for librarians at Columbia College, one that admitted women—well, attractive women, they had to submit a photo with their application—back when that was unheard of. Made a system for shelving books that was soon standardized. Made being a librarian into an actual profession.

"He also had a terrible, controlling temperament. Made enemies of his bosses wherever he went."

"I heard he was a ladies' man."

"Dear God, that's putting it carefully. Less like Harvey Weinstein, who terrified all his conquests into silence, more like Donald Trump. Instead of apologizing when scores of women complained about his abuse, he paid them the money the courts decreed, then said something to the effect of, 'Gee, Ladies, I'm a typical man, taking advantage of women's beauty in a way every man wishes he could.' Didn't see anything wrong with what he'd done. And continued to do." Glenn shook his head. "Old Al should have thought twice before empowering women librarians. You don't mess with librarians."

"His wife jumped?"

"So the story goes. It's likely he gave her several nasty diseases. But you have to keep in mind, she wasn't some shrinking violet. She was a woman whose beliefs about consorting with only the right race, abstaining from liquor and tobacco, not being Catholic or God forbid, Jewish, were as entrenched as her husband's if not more so. And people of different ethnicities or those of different sexual orientations, waaaaallll, you didn't dare talk about them enough even to damn them.

"At one point, the Lodge was a town unto itself over there. They had farms that raised their own pigs and chickens, grew their own vegetables, made their own furniture, and when they made the place year-round, and seriously started winter sports—the Winter

Olympics never could have come here if we hadn't had the Lodge to help house everybody. So Pepper Porter held her nose and worked with them to get that first Olympics here. I mean, at the beginning, Pepper was known for being a prude, but even she couldn't have dinner with Alfred and Adelaide without being restrained from punching someone."

I laughed. "I would have loved to see that."

He smiled. "Yes, me, too."

"What you're saying is there was enough business for Appleton and for MacTavish's, too."

"What I'm saying is we've always had a damn fine bar."

"It is a damn fine bar. Oh, to double-check, we're open tomorrow?" Usually, the Battened Hatch closed on Monday, but the chef from Pepper's was participating in some fancy contest and Mac-Tavish's needed an open on-site restaurant for the tourists.

"If you can see your way clear," he said. "Kitchen will be set up for pub menu."

"Not a problem." I thought it was worth a try. "By the way, have you heard of something called Beulah?"

"Beulah? Nay."

After being up so early, I was more than ready to go when we closed at eight. I was the last one out, locking the door to the lobby. An older, wiry man named Ivan was the nighttime security guy. Most (read: nearly all) nights were calm at MacTavish's, so his main source of entertainment was listening to the police band.

"Did you hear about the jumper over at Appleton Lodge?" I asked him at his desk in the corner.

"Crazy," he muttered. But he was laser-focused on what was currently coming over the airwaves.

"Something else happening?"

"Yeah," he said. "Some hunters—oops, I mean hikers, it isn't hunting season yet—found a body in the woods up Anvil Mountain."

My heart stopped.

"Have they given any information about who it is?" I asked.

"Naw. They wouldn't on the band," he said.

He went back to listening. I headed for the employee parking lot.

All I could think about was the suitcase locked in the storeroom.

I tried to breathe.

I didn't know for sure it was her.

For that matter, I didn't know much about the jumper, or the knocker or the footsteps that preceded the jump.

All I knew was, I was tired and overwhelmed.

BACK ON EARTH

Ingredients

Honey Simple Syrup

> ½ cup honey
> 2 cups water

Cocktail

> 1 ½ oz gin
> 2 oz iced chamomile tea
> ½ oz honey simple syrup
> Few dashes of orange bitters
> Fresh orange, cut into slices
> Ice
> Coupe glass

Method

Honey Simple Syrup

> In medium sauce pan, add honey and water. Bring to a slow boil, stirring often until honey is dissolved. Remove from heat and bring to room temperature before making cocktail.

Chamomile Tea

> Steep 2 chamomile tea bags in hot water and bring to room temperature.

Cocktail

In cocktail shaker add ice, chamomile tea, gin, honey simple syrup, and orange bitters. Shake contents together and strain in coupe glass.
Add fresh orange slice to side of glass for garnish.

7

MEN, UNEXPECTED

B Y HABIT, I drove up to Philip's. I parked in his driveway. In normal times, the Craftsman-style house was warm and welcoming. It was made from local stone with a gracefully rounded arch turning the porch into a picture frame.

The porch once again sat dark. I had a key. I let myself in.

The door to the studio was closed, but music reverberated through the front of the house. Not knowing what to do, I sank down onto the sofa in the living room.

I don't know how long I sat there before the studio door slammed open and Philip traipsed past me to the bathroom. He saw me on the way back. He didn't even stop.

"Rachel said she couldn't stay with you because you do this," I said.

"I can't be with someone who doesn't let me work," he answered.

The door slammed shut.

I sat in the dark.

I couldn't go home and be by myself all night, not without talking to a friendly person.

I texted Hannah. *Can I stop in for a minute?*

Yes, please, came her response.

I dragged myself up and out to the car.

Thankfully, traffic was nonexistent. Hannah lived in a bright, sixties-style parsonage next to the Episcopal church. In fact, most of the back facing the walled garden was glass. I wasn't paying close attention, so I didn't notice there was another car in the circular driveway until I pulled in.

She saw my headlights and opened the front door. Hannah was about my height, with muscles well-toned from working out at the Golden Ticket, our local gym. Her hair was jet-black and her skin was a soft tan, even though she was from a Black family. It was kind of an issue for her. She didn't want people to think she was pretending to be something other than what she was because she didn't look Black. At the same time, she didn't want to parade her lineage and be known solely as her famous father's daughter. As the offspring of two well known (if never married) parents myself, I understood.

"Avalon! I'm so glad you stopped by. There's someone I want you to meet."

Damn. I wasn't in the mood to meet anybody, especially not anybody belonging to the hulking hybrid SUV. I had a brief flash that it might belong to the Men in Black.

I wasn't wrong.

Two gentlemen seated in Hannah's living room jumped to their feet at my arrival. One wore sunglasses—inside at night—but he quickly shoved them into his pocket.

Both were tall with dark black skin, one in a black suit, white shirt, the other a silver gray suit, white shirt. Both had loosened their ties and undone their top buttons.

Mr. Gray Suit shook my hand first. He'd been wearing the shades. "John Mark," he introduced himself with a firm handshake and stepped back, a practiced moved I'd seen used before when you were used to traveling with someone better known.

"And this," Hannah said, "is my brother Zachariah."

"This is Avalon? Our Avalon? Zachariah Malachi. Sister!" he said, claiming me.

And he pulled me into a bear hug that shook the floor. He was maybe six foot three to my five foot seven, and he, too, worked out. His arm muscles were rock hard, though he was lean.

I turned to Hannah. "Your brother? I thought you said you were an only child?"

Zachariah threw his head back and laughed. "Not if Dad Almighty has anything to do with it," he said. "Sit, sit."

The man exuded charisma and self-confidence. His dark hair was shaved, his head was oval.

"They were in Montreal for a conference over the weekend," Hannah said. "Well, Zachariah spoke at the conference. They're spending the night here to break up the trip home."

"Dad Almighty can't be everywhere," he said.

Hannah's father was Samuel Bricksford, a well-known pastor and civil rights advocate, called The Reverend Almighty Samuel Bricksford in some circles. When Hannah had said she simply called him Dad Almighty, I thought she'd been joking.

"No, he can't," said Hannah, then, to me, "I just opened a bottle of Chardonnay." She went across to her drink cart and brought forth a wine glass. "Sit," she instructed, and I did. She poured and handed me the wine goblet.

They talked for a while about the conference and about Hannah's church. When there was a brief lull, I stood to make a break for it.

"You must have a reason for stopping by," said Zachariah, "and I bet there's a reason we're supposed to be here to hear about it."

I didn't know what to say in front of the two strangers.

"It's just been a heck of a day," I said. "Wanted to see a friendly face. That's all."

"Heck of a day," Zach said. "Okay, unpack."

I looked at Hannah, who gave me a warm smile, which was no help whatsoever. "My friend Marta and I saw someone either fall or be pushed off the belvedere at Appleton Lodge," I said. "We thought he died. Then, a woman left a suitcase at the Battened Hatch on Friday, said she'd be back within the hour. She never came back. I just heard they found a body in the woods on Anvil Mountain. I don't know it's her...but it's been a heck of a day."

The next thing I knew, Zachariah Malachi had one arm around me, and one stretched heavenward. He called on the name of Jesus to be with the families and the people involved, and he prayed that my spirit of pain be replaced with a spirit of peace.

Hannah had her eyes open, looking at me. She knew I have a thing about forced religion. But to tell you the truth, if Jesus was looking down on this, I figured he was highly amused.

When Zachariah finished, Hannah peeled me away, put her arm around my shoulders, and walked me to the door. "Sorry about that," she whispered. "The guys are hitting the road early. I'll see you in the morning, regular time."

I felt oddly peaceful heading out to the car.

MEN, UNEXPECTED

Ingredients

> 2 oz Cabernet Sauvignon
> 1 ½ oz Bourbon
> 1 oz simple syrup
> Few dashes angostura bitters
> Luxardo cherry for garnish
> Ice
> Martini glasses

Method

> Chill martini glass by adding ice and a small amount of water.
> In cocktail shaker, add ice, bitters, Bourbon, wine, and simple syrup. Shake all ingredients together.
> Discard ice and water from martini glass. Strain contents of cocktail shaker into chilled martini glass.
> Garnish with Luxardo cherry.

8

THE NEXT PART

HANNAH ARRIVED AT my place the next morning as promised, bearing gifts of lattes and breakfast wraps from the Cardamom Café. Just seeing the items brightened my mood. "Let's eat in the living room," I said, turning on the gas fireplace.

My cottage was designed and decorated by a Hollywood set designer back in the day, added as a guest cottage for the imposing wood lodge built for star Sally Allison, which sat across the small waterfall from my place. Sally was older now and away with her husband and family, sometimes in Southern India, sometimes in Paris, for long stretches of time.

For twenty years my dwelling had been the family home of Sally's daughter, son-in-law, and two sons—one of whom was Philip Young. After the family had no need for it, Sally turned it back into a guest cottage, using copies of the original wallpapers and chintzes. Not my style—at all—but so nicely chosen it never occurred to me to do anything more than add a sofa pillow.

We plated our wraps in the kitchen and settled our lattes on the coffee table before claiming the two pillowy chairs that faced the fireplace. "How did you not mention you have a giant of a brother named Zachariah Malachi?" I demanded.

"I prefer not to talk about our family dynamics much—as you may have noticed. You're right, he's not my blood brother. His dad, The Reverend Dr. Willard Jackson, is Dad's right-hand man. Zachariah arrived, even as an infant, fully camera-ready. He loves being in a crowd. He loves speaking—exhorting, even better. He

59

loves singing. He loves revving folks up. He loves all of it. He has become the anointed heir of Dad's kingdom."

"Wow," I said, though I could see it. "And...how do you feel about that?"

She expelled a breath. "Relieved. So relieved. As you know, I'm more the hands-on faith kind of person than a lead-from-the-stage kind. I love having a church and a community and working here to 'be the change.'"

"You're really all right with it?"

"I am SO all right with it. My gratitude knows no bounds." She sat for a minute. "What's up with Philip?"

She always knew the hard questions to ask. "How do you know there's something up with Philip?"

"You turned up at my place at 10:00 PM last night."

She had me there. I tried my best to explain what was going on with him. Which I didn't understand, at all.

"Rachel says it's part of why they broke up?" she asked.

"And I can understand why. He's like a different person."

"Well, you did say you were worried that he was too perfect."

"I guess I did."

"How long is he usually in this zone...painting, I mean?"

"I don't know. A week, maybe? I wasn't paying that much attention last time it happened."

"Okay, let's think about this another way. Let's say there's a regular person who, I don't know, sells roof shingles, and he has to be gone on a business trip one week a month—would that be a deal breaker for you?"

"At least then I could plan."

"Plan what?"

She had me again. My life was pretty much here in Tranquility, with or without Philip, and we didn't have kids who needed picking up after sports or formal events to which we'd RSVPed, which I'd now have to attend alone.

But we might, someday.

"He paints sometimes without disappearing from the world?" she asked.

"Yes, he does, most of the time. And those paintings are great. It's not like he's accessing some inner genius now that he doesn't have otherwise. But the paintings he's doing now are maybe more...dramatic?"

"My guess, and it's only a guess, is that he's working something out."

"Why doesn't he talk to me about whatever it is?" I said. "That's partly why I resent it. I feel shut out. Like, if he really trusted me, he'd tell me what's going on."

"Maybe, eventually, he'll feel he can."

"If I hang in."

"If you hang in." We sat, lost in thought. "Have you heard any more about the body they found last night?" She asked.

"Not a thing."

"What about the missing woman? Any news on her?"

"This part is interesting. She came into the Hatch on Halloween Eve. She graduated from Tranquility High School. Marta knew her from church, back when she was he. Said back then, she was really nice to the little kids at church. Played football, was well-liked. Left town for pretty obvious reasons. Came back this year to see her parents and because her high school class was having its ten-year reunion—which they have on Halloween instead of linked to homecoming or something."

"Okay. Interesting."

"She left a suitcase at the Hatch, saying she'd pick it up later, but she never did. It had her parents' address on it. I tried to return it on Sunday morning. Got there as they were leaving for church. They told me quite emphatically they have no daughter." I paused a minute to catch my breath. "I. Can't. Even."

"Heartbreaking," she said.

Whistle jumped up from where she was sleeping on the sofa that faced the picture window, barking like an eighty-pound watchdog.

The doorbell rang not twenty seconds later, making her really more of a notification dog.

First off, it was unusual that anyone came to my door at all. Second, if they did come up through the dale, it was a friend, who'd come to the kitchen door. Third, I was disconcerted because whoever it was had climbed the hill completely unnoticed and now stood on the other side of the front door. For the first time in a very long time, I had no idea who was at my door.

"You going to answer it?" Hannah inquired.

"I guess."

I walked over, Whistle joining me, lifting and replacing her paws and whirling like a member of the Riverdance troupe. There wasn't a peephole, since the only folks who came up originally had to be invited by Sally.

I opened the door.

There stood Inspector Mike Spaulding of the highway patrol. He wore a long black jacket, khakis, shirt buttoned up, no chain. Definitely on duty.

"I hear you have her suitcase," he said.

"Come in," I said. "What's going on?"

Mike came in and nodded toward Hannah, who stood up. "We're finished with breakfast," she said. "I'll be on my way."

"Stay, if you don't mind, Reverend Bricksford. I might need your expertise."

I motioned to the sofa. Hannah and I moved the side chairs to face him.

Inspector Spaulding looked at me, seemingly without malice, like I was merely a townsperson with whom he was familiar. Last time we'd spoken one-on-one, that hadn't been the case.

"Sandy Wilcox. Her body was found yesterday on Anvil Mountain. Her parents told me you had her suitcase."

I nodded. "Friday night. She was going to walk up to her parents' house and pick up the suitcase later. I tried to return it yesterday, but they declined to take it."

He was making notes. "Where is it now?"

"I locked it into the storeroom at the Battened Hatch, still hoping she might come back. If I can ask...what happened to her?"

"It's being treated as a suicide. Shot herself. She was alone. There was gunshot residue on her hand."

"Shit," I said.

"Shit," echoed Hannah.

"Did she say anything else to you when she was at the Battened Hatch?"

"Only that she was going to her high school reunion the next day."

"We're in the process of putting together a list of those attendees," Mike said. "She didn't mention anyone specific?"

"No. Marta used to know her from church. Said she was well-liked, back in the day."

"Yes, I got that they went to Marta's dad's church. As a matter of fact, that's what I wanted to talk to you about." Mike shifted to face Hannah. "I was wondering...well, truthfully, I was wondering if you might come with me to the morgue. I'm supposed to meet her parents there in an hour. They didn't want us to contact Tim Layton, their pastor, but I thought it might be good to have someone there. They have agreed to identify the body, but not to claim the body."

Monday was usually Hannah's day off, but I knew she'd agree, which she did without hesitation. She also sometimes acted as a fill-in chaplain for the police.

"Mike, have you heard anything about Jarrett Banks who fell over at the Appleton Lodge?" I couldn't help but ask.

Mike raised his brow. "Yeah, they've taken two statements from him. First, he said he saw the ghost of Adelaide and he fell or jumped to get away. Second time, he said he had no memory of how he got up there or why he would have gone."

I pondered this information. One statement seemed to make less sense than the last.

"Why?" Mike said. "Did you hear something?"

"Not exactly. But I was there, on the front of the property, when he came down."

"Dear God, Avalon. Can nothing happen in this town without your involvement?"

"Sure. Most of the things I'd like to be involved with happen without me quite happily."

"Tell me more. About Jarrett."

Oh, sigh. I really didn't want to get Marta and the others involved. But I didn't want to hide information, either. "I was with Marta and her friends Colin Keene and Toby Cabinau. Toby's girl-friend was talking about the Lodge out front when we heard a scream. By the time we turned around, Jarrett was...landing."

"And you didn't go find out how he was?" Mike sounded gen-uinely surprised.

"If I tell you something, could you not talk it around unless it's absolutely necessary? I don't want to get anyone in trouble, but I also don't want...to keep anything from you."

Our eyes locked.

"You know I won't," he said. "Unless absolutely necessary."

"Toby's brother Dwayne was there," I said. "He's a cop in North Pass. He told us, since we weren't involved, to leave. He took over handling the situation."

"Okay. So since you didn't hear or see anything, or since you weren't inside, that makes sense. I guess."

"We did not hear or see anything," I repeated.

"And you weren't inside, especially not anywhere near the entrance to the cupola."

"We did not hear or see anything," I said.

"Damn it, Avalon!"

"Well, it's not being investigated as a crime, is it?"

"He was trespassing. *As would anyone be who was in the Lodge.*"

Fudge.

"But no. It seems one way or the other, he jumped."

"When do you want to pick up the suitcase?"

"I'll send an evidence guy around this afternoon. I hope it will help us find who to notify, since Sandy Wilcox had obviously not been in touch with her parents."

Again, I was biting my teeth together to keep my mouth shut. The police would take her suitcase. They'd find the oxy. And whatever else.

"The Battened Hatch will be open today because Pepper's is closed. So I should be there to hand it over."

He sighed. "Good enough. Don't touch it between now and then."

"Got it."

He sighed again. "Thanks again, Reverend Bricksford. It's hard enough to meet with parents of someone deceased. Having you there will help."

"I'm not sure about that, but I'll do what I can," Hannah said. "Especially with suicide. It's so hard."

"I wish I was sure it was suicide," Mike mumbled.

"You said they found her alone, with gunshot residue on hand," I said, not understanding his confusion.

"Yes," he said. "It's been logged as suicide. But if it was...what happened to the gun?"

THE NEXT PART

Ingredients

2 oz citrus vodka
1 oz lime juice
½ oz Aperol
Splash of white cranberry juice
Fresh lime cut into wedges
Ice
Martini glass

Method

Chill martini glass by adding ice and a small amount of water.
In cocktail shaker, add ice, citrus vodka, lime juice, Aperol, and white cranberry juice. Shake contents together until nice and cold.
Discard ice and water from martini glass.
Strain contents of cocktail shaker into martini glass.
Add fresh lime to side of glass for garnish.

9

REALLY GOOD WHISKEY

Not long after I arrived at the Battened Hatch, the evidence guy came, impeccably credentialed, and took the suitcase away.

I was sad to have it gone. It tied me to Sandy, and made me feel somehow she might return, even though I knew she wouldn't.

Marvin, one of our older regulars, was happy to find we were open on a Monday. He sat at the bar and ordered whiskey. "Keep 'em coming." Of course, he meant the cheapest whiskey, and I'd only keep two of 'em coming before I cut him off. He was a lightweight, and he depended on me to monitor his intake. Still, he liked to say the line, and to have a bar where we knew him and knew his order.

"Did you hear about crazy Jarrett jumping off the tower at the Lodge yesterday?" he asked with his first round.

"I did," I answered.

"You should have seen them lodges in their heyday," he said. "It was really something spectacular. I 'as sorry when they burned two of 'em down."

"It was arson?" I asked.

"Sure enough. There was ack-cell-er-ant," he said, under his breath.

"Why'd they leave the main Lodge, then?" I asked.

"If I knew why one was left, I'd know why two were gone," he said. "Insurance, most like. Can't tell ya. But the lodges were really something. Say what you will, they employed the whole town, just about."

"They got shut down because of their exclusionary policies?" I asked.

Marvin snorted. "That's one way to say it. But, you got to know, thousands of clubs and country clubs and lodges and civic groups, swimming pools, beaches, neighborhoods, if they were private, they didn't have to let them Catholics in, or Jews, or them Coloreds. It wasn't just here. It was all over the place.

"A feisty Jewish lady tried again and again to join the Appleton Lodge, and every time they turned her down, she told the newspapers. That was way back before World War Two. They always said, 'You need a sponsor, we don't accept anyone without a sponsor,' and of course no one would sponsor her. But there was this Black fella, what was his name? Marvin Johnson. He had a friend who was a member, who sponsored him, for real or just for fun, I don't know, but they let him in. A lot of folks said it was so they could prove they let all kinds of folks in. But why? When it said right there in the booklet you had to be educated and White and Christian. Why disprove your own policies?"

I couldn't take much more of Marvin, and orders were coming in, so I moved on. Marta wasn't in today, and Davros and Manuela and I were handling the lower volume of customers.

The crew in the kitchen did great with the pub menu; in fact, they seemed to be enjoying the absence of their chef. Food came out fast, orders filled correctly.

At some point, my old friend Troy stuck his head in. "You open?" he asked, surprised.

"Yep. Not usually on Mondays, but we are today."

"Great!" He came in with Dani Rice, who worked with him at the new Pepper Porter/Sally Allison Theater Complex. I knew Troy from the olden days of high school back in LA. I was thrilled when he accepted the job as artistic director of the new theater, leaving his longstanding gig at the Old Globe in San Diego. Dani was the dramaturge who oversaw what was becoming a very robust emerging playwrights program.

They took a booth. Troy was Black and Dani was trans, and just their presence made me feel more comfortable—and more concerned—than I had before they came.

I, in all my blonde, White, heterosexual glory went over to talk to them.

But I had no words.

"We have a cheese-topped marinara that's really good today," I said. And I returned to the bar.

About ten minutes later, after they ordered and Dani was busily texting, Troy came over.

"So, what's up, Av?" he asked.

"I'm sorry," I said. "I realized I was being reductive. I have no idea what I meant to say. 'I met a trans woman on Friday here in the bar and now she's dead and she maybe killed herself because no one accepted her and I want someone to be sad with me'? That's stupid. Or, 'It feels like Tranquility really isn't safe these days for anyone LGBQ+ or of different ethnicities, so be careful?' I think you both are aware. I realized I had nothing to say. And the marinara really is good."

"Av," he said, and I loved the sureness and familiarity of his voice, a voice I knew well and had for a very long time. "Nowhere is safe as long as there are people who hate, whether they're White Nationalists or otherwise. As you know, I'm still trying Tranquility on for size."

"I know. And it's not just you, it's your kids. I love those guys. Let's get together again soon."

"Yep. Will do."

"Meanwhile, what's up at the theater?" We talked for awhile and I started to feel like my feet were firmer on the ground.

After they ate, as Troy settled up with Davros, Dani came over to the bar. "Troy told me why you came over," she said. "At first, I was annoyed. No, I don't know every trans person, no, I don't know how to find her friends, no, I don't know the particulars of her story, and no, I'm not going to lead the funeral choir. But I do want to say this. If she did kill herself, I am angry at whoever drove her to it. Because one thing I can tell you is this: she didn't 'become' a transgender person because she hated herself. She transitioned because she loved herself so much that she was willing to fight to be her true self. What business that is of anyone else's, I do not know. Whoever would have driven her to do it, well, no words. That's all."

"Thank you," I said. "I admit I'm feeling a bit lost. So, thanks."

And they left.

Usually, I love hearing people's stories and fitting them together in a way that somehow makes sense. It's why in the past I have enjoyed working with Mike Spaulding to solve crimes. And if a crime had been committed in Tranquility having to do with either Jarrett or Sandy, I was ready to get on it.

There just didn't seem a clear commission of any crime. Except maybe trespassing on Lodge property. I had that one solved already. It was us.

Around two o'clock, a man I didn't recognize slid up to the bar. He was White, medium height, with a good head of brown hair, neatly trimmed mustache and beard, and large brown eyes, wide-set. He looked like he was an off-duty newscaster.

"Hi," he said. "I'm Anders Evans. I'm looking for someone."

The usual bartender response is, "Aren't we all, pal?" but I suspected this was different.

"Try me," I said.

He found a photo on his phone and turned it around to me. "Sandy Evans. The last text she sent me came from this bar."

And yep, Sandy Evans was the person we'd all been calling Sandy Wilcox. In the photo, she was laughing, her hair falling backwards, a shadow across her face.

A five-hundred-pound weight dropped into the pit of my stomach.

"Yes," I said. "She was in here on Friday night."

"Have you seen her since?"

I have never wished harder for the company of Hannah or even Mike. Or, frankly, anyone.

What's the best way to give someone truly bad news?

"She, um...she died," I said.

Anders sat there, looking at me. His response turned from an annoyed *Why are you saying this?* to a different expression. It was a terrible, pleading look. *Please be wrong. Please let me have misheard you. Let it not be true.*

"I'm so sorry," I said. "And I'm so sorry to be the one to tell you. I don't know much about how to do this. Would you like a drink? I mean, on the house?"

He dropped onto the bar stool. He turned his phone around and looked at the photo, then brought up the numbers to dial. But then he turned it off and put it down.

"Yes," he said. "Whiskey."

I got our best whiskey and poured him a shot. He took a dram.

"Wow, good stuff," he said. I was surprised he even noticed.

"How did you know her?" I asked.

"I'm her husband," he said, and finished the pour. I refilled the glass. It was all I knew to do. "What happened?" he said.

"All I know is, apparently she went to her reunion. A day later some hunters found her body in the woods on Anvil Mountain. They...they think she committed suicide."

He immediately sat up very straight. "Hell, no," he said. "No, absolutely not." He pushed the whiskey glass back. "Where is she?"

"Uh, the morgue, I think. Her parents agreed to identify her, but not claim the body," I said as gently as I could.

He took out his phone again, scrolled through some items, and put it back. "I need to talk to someone. The police or someone. She wouldn't have committed suicide."

I pulled out my own phone and dialed Hannah. It took several rings, but she picked up. I drifted away from the bar and from Anders's hearing. "Where are you?" I asked.

"I just arrived at the morgue," she said. "I was about to enter the building. I see Inspector Spaulding at the door."

"Let me talk to him," I said.

"What is it?" she asked. "What's up?

"I've got Sandy's husband here. And her name is Sandy Evans."

"Wow. Holy smokes. Hang on."

I heard her car door shut, and within a few minutes, she'd gotten her phone to Mike.

"What is it?" he asked. There was still a slight edge in his voice. We weren't back to our easy camaraderie, but he was ready to listen.

I told him about Anders and his request to talk to the police.

"If he's the spouse, can he get over here?"

I turned around and asked, "Do you have a car?"

Anders nodded.

"I'm talking to Inspector Mike Spaulding, who is handling the case. He wants to know if you can come to the county morgue, now."

"Yes," he said, and he choked back his emotion. Then, to me, "Do you know where it is?"

"Yes, I believe it's one and the same as the local hospital morgue. We don't have lots of specialized services around here."

"And the local hospital is...?"

It was the midafternoon lull. The least I could do was drive him over. I offered and he accepted before I could finish the sentence. Granted, it is hard to find your way around when you don't know the area, you've just received terrible news, and you've been drinking. Although he only drank the first round.

I put Manuela and Davros in charge and grabbed my car keys.

REALLY GOOD WHISKEY

Ingredients

> 2 oz honey whiskey
> ½ oz lemon juice
> 1 oz orange liqueur
> Sugar on a small plate
> Lemon slice
> Ice
> Coupe glass

Method

> Chill coupe glass by adding ice and a small amount of water.
> In cocktail shaker, add honey whiskey, lemon juice, and orange liqueur. Shake all ingredients together until very cold.
> Discard ice and water from coupe glass.
> Rim glass with fresh lemon slice and dip into sugar.
> Strain contents of cocktail shaker into coupe glass.

10
THE REST OF THE POUR

"Inspector Spaulding is a good guy," I said, once we were in the car. "He'll listen to what you have to say."

"She wouldn't have killed herself without saying goodbye to the kids," he said. "She was being very purposeful about her goodbyes. She had terminal cancer, colon cancer. We'd done all we could do. She wanted to come and say goodbye to her parents, and see the kids she'd grown up with, maybe help them understand a bit.

"She was in a lot of pain. A lot. But she had some prescriptions to help so she could return here, just for two days.

"But then she was coming home to Brooklyn. She was going to talk to Liam and Meg, our kids, about her life, about their futures. She was going to make recordings for them, for them to listen to during important milestones. She had it planned out. She'd chosen a death doula. Saying goodbyes, the way she wanted to, assuring everyone of her love, it was so important to her. So important..." He broke down crying. I drove.

"And her friends. I mean, she had a great group of friends, but she worked for a nonprofit and everyone who came in for help became her friend...She wouldn't do this to us."

"How long have you been married?"

"We've been together for seven years now. But we've only been married for six months. We never thought it was necessary until Sandy got cancer. Then...then it became clear that for a myriad of medical and legal reasons, it would make everything so much easier."

We drove in silence the rest of the way.

At the hospital, I drove around to the back, to the small entrance marked *County Health Services*. Anders and I got out of the car and stood a minute.

"Are you okay?" I asked.

"No," he said. "In no way am I okay."

I waited for him to take the first step, and then we walked together into this hallway tucked away from anything people want to think about.

As we entered, Hannah was exiting the outer door that said *Morgue*, holding the door for the couple I'd seen outside their house on Sunday.

"Those are her parents," I said to Anders, and he shook his head. We let them pass and walk on down the hall.

"They're with Reverend Bricksford," I said. "She is someone who can likely help in many ways, if you need it."

The hallway we were in was functional and cold, the concrete walls painted in institutional green, the floors an ecru tile that might have started out white. Since this part of the building was lower on the hill, the only windows in the corridor were small and far above anyone's sightline.

We arrived at the glass door of the lobby that leads to the morgue. Mike was there talking with the coroner. He stood tall when he saw us and opened the door. "Mr. Evans," he said, extending his hand. They shook. Anders entered the outer banks of what amounted to many people's personal hell.

I stood in the frigid hallway, not knowing what to do.

Within a couple of moments, Hannah returned from the parking lot. There were no benches, so she leaned back against the concrete. I stood next to her.

"How did they take it?" I asked.

"They are shattered," she said.

"And guilty? I hope they feel so freaking guilty."

"I'm sure they do. But your heart has to break for them. They honestly believe they were doing the right thing, disowning their child. They honestly thought letting her come in and stay there would mean they were letting evil into their home. They've been taught to believe their beloved child has gone to hell. And no matter what you say about disowning your child, you love them in a deep and complex way. Your heart is broken. And you do feel guilty, wondering what you did wrong." She sighed. "I feel for anyone whose bad theology shatters hearts and tears parents and children apart."

"But if they'd questioned it, if they'd read the Bible and done their research, not just blindly accepted..."

"I know. But still, I feel for them. They've paid the ultimate price."

I sighed. "There is no way around it, you're a better person than I am, on every level."

Hannah's response was a pastor version of a dad joke: "Well, I'm paid to be good, whereas you're good for nothing!"

We both broke into laughter, mostly because we needed the release. Fortunately, we gathered ourselves before Mike stepped out into the hall.

"He's in with her," he said. "And here's a question. He asked, if he talks to their family and they decide they want to have a funeral here, is there a funeral parlor that would be appropriate?"

I remembered the signs that were put up in the auto repair places, and the fact Sandy's parents didn't even want Marta's dad notified. It was a fair question.

"Yes, I think that can be handled," said Hannah. "Let me make some calls."

Mike nodded, and Hannah headed out to the privacy of the back parking lot. "Your friend is a good one," he said.

I nodded. *You're a good one, too*, I thought. But I didn't dare say it.

The funeral parlor Hannah found was R. Richards and Sons, which the sign in the photo on the website announced was established in 1972. I took Mr. Evans back to MacTavish's after he gave his statement to Mike. I hesitantly asked Glenn MacTavish if he'd consider comping him a room for a couple of nights, and much to my shock, he agreed without hesitation. Anders went to his room to make calls.

He reappeared in the Battened Hatch just before supper.

"We're going to have a remembrance ceremony for her back in Brooklyn, but we want to have one here, too. We're not going to slink out of town. I talked to the funeral home. They sounded like understanding folks, and are keeping up with the times as far as their services offered, green burials, etcetera. I'm going to meet with them tomorrow morning, and if all works out and the body is released, we can have a visitation as early as day after tomorrow."

I nodded. "That all sounds good." What did I know?

"Avalon, I know we've just met, but the fact you met Sandy makes a difference to me. Is there a chance you can drive me to the funeral home tomorrow morning?"

"Sure," I said, feeling a bit off-center.

"And one other question. Do you still have that whiskey pour I didn't finish?"

In fact I did, as I wasn't about to dump it and I hadn't yet found another use for it. This time, he sat at the bar and nursed it, busily texting to family and friends.

Trying to turn my mind to something else, I went into the kitchen. "Hey, Stormie," I said to the sous-chef. "If I was going to order something that you wouldn't mind making, what would it be?"

She smiled. Supper rush was over. "What do you like?" she asked.

"It's for a friend. A pretty adventurous friend."

"When do you need it?"

"Just before closing."

"Leave it to me."

When I returned after closing, the kitchen was spotless and three takeout bags sat on one of the gleaming metal tables. "Thanks!" I said. "How much?"

"Not on the menu," she said. "My version of leftovers."

I walked to my car, into the world that seemed constantly about to unravel at all the seams. I pretended I didn't notice. I drove up to Philip's house and let myself in. I put the bags on the kitchen table with a note that said *In case you get hungry.*

Then I turned on the kitchen light just so he'd know someone had been there. Otherwise, the food might sit there for days.

I had no sooner pulled into my glade than my phone buzzed with a text.

Can I stop in for a minute? Hannah's text echoed mine from the night before.

Yes, please, I answered, echoing her response.

I went inside, saw to Whistle, and turned on the light by the kitchen door.

Then I put on the kettle and turned on the fireplace.

Hannah came in the back door, sloughed off her coat, and sat down by the fire.

"How do you do it?" I asked. "This is your day off. How are you still standing?"

"Oh, Avalon," she said. "What I didn't tell you is that Zachariah has cancer. That's the reason they were driving back from Montreal. He's had a lung transplant, and it bothers him to fly."

"What kind of cancer?"

"It started as lung cancer. So unbelievable, since neither he nor anyone in his family smokes! The doctors thought they'd gotten it all, he went through this complicated transplant, and even though his body didn't reject the lungs, the cancer has reemerged. Just about everywhere. His family is sure God will heal him, his friends are sure, my father and his father are sure God will heal him, but he's so sick."

"Oh, Hannah, I'm sorry," I said. And I hugged her. I'm not a big hugger, or even a little hugger, but this had me worried. She was my rock. She was everyone's rock. But suddenly, she sounded...unsure.

"That's why he stopped in. I'm not really on a direct route from

Montreal to New York City, but he wanted to talk to me alone. He said I was the only one who'd listen when he talked about the possibility of his death. I'm glad I could be there for him."

The plug-in kettle whistled. I poured two cups of tea. They both sat in front of us and went cold as we sat and stared into the fire.

THE REST OF THE POUR

Ingredients

1 ½ oz Bourbon
1 oz sour mix
½ oz maple syrup
1 oz aquafaba (garbanzo bean liquid that creates a vegan foam)
1 oz red wine
Fresh orange slice
Luxardo cherries
Ice
Rocks glass

Method

Add ice to rocks glass.
In cocktail shaker, add Bourbon, sour mix, maple syrup, and aquafaba. Shake ingredients together.
Strain over rocks glass
Take a spoon and turn it over. Slowly pour red wine over back of spoon into drink.
Add orange slice and Luxardo cherry as a garnish on a cocktail pick.

11

GARDEN OF BRIGHT MEMORIES

THE NEXT MORNING, I allowed myself to go down to the Cardamom Café and eat in. I wanted to feel part of the community, of the flow of people who weren't involved in a potential murder investigation.

I got my usual curried banana wrap with coconut and almond and a masala chai latte and sat in the dining room portion of the establishment. Avantika Azni, who owned the establishment, loved to invest in local artists. I happened to be seated under a large, vibrant canvas painted by Philip Young. This canvas had spoken to me even before I knew who'd painted it. The colors and movement of the strokes had pulled me in and evoked emotions I hadn't realized I had.

Damn Philip anyway.

Instead of displaying the artwork with "for sale" prices, Avantika herself purchased all the art at top dollar from the artist, then displayed a QR code that took you to the artist's other work. I wondered, given what had happened with Philip's art in Paris last summer, if Avantika might not be sitting on a small fortune with this painting. If so, she deserved to be.

I also wondered what was creating such internal churning in Philip to drive him to his current state. I hoped he'd tell me someday soon. I hoped he'd work it out.

The Cardamom was the place the locals hung out. We'd make room for a few in-the-know tourists, but in general, it was just folks. I noted that even Arthur Bristol, our current mayor, stopped in for an all-American bacon, egg, and cheese wrap, though he took it to go. Avantika was running against him in a hotly contested race that would be decided in a week, next Tuesday. Avantika wasn't the original candidate to square off against Art. His original opponent was Joseph Emberg, my predecessor at the Battened Hatch, and a beloved member of the community. Could Joseph have beaten Art Bristol? Even that would have been a tough fight. Like many communities, Tranquility had a wide rift between those who wanted to keep things as they'd always been and those who wanted to move things forward.

To the stalwarts, the new arts center—and those it would attract—served as a stark warning. Mayor Bristol and his crew were reminding us on every corner how we needed to hold onto our old values, our families, our religion. I'd read somewhere that folks will fight harder to keep what they have than they'll fight to get something new that they want.

But then, I'm not a psychologist, I'm a bartender.

I know, I know, often much the same thing.

Still, popular wisdom had it that Avantika stood for everything Old Tranquility was fighting against—an actualized woman of color who would welcome those artist types with all their crazy ways. Could she win? Would it have taken a younger White man to beat an old White man? With Joseph gone, we wouldn't soon know.

But then, if Joseph wasn't gone, everything would be different. I would have had lunch while changing trains, caught the next train into New York City, and never known life here in Tranquility. I'd be living in Brooklyn, possibly still in a brownstone belonging to my family for over a hundred years.

Okay, couldn't go down that rabbit hole.

In any case, I had personally taken advantage of the availability of early voting.

I checked my watch. Time to go home, prepare for the day, and pick up Anders Evans. But first, to clear my thoughts, I walked half a block down to the library.

The Tranquility Library was a beacon of books and information. From the street, it looked like a simple cottage, but it stretched out behind and below towards the lake. It's like walking into a magical house filled with books. Well, it is a house filled with books.

I didn't have much time, so I zeroed straight in on Agnes the librarian. She was at the checkout desk, which was just inside the front door. She wore a gray skirt, a beige blouse with little red books floating on it, and a gray vest.

"Good morning, Avalon. May I help you with something?"

"I have an odd question."

"Those are the most interesting."

"Have you heard of anything around these parts called Beulah? A place, maybe, or a contest that gave out medals?"

She looked thoughtful. "No. Any other clues?"

"A friend saw a picture of a well-dressed Black woman from decades ago, holding a necklace or a medal that had farmland and said Beulah. It made my friend curious."

"Still nothing, though I'll poke around in the local history books. Have you talked to Edison, the curator over at John Brown's farmhouse? The mention of farmland makes me wonder if it could possibly have something to do with Timbuctoo."

"Timbuctoo?"

"The farmland."

Another patron came in looking for a book. Agnes apologized with her eyes and moved on. I'd used this library before when trying to solve a riddle. In fact, the high school yearbooks had been very helpful then.

Did I have time?

"The local high school reunion last weekend. It was their tenth?" I asked.

"That sounds right," said Agnes.

I danced down the steps to find their yearbook.

It was the tenth. I looked at the posed photo of Frank Wilcox in the senior portrait section. Full, curly hair, open smile, secrets behind the eyes.

I'd promised to pick up Sandy's husband not long from now, so I sprinted back up to the main floor.

"I'll let you know if I find anything about Beulah," Agnes said.

That's the great thing about a librarian. Other folks might say, "Nope," and that's the end of it—but give a librarian a mystery and he or she is like a squirrel with a buried nut.

R. Richards & Sons Funeral Home was about a mile outside of town, up toward the mountain peaks that became a skier's paradise in winter. The parking lot was large and ran along one side of the building, the side away from the hearse driveway. The lot was surrounded by stately pine trees, giving a sense of sanctuary, of time passing, but things staying the same.

There were three other cars in the lot when we arrived, one of which was Inspector Spaulding's unmarked vehicle. Anders got a phone call as I turned off the car, so I got out to give him privacy. As I did, the back doors to the funeral home opened, and Mike Spaulding and one of his fellow inspectors headed my way.

The man with Mike was three inches shorter, not heavy, but compact. You wouldn't want him body blocking you. Although he, too, was in civilian clothing, his hair was brown with a receding hairline. He sure looked like an officer of some sort to me. He was White, mid-fifties, and no-nonsense, even in the way he walked.

He and Mike came to a standstill in front of me. "Avalon Nash, Inspector Cal Becker," Mike said.

I extended my hand and Inspector Becker gave it one serious downward shake before stepping away.

"I'll call the morgue," said Becker. His voice was low and a bit stubbly, like his hair. He headed for their vehicle.

"There are two of you now?" I asked Mike.

"I need a partner if it could be murder," he said.

"Did Anders lead you to believe it might be?" I asked.

"And..." he lowered his voice, although there was no one else even close. "There's something not right about the scene. Even if someone came along and helped themselves to her firearm. It's not quite right."

"Her firearm?" asked Anders as he joined us. "Where the hell would she have gotten a firearm?

"She didn't own one?"

"Never had, never would. She wasn't a weapons kind of person. Which makes it even crazier. If she had decided to off herself, that's not how...not how..."

"Again, I'm sorry for your loss," Mike answered. "The body will be released this afternoon. The funeral director can call and make arrangements."

Anders nodded. Mike continued to his car and they pulled out.

"Let's go and see if I choose to go with R. Richards," said Anders.

A thirty-something man in a nicely fitted navy blue suit opened the door for us. His nametag read Hector. His hair was jet-black and combed to one side. His shirt was light blue, tie navy, and he wore a wedding ring.

"Mr. Evans," he greeted my companion. "Please come in. We are so sorry for your loss. Let us know how we might help you."

He led us through the hallway, warm with thick royal blue carpets, and soft yellow walls with ecru trim surrounding long panels of expensive blue wallpaper. The chandeliers also had blue shades. It gave an air of being in the entryway of the house of a trusted friend who was richer than you.

Hector led us to French doors, trimmed in ecru with the same wallpaper pattern in place of what would usually be the glass panels. In a practiced move, he opened both doors inward.

I didn't know what to do. I wasn't family, I was Mr. Evans' ride. I had no say in any decision-making process—nor did I want any.

But Anders swept his hand in front, indicating I should precede him into the room.

I didn't have the wherewithal to excuse myself. I did love being in the midst of and collecting people's stories. And, I told myself, someday I might need to know what my options were. Like if my eighty-two-year-old husband Philip Young died. Or my twenty-nine-year-old boyfriend of the same name, perhaps soon, and murdered by me.

Rosa Santiago was a shorter woman—fifties perhaps, nicely dressed, black hair pulled back into a bun—who introduced herself as the proprietor. "Sorry to meet under such circumstances. Let's see how we can help carry the burden, even a little."

She led us into the nicest office I'd ever seen. There was a fireplace with a loveseat and two rounded, padded chairs in front of it, as well as a café-style table with four chairs. In the corner, she had a desk facing out with comfortable chairs in front.

"Coffee or orange pekoe tea?" she offered.

We both asked for tea and sat in the two rounded chairs in front of the fire. I breathed a sigh of relief, because this way Rosa would have to face Anders and I could be relegated to interested bystander.

"You're the proprietor?" he asked, "Rosa Santiago? The name of the business is R. Richards and Sons."

"When we bought it, we chose to keep the name as it's been known for fifty years," she said, informationally. "It's actually R. Santiago and Daughters—though I think you met my son-in-law."

"Interesting," he said, leaning forward.

As they talked, I noticed there was a security camera up in the corner. I wondered if Rosa had it installed, or if it was left over from the last owners. Or if it was one of those that looked good and didn't work. I made a mental note to notice any other cameras.

Anders continued, "May I ask what brought you to this business?"

She smiled. "My husband and I moved here thirty years ago. My husband's family was in farming. When my husband died, we had a hard time finding a funeral parlor that treated us with respect. In fact, many migrant families we know, although performing a necessary service, are hardly treated as equals. My son, here legally, chose to return to Mexico as soon as he graduated high school. He couldn't get away fast enough. I can't imagine him wanting to return for a high school reunion, after how he was treated.

"In any case, after my husband's funeral, my daughters and I sat down and discussed what to do with the insurance money. Myself and one of my daughters decided to train to become funeral directors. Most funeral homes in this part of the state are still traditional. We saw an opportunity. Depending on how you would like your wife's remains handled, I would either take you through these doors"—she nodded toward two tall wooden doors to her right—"to choose a casket, or I will take you through these doors" —she nodded the opposite direction—"and show you the various possibilities for green burials, cremation, and the like."

"Wow," he said. "Okay."

"We also pride ourselves on offering our services, and our respect, to folks who might not find as much at a traditional home."

"I'd like to see your less traditional room," said Anders.

"Now?"

"Yes."

"We're doing things a bit out of order," said Rosa. "But sure."

As we stood, there was a knock at the office door and Hector admitted Hannah. She joined us as we walked through the newer doors into the Green Burial Choices. It was, admittedly, beautiful and interesting. Instead of lines of caskets, there were biodegradable shrouds you could handle, small waterfalls, actual trees growing, and things I didn't have the time to explore.

Now that Hannah was here, I left Anders in her care. I gestured to doors that headed outside under the heading *Garden of Bright Memories*, and Rosa nodded me out.

Adirondack sun shone over a huge Edenic garden that had clearly been added after the original building. It was two acres at least, the perimeter enclosed by a fence hidden behind trees and bushes. You heard nothing from the road. There was the gurgle of the brook, the splash of a waterfall in some hidden glen, the low tones of a wind chime through tall, strong oak trees, Japanese maples, weeping willows. Sheesh, I'd consider spending eternity here even if they were getting up a group to go now.

"Oh!" came a cry, as a woman exited a copse of trees not three feet from where I stood. "Sorry," she said, "I thought I was alone."

"I didn't mean to startle you," I said.

"I was visiting my mother's tree. I mean, the one where her ashes are buried."

I nodded and went back to sit on a bench I'd passed. "I'm Joy Basking," she said. "I don't think I recognize you."

"Avalon Nash. I live in town and work at the Battened Hatch."

"Oh, nice. I grew up here, still have friends and family. I mean, living ones as well. I'm back for a class reunion."

She did look to be the right age. She was my height, her chin-length blonde hair in a blunt cut. Nicely dyed, but dyed nonetheless. Not that I'm a snob. "Ah," I said. "Last Saturday."

"Yes. Why are you here? Have you lost a loved one?"

"No, I drove Anders Evans over. Sandy Evans was his wife."

"Sandy Evans? I'm afraid I don't know her."

"Oh. I thought she was at the reunion." To her confused look, I added, "Wilcox. Used to be Frank Wilcox."

This computed. "Oh, yes, sorry. But why are you here?"

I guessed word hadn't gotten out.

"Um, she died."

Joy stared. Her mouth actually dropped open.

"No, she was fine. On Saturday afternoon, she was fine. She was the talk of the reunion, as you might guess."

"Well, she wasn't fine, she had cancer, but between then and now, she was shot."

"What? No!"

Why was I doing this? Shocking Joy? "You hadn't heard. I'm

sorry. Yes, her husband is here arranging the visitation and the funeral."

"*No.*"

She sat next to me.

"You said she was the talk of the reunion. How did it go over, her being a woman now?"

"Fine, I mean, lots of us were surprised, but when we thought about it, not shocked. She was...still herself, you know? When you talked to her, he—she—was who she'd always been. Friendly. Chatty. She'd always stood up for people who were different, and now she had no trouble standing up for herself."

"I'm glad to hear it," I said. "Were there those who didn't take it very well?"

"I'm sure there were, but they didn't dare...didn't dare...*she's dead*?"

I nodded. "Surely you've seen the signs at the auto repair? You know this town doesn't take to change very easily."

"I do know," she glared. "You said there will be a visitation and a service?"

"Yes."

"Do you know when? I've got to call everyone!"

"I don't know when. They will know inside, of course."

"She was shot? Oh, my God!"

She stood and headed for the main building.

What had I done? Should I not have said anything?

I still had Mike Spaulding's number in my phone. I texted: *Met one of the classmates who was at the reunion with Sandy on Saturday. I had to tell her what happened. I'm afraid she's going to tell everyone and perhaps they'll circle the wagons.*

It was a few minutes, but he responded: *We were hoping to talk to as many of them as possible one-on-one, before they had a chance to get their story straight. Thanks for letting me know.*

I stayed on the bench.

To reach the Garden of Bright Memories, you had to go through the funeral home, but once outside, there was an exit door to the parking lot. I exited.

I texted Hannah: *I need to get to work. Any chance you could give Anders a ride when you're done?*

Okay, she replied. For the record, with Hannah, "sure" means "yes" and "okay" means she's crazy busy and she'd really rather not but of course she would. Usually, I'd wait around but I really didn't want to. She sent another text: *You know Brent Davis, right? Can you contact him about putting info on the newspaper website? He can contact Rosa. I don't want to leave it to her with things happening so fast.*

In the parking lot, I found that Inspector Becker had corralled Joy. The two now stood looking over a piece of paper and circling things. "So these are the classmates who were in attendance?" he finally said as she nodded.

I got into my car and took off before anyone could stop me. Where was Mike? Why had he sent Becker back alone to talk to Joy?

Was it too late for me to become just a normal person who minded her own business?

Yes. I was pretty sure the answer was yes. It was too late.

GARDEN OF BRIGHT MEMORIES

Ingredients

1 ½ oz Hendrick's gin
½ oz elderflower liqueur
1 oz iced green tea
1 ½ oz fresh honeydew juice
Chunks of fresh honey dew in small cubes
Fresh edible flowers from your garden or can purchase at
your local market
Ice
Nick and Nora Glass

Method

Clean and cut a honeydew melon into small pieces. Save a
few for garnish. Blend the rest in food processor until it
becomes a juice.
Steep hot water with two green tea bags and let chill.
Chill Nick and Nora glass by adding ice and a small
amount of water.
In cocktail shaker, add ice, Hendrick's, elderflower
liqueur, iced green tea, and honeydew juice. Shake all
ingredients together.
Discard contents of glass and strain contents of cocktail
shaker into glass.
Add a couple chunks of honeydew to a cocktail skewer
and fresh edible flowers for garnish.

12

SUDDENLY SUSPECTS

B RENT DAVIS, THE editor of the local newspaper, came into the
Battened Hatch midafternoon. "Thanks for calling," he said. "I
did speak to the funeral home, and we've put information about the
visitation and a celebration of life on the website."

"Thanks," I said. "So what brings you in?"

"Avalon," he said in mock exasperation. "When I asked the police
about Sandy Evans' cause of death, the only answer was, 'The investigation is ongoing.' Which, to me says 'Why don't you mosey on
over and talk to the bartender at the Battened Hatch?'"

I trusted Brent to know when to share information and when
not to. He'd been a help on investigations gone by.

I told him what I knew that was discussable. As we spoke, Joy,
the woman I'd met at the Garden of Bright Memories, wandered in
and asked for a booth. She was soon joined by another woman who
slid in across from her. Both leaned in and started talking.

I excused myself from Brent and texted Mike, as if we were still
friends working a case together: *And so it begins. Two reunion attendees have arrived here and are urgently discussing something.*

Manuela hadn't taken their order yet, and I signaled her that I
would take care of them.

"Hi, Joy, welcome," I said at the table.

"Oh, hi, Avalon, is it? I thought this was where you said you
work. We're expecting several more people."

"Gotcha." I gave them menus, then leaned farther across the
table than needed to put down the silverware, because I wanted
to see the list they had. It was printed, maybe thirty or so names,

most of them circled in blue pen. At the top of the paper it said *REUNION RSVPs*. Of course, I had no non-suspicious reason to openly stare at it. But I did see one circled name that stopped me cold.

"Anything to drink?" I asked perkily.

"Are we doing this?" asked the new person.

"Cynthia, we said we wouldn't."

"But what we say and what we do…"

"Okay, okay, what have you got on tap?"

I named the beers, they ordered, and I headed back for the bar, glad to see Brent was still there.

"Do not leave," I mouthed, then brought the brews back to the table. "So you're staying in town?" I said to Joy, as if making small talk.

"What? Oh, yes. Might go to his, um—her…"

"Sandy's," I said.

"Sandy's visitation, if I can. Don't want the room to be empty."

"That's thoughtful," I said. "Want to order now or wait for the others?"

"We'll wait."

Once behind the bar, I texted Mike again: *Sorry to bother you and you probably know this, but Jarrett Banks was at the reunion. The guy who plummeted from the belvedere.*

Holy smokes. That told me there was more going on here than met the eye. And also, if you wanted to get my adrenaline pumping, this was the way.

Brent sat patiently.

I turned to him. "Jarrett Banks, of Appleton belvedere fame, was at the reunion just the afternoon before," I said. "It seems a mighty big coincidence."

"A coincidence," Brent said. "Nothing you could put in the paper."

"Can I ask you about the Appleton Lodge?" I said. He was a walking encyclopedia of knowledge of Tranquility and environs, past and present. I told him what I knew, and he made a few corrections and added some other interesting facts.

Apparently, a land company had purchased the acreage after the Lodge closed and had been trying to sell it for years. Every time a deal nearly went through, something big happened. Like a fire.

"I also heard they actually let a Black man into the club," I said.

"That was a bizarre story," said Brent. "Marvin Johnson. Maybe forty years ago. I don't think Marvin really wanted in. He wasn't stirring up trouble or making a stand. But he was a great sportsman and a fast runner. It was at a time that the club was having competitions with other organizations. I think Marvin was brought in as a ringer."

"Is he still around?" I asked. "He'd be pretty old by now. Has anyone talked to him?"

"No. I think he got tired of the hassle. One day he up and left town."

"No forwarding address?"

"My guess is he wanted to leave the Lodge behind. Wanted everyone to leave him alone."

"Don't blame him. Back to the story at hand, I know it's coincidence, but does Tranquility usually have reunions that end up with two people dead, or attempted dead, within the next twenty-four hours?"

"Not usually, no. If you hear of anything else that leads down an interesting path, do let me know."

"Will do. Oh, hey—" It occurred to me, if there's one thing as good as a librarian, it's a newspaper editor. "Does the name Beulah mean anything to you?"

Brent shook his head. "What's the context?"

"It was a word on some sort of medal or necklace that also depicted farmland. I think it belonged to a Black woman in times gone by. Not much to go on."

"Was Beulah part of Timbuctoo? Or someone who owned a farm there?"

It was the second time I'd heard the name Timbuctoo. "What, or where was Timbuctoo?"

"Back in the 1840s, the way states kept Black people from voting was to add a land requirement. Here in New York, you had to own $250 worth of property. It disenfranchised just about every Black landowner. In response, a White New Yorker named Gerrit Smith gave away tracts of land to Black famers up here in Essex and Franklin counties. They have an exhibition about it over at the John Brown Farm just outside of town."

"The John Brown, whose body lies a-molderin' in the grave?"

"Yes. Though apparently his soul goes marching on."

I'd heard of the reformer who'd started a slave uprising in Virginia that ended badly but many said was the kickoff that led up to the Civil War. I had no idea his farm was nearby.

When Brent left, I went into the storeroom that once held Sandy's suitcase just to catch my breath. When I came out, I ran into Marta in the hallway. She glared at me.

We were back at that. "Can we talk?" I asked.

She shrugged. No one else was in listening distance. I took a deep breath.

"You're a great friend and a great person. I count on your friendship. It means a lot to me. Philip Young is also a great person. Your relationship with him is your relationship. You should talk to him. He'll date who he wants to date. It's up to him. Right now, good luck to anybody. But I mean it. If you want to tell him how you feel, you should. You don't want to go through life feeling like there was a chance and you missed it."

Marta stared at me. "You don't just ask somebody if he likes you."

"It seems like this might be the time. He and I have been dating, but he's not engaged or anything, and some day he might be, to me or somebody crazier than you or me."

"But if he doesn't like me, I'll feel stupid. It will change things between us."

"That could happen. But I know how much he likes you and how much he respects your art. You might start with that, and calmly ask if he might ever see anything between you. Ask as peers, not as someone who will fling herself from a belvedere if he says no. That way, you can continue to be friends either way."

"You wouldn't mind if I asked?"

"Like I said, I think you're great. You're a sister to me. I don't want a boyfriend who's chosen me only because I'm handy. I also don't want a friend who resents me for having Philip as a boyfriend. Don't do it if it doesn't feel right. I only want our relationship—yours and mine—to be transparent."

"You wouldn't be mad if he left you for someone else?"

"If he leaves me for someone else, he isn't really mine."

She nodded and continued back to the bar.

What a crazy world this was.

Was Philip my boyfriend? We'd had a rocky start, stacked with wonderful moments. I was afraid my feelings for him ran too deep, exactly the same fear it seemed Marta had.

And yet our time together immediately after his return from Paris had been great.

Did I purposely choose people who would explode the relationship? Break up with me, go off to Paris for the summer, disappear into a sinkhole of art, both of which Philip had done?

I didn't know.

To change the tone between Marta and myself, I asked if she'd found out anything about Beulah, or if she'd heard of the farming collective called Timbuctoo. She'd heard of the collective in school but didn't remember much.

"There's an exhibition about it in John Brown's barn, apparently. Maybe we can stop over and see if we can find any clues. Do you know where John Brown's farm is?"

"Yeah, of course. It's right next to the Olympic ski jumps."

"Really?" How had I missed that?

A few minutes later, a woman walked in. She was petite with chestnut brown hair, some of it pulled back with a decorative comb.

She looked around the pub, saw the two women at their booth, hesitated, and instead came my way and slid onto a stool at the bar. "Hi," I welcomed her. "What would you like?"

"I want to look like I'm drinking, like I'm part of the gang, but I don't really want to drink," she said.

"Sure," I said. I made her a lemon drop with seltzer instead of vodka. She took a sip. "Wow, good. I should have asked for this a long time ago."

I smiled. "Let me guess. You're from the reunion. Gearing up to sit with Joy and friend."

"I think it's Kim. Joy and Kim."

"Got it. I'm Avalon, by the way."

"Cynthia. Wright."

"You heard about Sandy?"

"Yes. I haven't yet wrapped my head around it. I don't know that I'm up to everyone else's thoughts and opinions."

"I hear you. Did you know Sandy?"

"No," she said. "I knew Frank." She sipped. "I'm getting different stories about how he died."

"They're not sure yet."

"Maybe someone killed him?"

"Could be someone killed her. Do you know anyone who was angry at her?"

I was surprised at the speed of the reply. "Me. I was mad at her. Furious, more like."

"Okay," I said. "There has to be a story behind that."

"Not that I killed her. Of course not! I'd never kill anybody."

"Good to know."

"I just...I just..."

I let her sit.

"I miss him so much. Frank. We went out our junior and senior years. He was...great. Kind and funny and smart, the guy you seldom meet. I mean, he played football, but he wasn't in with the jocks. He helped fundraise for charity and stuff, but he never ran for student government. And he never went off on anybody, you know? The jocks would bait him and other people, but he was so even-keeled. He'd stand up for the weird kids and the gay kids if anyone came after them. It kind of shamed people into behaving.

"He was different, too, in that we made out and stuff but he never tried to get into my bloomers, if you know what I mean. I took it he was a gentleman. But the beginning of senior year, he said we had to have a talk. He said he knew he would leave town at the end of the year, and not with me. That I was special, I should go to college and do everything I'd been talking about. But we weren't meant to be together. He couldn't be with anyone from Tranquility. It was up to me, he said: We could date senior year, or break up and I could look for someone who might want to get serious."

A tear ran down her cheek. "It's obvious now. Duh. But back then, I was so hurt and so mad. Why wasn't I good enough? Why didn't he love me like I loved him? I thought we could have a life together, I really did." She was crying harder now. "Could I have done something different?"

I pulled some tissues from the box behind the bar and handed them to her.

"No," I said quietly. "It wasn't you."

"It's stupid, I know, to be mad at Sandy for taking Frank away from me. But I couldn't even talk to her at the reunion. Now, I wish...I wish..." She went back to her mocktail.

The outer door opened and another woman came in, one of those people who took up a lot of space and a lot of oxygen simply by walking into a space. She flounced over to Joy's table.

"Oh, God," said Cynthia. "That's Doria."

"Was she at the reunion?"

"No," she said, then lowered her voice and gave it a dramatic flair. "Her husband found out there'd be a trans person there and didn't *let* her come."

"Geez," I said. "Who's her husband?"

"Roscoe Cone," she said.

That's a name? I almost said. "Was Roscoe in your year?"

"No, he was a year older. We let spouses come and stuff, but they weren't there."

"Did you know Jarrett Banks?" I asked. Cynthia was turning out to be a real font of information.

"Sure. Everyone knows Jarrett."

"Did he seem mad? Or anything?"

"Oh, I don't know. I don't hang with his crowd. He was a jock. Hung out with the other jocks."

"So he played football?"

"Sure."

"How did the guys feel? The ones who were on the football team with Sandy? It must been an unusual experience for them."

"I don't know. Who cares how jocks feel?"

Her virgin lemon drop was almost gone. It felt like she was getting tipsy, even without the alcohol. An interesting syndrome I'd seen before.

Apparently the reunion table had placed food orders when I was back talking to Marta, and the food came up.

"You want to serve?" Manuela asked me.

"No, it's okay," I said, though I followed behind her and started bussing a newly empty table. As I did, Inspector Cal Becker sauntered in. Mike Spaulding was nowhere to be seen. I was reading too much healing into the rift in our relationship—another current failure. He sent Inspector Becker wherever I was.

Inspector Becker saw me, then saw the women at the table. I gave what I hoped was an almost undetectable nod in their direction and continued fussing at the nearby table.

"Hello, ladies," he said to them, flashing his badge. "I'm Inspector Becker. I came in to talk to the bartenders here, as it's where Sandy Evans left her suitcase. But then I saw you folks, all of whom are on my list of people to interview. I'm sure you all know much more about what's going on than almost anybody, and this seems like a more comfortable place to talk than going back to HQ."

"Inspector Becker, you have got that right," said Doria. "I just got here and my food hasn't come yet. I'll give my statement!"

"Surely," he said, and took down their names.

"But you weren't even at the reunion!" Joy said to Doria, hoping to jump the line.

Inspector Becker motioned, and she stood up, made a face at Joy, and followed him over to the opposite wall where he claimed a table. He pulled out a notepad and a recorder. Doria started talking before she even sat down.

I relinquished the dirty table to our busboy Andy and returned to the bar to find Cynthia gone. She apparently had decided that if sitting with her old high school friends was objectionable, giving a statement to the state police put it over the line of what she could handle.

The surprises kept on coming. A few minutes later Anders Evans entered the Battened Hatch and came over to chat.

"Some friends and relatives are coming into town today and tomorrow," he said. "In fact, a carload arrived a few minutes ago. They're checking in, but we're meeting for lunch. Can you put together a table for six in about twenty minutes?"

My eyes scanned the room. Between the reunioneers and the local authorities, it felt like this might not be the place. "Have a seat," I said, motioning to a stool in front of me. "I'm not sure this is the best place at the moment." I explained to him what else was happening in our establishment. "Let me see what I can set up for you next door in Pepper's."

"I'd appreciate that."

"In the meantime, can I get you a drink?"

"I'm now a paying customer," he said. "I don't need your best whiskey. How about a Vesper?"

I poured the drink early associated with Bond, James Bond, then swung through the kitchen to talk to Mindy, the hostess at Pepper's. Happily, they would be able to accommodate.

Back at the bar, I gave Anders the good news. Then, as a person who collected stories for a living, I asked, "Did Sandy tell you there was anyone she especially wanted to see at the reunion? It sounds like this was her time to say goodbye. Was there anyone besides her parents she felt she wanted to make things right with?"

He looked thoughtful.

"Her parents, yes. She mentioned a few friends she wanted to see in town, I'm not sure they all would have been at the reunion. A few places she wanted to visit, places she wanted to eat, stuff like that. She said she'd have to see how the weather was. With all the painkillers, she couldn't drive, so they'd have to be in walking distance. She took a Megabus up from Manhattan. It took over seven hours, but she was determined."

"So, besides her parents, it was all happy memories she wanted to revisit?"

"Now that you bring it up, she did say there was someone she hoped to see at the high school. Someone with whom she needed to tie up some loose ends. Something that hadn't ended well."

"Did she say what?"

He looked uncomfortable. He lowered his voice. "There was one guy on the football team who kissed her once, back when he was Frank. That first time, he let it happen. He figured maybe this guy was trying to figure out if he was gay. But the next time they were alone in the locker room, it was full-on assault. Sandy barely got away. The guy never spoke to her after that."

"Shit," I said.

"Yeah. I think she wanted to see if the guy had matured at all, if he wanted to own up and apologize."

It didn't seem to me like those were the actions of the kind of guy who grew up and apologized, but I didn't say anything. I guess if you're dying and a good person, you maybe try to give everyone a pathway to healing.

I changed the subject. "Does the name Cynthia Wright ring a bell?"

He thought for a minute, then nodded. "I think that was her

girlfriend. I think she felt bad for Cynthia, but it was something that would never work out. She made a decision—I'm not sure if she later thought it was the right one, to keep her true identity to herself until she left town. She knew her parents would never accept it, nor would most of her friends or her fellow athletes, or her friends at church. There didn't seem a point. This was her plan all along, to come back, happy, with her own family, if only to show younger people other lives are possible."

I snuck a look over at Cal Becker, wondering if he was filling his notebook with information as interesting as what I was hearing.

"Thanks for the tip about Pepper's," said Anders, finishing his drink and leaving a twenty dollar bill. "You'll be at the visitation tomorrow?"

I nodded. "And I'll be here if you need anything before that."

SUDDENLY SUSPECTS

Ingredients

Poblano Simple Syrup

    1 poblano pepper
    2 cups of sugar
    2 ½ cups of water

Cocktail

    1 ½ oz vodka
    ½ oz Ancho Reyes Verde
    2 ½ oz lemonade
    ½ oz poblano simple syrup
    Fresh lemon slices
    Ice
    Collins Glass

Method

Poblano simple syrup

Cut the pepper in half and discard top and seeds. Cut remaining of pepper into small squares.
In a medium sauce pan, add sugar, diced peppers, and water and place on medium heat. Stir occasionally until all sugar is dissolved. Simmer over medium heat for an additional 10 minutes to let peppers absorb some of the sugar water. Take off heat and let stand until room temperature. After simple syrup has cooled down, separate peppers from the simple syrup and set aside for garnish.

Cocktail

Add ice to Collins glass.
In cocktail shaker, add ice, vodka, Ancho Reyes Verde,
lemonade, and poblano simple syrup. Shake ingredients
together until cocktail shaker is cold.
Strain over Collins glass.
On a cocktail pick add some pieces of the sweetened
poblano peppers and a fresh lemon slice for garnish.

13
CLOSING TIME

IT WAS LATE when Mike Spaulding came in. We'd announced last call, and the few patrons left were taking advantage. None of them were involved in the investigation.

Marta, Manuela, and I were closing up. When I saw Mike, I couldn't help it—my heart sank. Why was he here, if he wanted no help from me, wanted nothing to do with me, if our friendship was over, *fini*?

"Can I get a drink?" he asked.

His top button was open, so off duty.

"Sure."

Marta saw who it was and added my closing duties to her own.

Mike ordered a beer. I chose one on tap and slid it over. "Sorry if I've been bothering you with texts," I said. "I realize someone like me who thinks they think like an investigator isn't always helpful."

"You've been helpful."

"I know when it became clear Sandy might have been killed that it was important to bring in another investigator. But why Cal Becker? Or didn't you have a choice?"

"Cal is our most by-the-book guy. If this goes the way I think it might, I need every *t* crossed, every *i* dotted—correctly."

"Okay," I said. "Why are you here? I mean, every time I text you something to look into, you send Cal. I know you're mad at me and I don't blame you."

He didn't say anything.

The room was dark, only small lamps along the bar and soft green lights under the rows of bottles behind me. Even in the dim light, Mike's face looked lined and worn.

I knew I should shut up right about then. I didn't.

"You're still angry at me?"

"Hell yeah," he said. He drank his beer. "But I don't have anywhere else to go."

"Where were you today?" I asked quietly.

"I waited until crime scene investigators all left the scene, then I went up there by myself."

"To Anvil Mountain?"

"Yes. Right where an old logging road begins. It isn't often driven; it's bumpy with deep ruts and things. She wasn't quite there. She was still in the woods. I had a feeling everyone was assuming she went up there, sat down, and shot herself. I didn't think so. It took me a very long time, but went tree to tree, bark to bark. And I finally did it." He looked up. "I found the bullet. They were looking at the wrong trajectories. I had a feeling she was standing up, and it was an impulsive act."

"I'm confused. Not to mention, she didn't have a car—wasn't supposed to drive if she had one. And didn't have a gun, or access to one, that we knew of."

"Exactly. What took so long was that I called CSI to come back. I didn't want to find—more specifically, collect—that bullet by myself."

"Why not?"

"Just crossing the *ts*," he started..

"What help will the bullet be?" I asked.

"Knowing the weapon gave us a clue—a direction, at least—that even I wasn't expecting." He sat up straight and looked around. We were both surprised to find the pub empty, the other lights turned off. Marta had finished and even locked up. We were alone. This gave Mike the confidence to continue. "It was a bullet from a SIG Sauer P226."

There was a moment of silence, as if that was a mic drop.

"I wish I knew what that meant," I finally said.

"It's a gun most often used around here as a police duty weapon. Not by state police, but by local precincts. There was a point when they were offered a deal."

We stood in silence.

"Maybe it's good news, because it narrows the suspect pool?"

"It's not good news, any way you look at it," he said. "And I certainly don't want to be on my own tracking down the owner of that gun."

Yep, I could see that. The only local Black investigator looking to implicate a White cop.

"Will Inspector Becker help?"

"We'll see."

"Do you know if any of the locals from the reunion class have become law officers?"

"Three, I think."

"Do you know their names? More specifically, was Jarrett Banks one of them?"

"No. Mr. Banks is, appropriately, in finance."

"How about Roscoe Cone?"

Mike looked surprised. "Yes, he's an officer. But I didn't know he was at the reunion."

"He wasn't. I only heard his name because his wife Doria, who is in their class, allegedly wanted to go, but he wouldn't let her because a transgender person would be in attendance."

"Okay, interesting." He took another drink. "You do talk to people."

"That was a case of overhearing."

He laughed. "You do overhear."

"I do my best."

He sighed. "Okay. Tomorrow's going to be a long day. I'd best get going and check in with my woman."

"You have a woman?"

"You'd know if we were still friends."

"You're going to make me earn it, aren't you?" I asked.

"Hell yes," he said, and threw a twenty-dollar bill on the bar. He wouldn't accept a free beer, even when he was off duty.

All the back doors were locked and alarmed, so I had to head for my car through the lobby. As I did, I found Anders Evans, along with a couple of his newly arrived friends and family members saying good night to each other and to Hannah. I waved as they started back towards the rooms.

Hannah saw me and fell into step. "Talking to them about the Celebration of Life?"

She nodded.

"Your days start early and end late," I said.

"You're just now noticing?" she asked. "I don't know how clergy members with families manage it."

"You must be tired."

"Ready to drop."

Just then her phone buzzed.

"Really?" I asked. "Still?"

She fought with herself, given the late hour, but then looked at it. It was a FaceTime.

Hannah grinned.

"I'm going to take this," she said. She stopped where she was to initiate the call, then continued towards her car.

I continued towards mine. As I did, I overheard her say, "Hey, you, what are you doing up in the middle of the night?"

"Night shoot," came the reply. "Just thought I'd see if you were up."

And she was out of hearing range.

Really? *Really?* I knew the voice—as did most people in the world, as it belonged to a well-known actor named Landon Presser. Granted, I knew it from real life, as he'd recently stayed at my place during the Tranquility Film Festival, which was where he'd met Hannah. They had seemed to hit it off. I guess they had.

So Mike Spaulding had a woman, and Hannah was FaceTiming a well-known actor.

Where did that leave me? Telling my fellow bartender she could ask my boyfriend if he was available?

What the hell was I thinking?

On the way home, I made a decision. I picked up a few items and drove back to Philip's house.

As I had several days before, I made my way around to the back of the house. And there he was, once again, shirtless, listening to music, this time with earbuds. The canvas before him was maybe five by seven feet. He had to reach, to really elongate his torso to make the strokes.

All right. Now or never.

I knew how to get this man's attention. I knew what aroused him—not that he needed much help at this moment. I knew which of my undergarments were his particular favorites. I knew a lot of things about him.

I unlocked the side door and went inside.

CLOSING TIME

Ingredients

I oz mezcal
A few dashes of spicy bitters
½ oz lime juice
West Coast IPA
Fresh lime, cut into wedges
Ice
Beer glass

Method

In beer glass, add ice, mezcal tequila, spicy bitters, lime juice, and top off with West Coast IPA. Stir all ingredients together gently.
Add lime wedge for garnish.

14

TIMBUCTOO

WEDNESDAY I HAD the morning to myself, finally. Whistle and I made our own breakfast, read news on my phone, and sat around. Smiling. As a couple, Philip and I made love often, but last night was the first time I was...*taken*...on an art studio floor.

Worked for me.

I could wait for him to get through this time apart if I knew his issue wasn't with me. I had newfound courage we could work it out.

I was only slightly surprised to get a text midmorning from Marta. My first thought was, could she somehow know what Philip and I got up to last night?

Turns out we weren't on her mind at all.

I can't stop thinking about the lady in the Lodge, she texted. *Any chance you would be willing to stop by the John Brown Farm with me on our way in?*

Of course, the John Brown Farm wasn't on our way in. It was on the outskirts of town, in North Elba. But (outside of this week) Marta wasn't one to ask favors of me, as far as going places with her. And, I admit, I was curious.

We'd have to leave in like 10 minutes, I responded.

I'll be on the sidewalk.

She was indeed waiting on the sidewalk on Main Street beneath her father's church and the attached parsonage. She climbed into the car as I slowed down. "Thanks," she said. "I drew it."

"What?"

"The medal she showed me. So I wouldn't forget."

She held open a sketch notebook, which showed a pencil

drawing of a rectangular metal. She'd colored it in; the feeling it evoked was vivid. Etched into the metal at the bottom were rolling mountains and farmland. Above was the sky and the word *Beulah* in large, fancy lettering. In the very center was a step-cut emerald or green gem of some kind. I couldn't imagine an actual emerald of that size.

"That's what she showed you?"

"Yes. And she wanted me to do something about it, I just don't know what."

We drove past MacTavish's on our way out of town. I knew how to get to the Olympic Ski Jumps. I've had experiences there I could have lived without. But I had no idea that if you made a right-hand turn a half mile before the sports complex, you would drive straight to the John Brown Farm State Historic Site. It was incongruous to see the towering jumps rising from the landscape in the background.

We arrived at a simple farmstead from the mid-1800s. A two-story frame house sat overlooking a large pond. The wood on the house was whitewashed, giving it color but costing much less than paint. My guess was this was what the Brown family would have done back in the day. From the side, you could tell it was on a hillside; there was a basement floor below with two doors. A small top floor was likely a sleeping room with low ceilings.

The property was multiple acres. Past the pond, a pathway led to a brown barn, maybe twice or thrice the size of the farmhouse. Next to the front drive were monuments with tall iron fences around them, undoubtedly the graveyard.

Our car was the third in the parking lot. Emerging into the brisk November day, it was easy to imagine it was early autumn back in the 1850s. Large clouds billowed gray over the mountains, obscuring the sun. Together, Marta and I walked toward the farmhouse.

A man in modern clothes—khakis, dockers, navy blue coat—saw us coming. "Oh, hello," he said. "I'm sorry to say you're about two days late."

"For what?"

"Touring the house and the barn. The historic site is open May through October. Nothing is heated. We're here today, closing up, turning off the water, that kind of thing. You're welcome to walk around, however. The grounds are open."

I shot a look at Marta. She wore her determined look.

"Sir," she said, and she pulled out the drawing she'd done of the medal.

"Edison," he said, smiling.

"Edison. I ran into a woman who had a painting of this medal. She said it was important that I find Beulah. The woman holding it in the painting was Black, and it looks like farmland, and the woman said her family was from here. I wondered if it might be connected to Timbuctoo, or if you knew if there used to be a farm called Beulah."

The man was wearing a cap, and he actually took it off and used it to wipe his brow while looking at Marta's drawing. Marta had added a bunch of facts she hadn't shared with me. My guess was she was filling in some blanks herself, hoping for help.

"Why didn't this woman come herself?"

"I only heard about Timbuctoo, about the farms, after she was gone. I wanted to check it out."

"I don't recall a farm called Beulah, but then again, I didn't know folks named their farms. I guess they do. I've also never seen something that looks like this. However. Melinda Elliot is down in the barn closing up the Timbuctoo exhibition. She likely knows more about specific farms than I do."

We thanked him and moved down the path towards the barn.

The large barn doors were closed against the frosty November morning, but we were able to enter through a smaller, person-sized door in the side. It smelled of wood. In place of animal stalls stood tall panels telling the story of Timbuctoo with illustrations.

The woman working there, whom we pegged as Melinda, heard us and came over.

"Hi," I said. "We're on a mission, and the man up at the farm-house said you were more likely to be able to help us."

She had shoulder-length hair that was gray with attractive white highlights. She looked to be in her fifties. "You've piqued my interest, certainly," she said.

Marta showed her the drawing, asking if she'd ever seen anything like it. Marta gave the same circuitous explanation she'd given earlier.

"Folks did name their farms," she said. "The story is usually told that Timbuctoo was a failure, and from some angles, it might seem to be. Gerrit Smith gave away 120,000 acres of land in forty-acre parcels to Black families. While many of them never came to claim the land—they were city folks, and didn't really know farming, or they'd heard the locals up here weren't exactly welcoming—but many did come. They built homesteads, and made co-ops, and farmed through the harsh winters. Of course, some who did know farming were used to warm weather crops, so it was a learning curve. But, as I said, many were proud of their land, and their farms, and what they'd achieved. I do have a book back here somewhere, of the families that did claim the land. I'm not sure if it would tell if they named their property, though."

"So some folks did make a go of it?" I asked, knowing full well that if someone gave me forty acres to farm up here in the mountains, in the winter, I'd be gone by spring.

"Oh, yes. They became well-established families in these counties. As much as they might have heard that local citizens might not welcome them, Essex and Franklin Counties were a hotbed of dedicated abolitionists. We had—have—both ends of the spectrum."

She looked thoughtfully through the book. "If you go up to the Old Military Road Cemetery, in the old section you'll find the graves of the Epps family, one of the first Black families to come here to homestead. They arrived in 1849, made a go of it, and stayed. Lyman, Sr. was a teacher and helped found the public library. His son, Lyman, Jr., was the oldest living man in the county when he died in 1942. He was 102. He was celebrated for having sung at John Brown's funeral in 1859. So there is a lot of ongoing history here."

She perused the ledger in front of her. "Wait. I hadn't seen this before. Or, I should say I hadn't noticed it. She read, "John Brewster, thirty-six years old, wife and two children. Land in North Elba, Victory Farm. Winchester Franklin, wife Sarah, three children, Land in North Elba, Beulah Land."

"Really?" Marta was excited. "Does it say where the farm was?"

"It gives coordinates. Shall I write them down for you?"

"Yes, please!"

Back in the car, heading for work, Marta input the numbers into her phone. "I don't really know how to read coordinates," she said.

"That's why God created smartphones," I said, hopefully, since I couldn't have gotten us there, either.

"Can we try to find the property now?'

I sighed. "If we weren't both the manager and assistant manager who should have started opening fifteen minutes ago."

"I'm actually not on today," she said.

"Well, if I were you, my first step would be to find out if the family of Sarah and Winchester Franklin still owns that property. I mean, it's been nearly two hundred years."

"Good point," she said. "Who would know?"

"Maybe Google 'Essex County property search'? I'd also stop by the library to see if anyone there knows any oral history about the family."

"Good leads," she said. "Thanks."

I parked behind MacTavish's, and she headed down the street, already putting her phone to work to find the family of a ghost.

TIMBUCTOO

Ingredients

2 oz Boukha Bokobsa Fig Brandy
1 oz amaro
½ oz simple syrup
2 dashes of chocolate bitters
Luxardo cherry
Fresh orange peel
Ice
Nick and Nora glass

Method

Chill Nick and Nora glass by adding ice and a small amount of water.
In cocktail shaker, add ice, Boukha Bokobsa, amaro, simple syrup, and chocolate bitters. Shake together until cocktail shaker is cold.
Discard contents of Nick and Nora glass.
Strain contents of cocktail shaker into glass.
Add Luxardo cherry to cocktail pick and add to top of glass for garnish.
Twist a small piece of orange peel to release some oils over drink and also add to side of glass.

15
VISITATION

I OPENED AND worked the lunch rush at the Battened Hatch. Visitation at the funeral home was two to five, so I could stop in for a while and still be back for dinner service. One thing about wearing bartender black—it will take you almost anywhere.

Hector, in his fine suit, was once again at the funeral home, opening the door and welcoming people. Rosa Santiago and one of her daughters, Elena, also said hello and answered any questions. Things were set up in a side room. There was no casket, only a large photo of Sandy Evans. On a front table were many frames, photos of her with family and friends, most often laughing, several of her serving cookies. There were a lot of cookies.

Out in the hallway, there was a book to sign. I noticed that some folks were leaving sympathy cards for the family on the table with the sign-in book. I hadn't thought to bring one. There was also a brown lunch bag with a name on it, and I wondered briefly if someone had brought cookies.

Anders was there with their two children, Meg and William—called Liam—who were eight and ten. Anders told me he'd been married before, and his wife had died of breast cancer. Sandy hadn't felt the need to have her own biological children, but Meg and Liam were young enough when their mother died that Sandy was the only mom they'd ever known. Liam wore trousers and a suit jacket, and Meg did the same. "I let them pick their outfits," Anders said. "As a matter of fact, I let them decide whether they wanted to come."

He introduced me to half a dozen family members and close

friends who'd been willing to drop everything and come to Tranquility. Together they took on the job of providing hospitality. There were maybe twenty locals who came and went while I was there. Hannah stopped in and met everyone and stayed as long as she could.

Marta and Colin came by, Toby with them. Lily, they said, might come to the celebration the next day.

We were talking together when Toby's brother Dwayne came in. He was in uniform.

As he signed the book, Mrs. Santiago pointed the paper bag out to him. He checked the name on it and stashed it in his pocket. Not cookies, then.

When Dwayne saw me, he winked.

At the very beginning, another reunioneer was there, a guy named Chuck, who was maybe six foot two and had a big personality. He had a mop of blondish brown hair, still plenty of it, and he was happy to see just everybody, even high-fived Dwayne. Still, when he went into the remembrance room, he was appropriately somber.

As he did, I heard two women whispering that Chuck not only ran a large trucking company, he had a life-changing experience with 'natural' drugs and was now a guide for people on their own drug journeys.

I almost laughed. Was that what I did, too? And cut them off before the journey got too over the top? Most often, my part of helping with peoples' journey involved listening. I wondered if Chuck was the same way. In any case, he seemed open and together, not what I'd think of as a modern-day shaman.

According to them, there was another old schoolmate in attendance, Sheila, who had a successful hair salon in Plattsburgh, even though she was so shy she never said a word to anyone in all four years of high school.

I had a feeling Sheila talked a lot, just not to them.

Both inspectors were there in street clothes. Even streetier clothes than normal. Cal would never blend in with his haircut, and neither would Mike, not around here, although my old friend Troy came in before I left. He hadn't known Sandy. I was pretty sure he was there for me, and for the arts community, who stood by those who had a different calling.

Finally, her rounds complete, Hannah had a minute to stand next to my unobtrusive position against a side wall. We people-watched for a minute, and then I said, "Really? Landon Presser is calling you? When were you going to mention this to me?"

She smiled. "He's a nice guy."

"Becoming a good friend?" I asked.

"I guess."

"His mom is an Episcopal priest?"

"Yes. So he isn't put off by the collar."

"I want in on this kind of information," I said.

"I'll try. Didn't want to jinx our friendship, his and mine, by talking about it too soon."

"You believe in jinxes?"

"Only the kind we create ourselves."

"Anyone here from Tim Layton's church?" I asked about the congregation where Sandy grew up.

"Marta and Colin," she said.

"Can you imagine not going to your own child's visitation?" I asked, because I couldn't.

My mother, back in Los Angeles, is a well-known comedic actor and stand-up comedian who is openly lesbian. My father is a well-known conservative minister. He and Mom were together during his wild oats days before she'd decided to slide all the way in the other direction and before he'd found religion and become intolerable. Still, I was pretty sure he'd come to my funeral, if only to warn people onto the correct path in the afterlife.

Doria Cone was not in attendance. Only a smattering of folks from the reunion class were. Chuck and Sheila and the gossipers pretty much sewed it up as far as I could tell. Truth is, I wasn't so interested in Doria's attendance as I wanted to see her husband, the now mythic Roscoe Cone.

After Hannah left, Mike joined me in the same out-of-the-way place.

"Officer Cone isn't here," I said. "Did you get the other officers' names?"

"Yes. The other law enforcement officers from their class are Braden James, who's hit the big time and works in the city of Plattsburgh, Rick Norton, who works the next town over, and Dwayne Cabinau who works in North Pass."

"Any of them without alibis?" I asked.

Inspector Spaulding looked at me, as if wondering if I were serious.

"The moment word got out that she was killed by a bullet from a SIG, the Thin Blue Line circled around all of them," he said. "Apparently, the night after the reunion, they were each out with at least a dozen fellow officers in three different bars within a twenty-mile radius. Alibis put together by men who know how to question people. We'll never pick those alibis apart."

"Aren't there security cameras outside bars and stuff?"

"We will never pick those alibis apart," he said slowly.

Mrs. Santiago approached to ask if I knew where Hannah had gone. I admitted I didn't.

Mike took that opportunity to move on.

It was at that point Marta saw me and beckoned me out of the room. First, we went into the restroom to talk, but it was busy with women coming and going, so she led me across the hall into an unoccupied room. She looked about to burst.

"I found her," she said.

"Found who?"

"Letitia Franklin-Johnson. Descended from Sarah and Winchester Franklin."

"What? You did? Already? How?"

"You were so smart to send me to the library. One of the

librarians is very knowledgeable about the history of local families. The Franklins were prominent in town for a long time. As the generations passed, most of them left the area. No one wanted to keep farming. They sold the land. Letitia lives in town, back by the cemetery. She worked as a preschool teacher here."

"Did she know about Beulah?"

Marta's face clouded. "I don't know. She didn't want to talk to me. She kept insisting I tell her who told me about Beulah and showed me the medal. And if someone showed me the medal, why didn't I have it? I kind of had to admit it was a ghost. She sort of shut the door after that."

"Oh. I'm sorry. I'm guessing that's not what you were hoping."

"I don't know what I was thinking. In the movies, you know, she would have invited me in and showed me pictures of her ancestors, and I would have said, 'That's her! That's who I saw!' We would have gone back together to the farm and found the medal and it would have a map on the other side, and we would have found precious treasures."

"That was a specific set of expectations," I said.

"Yeah, I know. But she thinks I'm nuts. I should know better by now. I should know better than to go around telling people I see people others don't see."

"Well, shoot," I said.

"Yeah. She also said no self-respecting member of the Franklin family would be found, living or dead, in the Appleton Lodge."

"Damn."

It didn't seem like "Well, you tried," would be helpful, so we just gave each other a "Well, that sucks" look and she headed out.

It seemed like a good time to leave. I went to fetch my coat from the coat room. Just before the last turn, I heard a low male voice saying, "Be careful, Spaulding. Heard you been poking around about bullets and things you shouldn't care about."

No response.

"Yep, you just be grateful we let your slave-people ass hang here in peace. Would hate for things to get less peaceful."

"I am not descended from slaves," Mike responded, "but that doesn't mean it wouldn't be a pleasure to clock you."

"*What did you say?*" was Dwayne's retort.

"Okay, see you in a minute," I said to an imaginary companion and swung around the corner to see Dwayne Cabinau standing back from, but not unlocking eyes with, Mike.

Dwayne grabbed his patrol jacket and stomped away.

"Mike, WTF," I said under my breath. "You're going to let him get away with that?"

Mike didn't even look at me. "You choose your battles. And you let them show themselves."

He stalked away.

I was still shaking when I found Marta, Colin, and Toby, who were getting ready to leave. Marta and Colin both ducked into the restrooms, this time to use the facilities. When they did, Toby said to me, "Do you know Reverend Bricksford?"

"Yes."

"Is she...a real minister?"

It occurred to me he attended a conservative church that didn't have women serving on committees, let alone leading worship.

"Yes," I said. "She's a real minister, over at St. James Episcopal Church."

"Hunh," was all he said.

Out in the parking lot, we headed for our separate cars. Dwayne came barreling out as we did and threw his arm around the neck of his younger brother.

"I'll see you later," he said to Toby, mussing his hair in a gesture that seemed more threatening than little brother buddy-buddy.

I really should have controlled myself better. I glared at him.

He didn't let it go. He stopped outside his cruiser and said, "What's up, Avalon Nash, 2 Cherry Lane, off Elm Street." He took a step closer. "Hope you haven't been trespassing any more lately. Or anywhere near a belvedere where a man might be pushed off."

My chin dropped. He turned back to get into his car.

"What is wrong with you?" I asked. Out loud. Couldn't help it.

He turned around and gave me a wide, crooked Tom Cruise grin.

Shit.

I'd known not everyone in Tranquility was nice. But I had never before come upon this obvious of a magma flow of hot hatred. And I wondered just what he knew about his fellow officers, who might have done what, and how he could best hold it over them.

On the drive back to work, I thought about the fact Sandy was killed by a bullet, likely from a police officer's duty weapon. That particular SIG didn't have to be a duty weapon, of course. Even if it was, it could have been 'borrowed' from the officer by a friend or relative. It didn't prove an officer shot her.

What reason would an officer have to be up in the woods with Sandy? Did she go willingly? Was it possibly someone helping her to end her pain early? It didn't seem that way.

If the police were all tightly inside the Thin Blue Line, we might never know.

Yet, if there was a non-suspicious reason for that gun to have been used, and to disappear, why wouldn't its owner speak up?

More to the point, did Dwayne Cabinau know anything? He was enjoying this a little too much. Was he perhaps lording his knowledge over a fellow officer the same way he seemed to be holding knowledge of my trespassing over me?

I hated the feeling that justice would very possibly not be served. I hated the knowledge of what Mike had to put up with as a Black inspector.

More than hated it. It made me nauseous.

I took several deep breaths, got into my Subaru, and headed back into town.

VISITATION

Ingredients

Rose Petal Water

> Fresh rose petals (reserve some on side to float in
> cocktail)
> 2 cups of water

Cocktail

> Sparkling rosé wine
> Fresh strawberries
> 1 ½ oz strawberry vodka
> 1 ½ oz rose petal water
> 2 cups of water
> Ice
> Large wine glass

Method

Rose Petal Water

> In medium sauce pan, remove rose petals from one rose,
> add 2 cups of water. Turn on medium heat. Let simmer
> for about 30 minutes or until rose petals lose their color.
> Remove from heat and let cool. Strain petals from water
> after cooling and discard. Put remaining rose water in
> cooler for storage.

Cocktail

Dice two strawberries. Put them into large wine glass and
fill with ice.
In cocktail shaker, add ice, rose water, and strawberry
vodka. Shake ingredients together until cocktail shaker is
cold.
Strain into wine glass. Top off with sparkling rosé wine.
Add whole fresh strawberry to side of glass for garnish
and float a few fresh, cleaned rose petals to top of drink.

16
NIGHTTIME VISITORS

I HAD UNTIL closing to think about the growl in Dwayne's voice when he had looked square at me and told me my name and address.

Turnabout seemed fair play. If he had researched me, I'd do the same. My attitude wasn't helped by finding internet photos of Dwayne Cabinau and Roscoe Cone, each receiving commendations from their police departments, each in groups of White men smiling and getting plaques, although Dwayne's plaque had been years ago.

Roscoe had gotten both a plaque and a general commendation badge thing. I had never met him, which was probably why he was becoming the boogeyman in my mind. Who doesn't let his wife go to a reunion?

After work, I sat by myself in the emptying employee parking lot, wondering if anyone was watching me. Wondering if anyone who had access to my address was waiting for me at home. Without Sally in residence, the place was well out of sight of any living being and deserted.

Fudge.

I felt I'd used up my one Insinuating-Myself-Into-Philip's-Art-World ticket the night before. Fudge.

Knowing how much was on Hannah's plate and not wanting to bother her, I couldn't help myself. I texted: *Are you still up?*

Barely.

Which meant no.

I'm sorry, but can I stop in to ask you a question. One question. I'm going crazy.

Of course.

I pulled out of the parking lot heading for Hannah's. All of a sudden I had a bad feeling about Whistle alone at the house and drove home as fast as possible while not exceeding the speed limit by even a breath. Despite my worst fears, she was alive and well. I loaded her into my car. I left all the lights on. If any were off on my return, I'd go elsewhere.

Where elsewhere?

Not to the police.

I had to get a grip. They couldn't all be like Dwayne. One bad apple and all that.

I pulled up in Hannah's circular drive, past the house, and parked in front of her garage. I didn't want it to be obvious I was there and bring bad luck on her. She saw me and was waiting by the back door.

"Come in," she said. She was in sweatpants and a T-shirt. "Can't wait to hear this."

"I am so sorry. I know you're beat. But you've ridden along with local police departments as chaplain."

"I'm a backup chaplain."

We sat on the sofa in the living room, comfortably, with only the light from the kitchen behind us.

"Dwayne Cabinau, who is from Tranquility but now works as an officer in North Pass, was at the reunion. Then today, he was angry at Mike Spaulding and angry at me. In the parking lot, he made sure I knew he had my name and address memorized. How threatened should I feel?"

"Oh, geez, Avalon. I'm sure he was trying to scare you."

"Well, yeah. He also insinuated he might be willing to frame me for pushing Jarrett Banks off the belvedere. Why would he even say that?"

"What had happened just before this run-in?"

"I heard him saying racist things to Mike Spaulding."

"So you've got something over on him that could possibly get him into trouble. Are you planning to report what you heard?"

"Mike doesn't want me to."

"Then you should be okay."

As she said that, Whistle's ears perked up. I grabbed her to keep her from running and barking. My eyes followed her sightline outside Hannah's large living room window to the front of the house.

A car had pulled off the road into Hannah's driveway. The moment it did, the driver cut the headlights and it proceeded up the hill in darkness.

"Is it too late to change my answer?" Hannah asked. "You. Go into the other room and be ready to call the police. Aw, heck, maybe call Mike? If necessary."

She went to stand to one side of the picture window, where she had a clear view of whoever would be approaching the door. We both stood ready to jump into action.

Hannah then signaled me to leave the room.

I took Whistle and backed into the kitchen. I looked for something to grab as a weapon, and settled on the base of a blender. Just in case. Not practical, but heavy. Could likely knock someone out if I hit him on the head from behind.

Outside, the engine was cut. The car door opened and banged shut. She squinted to make out the figure approaching the steps.

"It's that kid who was with Marta and her friend today."

"Colin?"

"No," she whispered. "Colin is the friend. The other one."

The kitchen had doorways on either end, one that opened into the dining room, the other into the living room. I stood closest to that end, only steps from the living room from where I could easily monitor the proceedings.

There was a hesitant rap at the front door. Hannah opened it.

"Hi," said Toby, "can I come in?"

Hannah opened the door and he slid through into the living room.

I stood quietly. Whistle knew something unusual was happening. She sat looking up at me.

In the living room, Hannah reached to turn on a lamp by the sofa.

"No!" Toby said. "Please."

She left the light off.

"I saw you with Marta today, right?" Hannah asked conversationally. She sounded calm.

"Yes. I'm Toby Cabinau."

"Dwayne's brother?"

"Yes."

There was a pause. Hannah let the space expand. Finally Toby continued.

"I, um, I need to talk to somebody and Avalon from the Battened Hatch said you were a real minister."

"I am a real minister," Hannah said. "What do you need to talk about?"

"Forgiveness, I guess. I'm not Catholic, but maybe I need to confess. I don't know. I don't know. But I think someone should know."

"Do you want to sit down, Toby?" she asked. "Do you want tea or something?"

"Naw," he said. "I can't stay long. I shouldn't be here. It's late. But I'm so...sorry."

"All right," she said. "Why don't you sit down here and tell me whatever it is that's got you upset?"

Usually at this point, I would quietly leave the room, if not the house. But it was Dwayne's brother. Instead, as Toby sat, I did, too, on the kitchen floor. I put the blender base beside me.

"What happened?" Hannah prompted again.

"Frank Wilcox," he said. He started to cry.

"Take a breath. Tell me from the beginning."

NIGHTTIME VISITORS

Ingredients

Honey Simple Syrup

> 1 cup water
> ½ cup fresh honey

Cocktail

> 1 oz rye whisky
> ½ oz cynar
> ½ oz Amaro
> ½ oz honey simple syrup
> Few dashes of orange bitters
> Fresh orange peel
> Ice
> Coupe glass

Method

Honey Simple Syrup

In medium sauce pan, add water and fresh honey. Stir over medium heat until honey is dissolved. Take off heat and bring to room temperature. Store remaining honey simple syrup in cooler.

Cocktail

In cocktail shaker, add ice, rye whisky, cynar, Amaro, orange bitters, and honey simple syrup. Stir all

ingredients together and strain over cocktail strainer into coupe glass.
Twist fresh orange peel over glass to release essence oils over cocktail.
Float orange peel in glass for garnish.

17

FROM THE BEGINNING

TOBY TOOK A deep breath.

"Back when he was Frank Wilcox, he went to school with my brother Dwayne. He went to the same church as me and Marta. He played football. He went out with girls. He was a guy. He was a guy I wanted to be like. I think Dwayne did, too. I think he was a teammate of Dwayne's. Not a member of his posse, but you know..."

"Dwayne saw Sandy at the reunion on Saturday," Hannah prompted.

"Yes. He and his friends planned to go to the reunion, then go out after, you know? Celebrate Halloween. Dwayne had traded a shift and gotten off work, which isn't easy on Halloween. But he was so mad after the reunion. He didn't stay for the whole thing. He came home to my mom's house with some of his old high school friends. They were all freaking out that Frank was Sandy. Freaking out. Saying...not nice things."

"Who else was there?" asked Hannah, casually.

"I don't know. And even if I did, I wouldn't say. This is me confessing. Only me. I barely have the courage to do this."

"Where was your mom?"

"She was there. Upstairs. These guys used to hang out in our basement all the time when Dwayne was growing up. Mom likes having the boys around, and Dwayne isn't around much anymore. They came in through the front door and came down. I heard them saying hi to Mom, just like the old days. Anyhow, I was down there playing games online."

"Got it. Okay. Go on."

"I guess S…"

"Sandy."

"Sandy wanted to talk to Dwayne at the reunion, but he wouldn't. She gave him her number in case he wanted to talk later. He had been too freaked out to set anything up, but after he and his friends started drinking, they decided he should say yes. In a way, it was kind of funny because Dwayne started to text her, but…" Toby shook his head. "Finally one of his friends grabbed his phone and texted—as Dwayne—that he'd pick her up."

Whistle, who had been sitting next to me, decided it was time to check things out further. She headed into the living room. I grabbed for her but missed. I cursed quietly as Whistle eluded me, joined Hannah, and hopped up on the couch. Toby jumped.

"Sorry," said Hannah. "Are you allergic?"

"No, it's fine, I just wasn't expecting a dog, is all."

"She'll climb into your lap if that's all right."

Whistle would do that. If she feels someone is upset, she will climb into that person's lap and lie down, absorbing any hurt she can.

Toby continued, Whistle the comfort dog curled up in his lap.

Only then did it occur to me that I should be recording this. Toby was talking softly, so I wasn't sure I could get a decent recording, but it seemed I should try. I didn't know the rules for confessing things to clergy. I also didn't know what he was planning to confess, but it seemed it had something to do with Sandy.

I grabbed my phone and hit record. I was sitting against kitchen cabinets, out of sight but still. I hid the phone face with my hand as it lit up and until the light once again gracefully bowed out.

"Anyway, a bunch more of the guys came over to my mom's house. The basement also has an outside door and concrete steps where you can come and go, and they came down those. I was trying to just concentrate on my game. Dwayne decided it was time for me to join them. He said he'd been much younger when dad took him. I didn't want to. I should have gotten out of there when I heard them coming down, but by the time I figured out what was going on, it was too late."

I guessed Hannah was wide awake by now. I know I was.

"They decided it would be a meeting. I assumed they meant Proud Boys, but they meant KKK. There's still everything, everywhere. I have no interest. So I didn't know much. But Dwayne gets this look on his face and he says it's time to make all our fathers proud. It's time to send a warning to this generation. That they would do to Sandy what their fathers did to Marvin Johnson."

I've heard the phrase, "My blood ran cold," but I had never experienced it until that moment. It was like my body temperature dropped by ten degrees.

"Who was Marvin Johnson?" Hannah prompted.

"This Black dude who joined Appleton Lodge. He was invited to join, for sports; he wasn't bothering anybody. He probably didn't even want to belong. But the Klan decided they couldn't have someone uppity like that in their own backyard, so to speak."

"What happened to Mr. Johnson?"

Toby paused, as if gathering himself. "I didn't know and I wasn't about to ask. They were all saying, 'Do we dare go over? Do we dare get the stuff?' 'No, it's Halloween, we'll go tomorrow,' stuff like that. I still didn't get it. They finally decided they could get chains from Oscar's.

"There was this weird energy in the room. I said, 'Look, whatever you're doing, I'm beat. I'll go next time.'

"Dwayne said, 'Naw, this was going to be one for the books.' I had to be there. Like our dad, who was only a kid at the time, was there for Marvin Johnson.

"The dude who was texting with Sandy, pretending to be Dwayne, asked what time to say they'd pick her up. They said in an hour. They divided up. Some of the guys went to Oscar's garage. Dwayne said he was going in, just him, because he could get in and out without being detected. He grabbed me by the shoulder and said I should come.

"I said no. Whatever was happening, it didn't sound good and I didn't want to be involved. I pulled away from him and ran up the inside stairs.

"Mom was watching TV. Dwayne came up after me and grabbed me. 'What's all the fuss?' she asked, and Dwayne goes, 'There's a meeting tonight, and Toby says he's too good to go along.'

"She says, 'That right, Toby? You're too good for this family?'

"Dwayne grabs me again and steers me to the closet to get a coat. Then he steers me outside to his mega truck. 'I can't babysit you all night, fucker,' he says, 'but if you run away like a baby, it won't go good for you.'

"You've got to understand that when Dwayne beats you, he beats you to a pulp. Learned it from Dad. So I got in the truck. We drove over to Appleton Lodge. I was shocked because it was Halloween and all and everybody's supposed to stay away. But he drove up in back and parked.

"He said, 'I don't know what kind of infant you are that I can't trust you out here on your own. So he opens the door on my side and grabs me by the collar, then forces me inside the Lodge through a back door I'd never seen. He had his police flashlight so we could see.

"He took me down the hall and into the old music room. In the back of the room is a closet, and in the back of the closet is a fake back panel that led to stairs. We went down. It was this whole room, like a meeting room with wooden chairs and stuff and old flags from the Brotherhood. It was freaky. 'You okay? You not running?' he asked, and when I said okay, he said, 'You'll grow into this. You'll make me proud.'

"'Did Dad belong?' I asked, and Dwayne told me he did, but Dad was kind of shamed when his partying got out of control and they all knew about it. But our grandpa was a big mucky-muck, so they didn't throw Dad out.

"Anyway, Dwayne took me over to the stage. Just below the stage on both sides were drawers. One was a long drawer that pulled all the way out. But the other one was a short drawer, less than half as long. But Dwayne knew how to throw some sort of secret latch, and the hidden drawer behind slid out. 'You are one lucky son-of-a-bitch,' he said. 'You aren't even a member and you are getting to see our trophies.'

"I thought they meant trophies like they played ball or something, but it was trophies from the men they'd...killed. There was a broken pocket watch from somebody and an old boot and...just a bunch of stuff. And there was the shirt he said Marvin Johnson was wearing, but it was all torn up and shredded and stained. Blood, I guess."

Toby took a deep breath. "I don't think I can do this," he said. His voice was trembling.

"You're doing fine," said Hannah. When she talked to you like that, her voice was so reassuring you'd tell her anything. At least, I would. (Well, no, I wouldn't, but that's for another time.) She gave Toby time to pull himself together.

"You've come this far," she repeated. "It took courage to come here. Finish what you came to say."

Toby cleared his throat. "'Why?' I said. 'Why do you hurt people? Are you going to hurt Frank Wilcox tonight? I thought he was your friend.'

"'Don't you get anything?' Dwayne snarled, 'That makes it worse!' He got what he needed and he grabbed me and herded me back out to the car. He kept saying, 'I can't believe it, my own brother is a moron.'

"His big hunkin' truck has a back seat and he put me in it. We met up with everyone in the back lot at Oscar's. There's like a bunch of cars, but everyone piles into three trucks. Dwayne puts me into one of those, I don't want to say who was driving. I'll talk about me and I'll talk about Dwayne, but...

"Anyhow, Dwayne goes off to pick up Sandy.

"The guys I'm in the truck with are hooting and drinking. There's some loud noise coming from the chains in the truck bed. I ask what's going to happen. They tell me they're going to do what they did to that Black man—that's not what they actually said—and I said, 'Oh, what was that?'

"'First we have fun!' said one of them. 'A tranny, that will be lots of fun!'

"'And then we drag!' 'Yeah, like a drag show," and they all start laughing hysterically. I finally put together that meant they killed someone by handcuffing them up and then chaining them to the back of a truck and dragging them over the roads till there wasn't much left."

Hannah said, "Oh, my God."

Toby said, "I know. So we all drive out to Anvil Mountain, back up to this old logging road that is all rutted and messed up. Most of the guys were all whooped up, but there were a couple of others, like me, who were just real quiet.

"The moon was nearly full. Out where the mountain has been logged, you could see pretty well. There were lots of stars. It was pretty. Before too long, we heard Dwayne's truck coming up the road. Then everyone got quiet.

"But then something happened. One of the doors on his truck flew open and Sandy jumped out of the cab. The high beams were on and she could see everybody. I could tell some of the guys didn't feel right about it being a woman, even if...

"Anyway, she started to run, but two of the guys got on the other side of her to block her way so she couldn't. Dwayne gets out of the truck and comes around, cussing her out. Then she says something, I think calling him over, and he comes to her, and he grabs her. But he's wearing his SIG and she grabs it and shoots herself in the head. Just like that."

Toby started to cry. "I've never seen anyone...die...before."

It took him a minute to recover himself enough to go on.

"Then everyone got all freaked out and came around her, but she was really dead—she'd shot herself in the head. Someone said they had to get out of there, and they all ran to their trucks. I didn't know what to do, so I got into Dwayne's truck. He grabbed his gun and we left.

"He didn't have much interest in me after that. He dumped me out, barely slowing down, outside Mom's and told me if I ever told anything, but he was too distracted to even say what. I hadn't seen him again until the next day when he found me at the Lodge. I'd promised my girlfriend Lily and Marta I'd show them around."

"And you were there when Jarrett..."

"I think Jarrett was one of the guys who was quiet, who didn't really want to be there. I don't know. I didn't know who it was who jumped at the time. Dwayne told us we didn't need to stay because we hadn't seen anything inside the Lodge and we didn't know who it was who jumped. I think he just didn't want me talking to the cops, or anybody, about anything. I don't know if he was more scared about what would happen to the guys that were there if I talked, or if he was scared about what would happen to me if the wrong people heard me talk."

I remembered Marta saying something was off with Toby that morning. That was an understatement.

Hannah was good at giving people space to think and to talk. She gave Toby space.

Finally he said, "I don't know what to do. I don't know how to get this horrible feeling to go away. I feel like nothing will ever be right again."

"Toby, do you believe in a just God?" Hannah asked.

I guessed this part was her work kicking in.

"I guess," said Toby.

"You've got to pray and tell God you're sorry, then make it right as much as possible."

"How do I make it right?"

"Tell someone. Besides me."

"Like who?"

"Like Inspector Spaulding."

"Oh," said Toby.

"Do you think you could do that?"

"I could...try. No one could know, though."

Hannah said, "How about tomorrow morning, first thing, we meet him at the funeral home? I'll make sure it's open. We can talk in Mrs. Santiago's office. No one will know."

"Okay," Toby said, "Maybe."

"How about eight o'clock? No one will be around then. The funeral isn't till eleven."

"Yeah, okay, I guess."

"Do you want to stay here in my guest room tonight?" she asked.

It was a fair question. I couldn't imagine going home to his mother's place. Or to his mother.

He stood up, and Whistle landed on the floor. "No," he said. "If I don't come home, they'll wonder. They'll look for me."

"Okay. Got it." Hannah stood, too, and headed for the door with Toby. "You sure you're okay?"

"Yeah. Nobody is really paying attention to me at the moment."

"You've done a very brave thing," she said. "We'll talk more tomorrow."

"Will you be there when I talk to Inspector Spaulding?"

"If you'd like," she said. "Sure."

Hannah's front door opened and closed. Outside, the car engine started, and the car left the drive.

FROM THE BEGINNING

Ingredients

    1 oz fresh steeped earl grey tea
    ½ oz fresh lemon juice
    ½ oz simple syrup
    ½ oz gin
    ½ oz vodka
    ½ oz white rum
    ½ oz tequila
    ½ oz orange liqueur
    Soda water
    Fresh lemon, sliced
    Ice
    12 oz mason jar

Method

Chamomile Tea

Steep 2 chamomile tea bags in hot water and bring to room temperature.

Cocktail

Fill mason jar to top with ice.
Add gin, vodka, rum, tequila, orange liqueur, lemon juice, simple syrup, and earl grey tea. Stir all ingredients.
Top off with soda water.
Add fresh lemon to side of glass for garnish.

18
THE NEXT MORNING

"ARE YOU THERE?" Hannah asked.

I stood up and put the blender back onto the counter.

"Holy shit," I said.

"Yeah, I know," she answered.

"Does this happen often? How do you ever get any sleep?"

"I don't know. Things aren't usually this dramatic."

"Do you feel safe staying here?" I asked.

"Do you feel safe at your place?" she countered.

"I don't know. If anyone figures out that Toby came to talk to you, and you now know enough to get them in trouble, you're suddenly more dangerous to them than I am."

We both needed to get sleep. Especially Hannah. She looked like she could pass out for a week, at least.

I called MacTavish's, got the night clerk, Billy, whom I knew. I asked for a room with two queen beds. I told him I'd have Whistle.

Hannah didn't argue. She grabbed a toothbrush, I grabbed Whistle, and we each took our cars the back way to the hotel. The lobby was empty. I used my key to slip into the Hatch, grabbed a bottle of white wine, and walked past reception. Billy handed me a keycard without saying a word.

"I don't know what's going on, but even if the FBI asks what room you're in, I have no idea," he whispered.

Admittedly, I'd paid for an Uber to take him home one night and never mentioned it. Nothing a normal bartender wouldn't do.

I let Hannah in through one of the back hall doors. The streets were empty enough. I was fairly certain no one had followed us.

Like Toby said, we likely weren't on anyone's radar, but if we were, they'd try our actual houses first.

I locked and bolted our room door. MacTavish's was Whistle's old stomping ground, and she happily settled in. I poured Hannah and me each a glass of wine, we talked about nothing for ten minutes because there was no way to even get started, and then we put ocean sounds on a sleep app and passed out.

The next morning, we both awoke at 6:00 AM.

I made coffee in the Nespresso there in the room, but neither of us drank much of it.

"Tell me," I said. "What is the deal with clergy? Is it like lawyers, stuff people tell you in confidence is privileged information?"

"I don't know about lawyers, exactly, but for clergy, once murder is involved, our vow of silence is lifted." She smiled at the idea of her taking a vow of silence.

"It wasn't murder, exactly," I said.

"Yeah, it was."

Billy at the front desk was going off shift. I told him I was leaving and promised to settle up later. He had gotten into the whole spy aspect and said it wasn't even on the books, even though he'd ordered maid service to make up the room.

Hannah and I left out one of the inn's many back doors, by 6:15. We each headed to our houses, which seemed less fraught as daylight took hold.

Hannah was able to arrange the covert gathering with both Inspector Spaulding and Rosa Santiago.

True to plan, Hannah arrived at R. Richards and Sons at 8:00 to meet Mike and Toby. Rosa opened up for them and let them into her office. She made coffee and turned on the fire.

By 9:00, it was clear Toby wasn't coming.

I knew this because around 9:15, Mike Spaulding knocked on my kitchen door.

I'd returned to my cottage in the glade that morning to find all the doors locked and the lights still on; everything was undisturbed, as far as I could tell.

Mike accepted a cup of coffee and we sat at my kitchen table, looking incongruous among Sally's flowery chintz.

"I hear you have a recording," he said. "May I listen to it?"

"I haven't played it. I'm pretty sure the quality isn't very good."

I found the file and handed him my phone. "I don't think I can bear to hear it again. I'll wait in the living room."

He nodded and pushed play.

I changed my mind, went into my bedroom, showered, and got dressed for the day. When I came out, Mike was standing by the picture window in the living room.

"Well?" I asked.

"The quality isn't very good."

"Will it help in any way?"

"Since Toby didn't know you were recording him, the only way it may help is that we know what the puzzle picture is supposed to look like as we fit the pieces together."

Toby.

"He didn't show up."

"No. Not surprising. Lots of people lose their courage in the light of day."

I reached for my phone and Mike put it into my outstretched hand. I sat and texted Marta, asking if she could text Toby something innocuous, just to see if he responded.

She said she would.

"What are you thinking is your next course of action?" I asked.

"I'll start by stopping off to see how Jarrett Banks is doing. He's still in the hospital. I'll arrive at the hospital at funeral time, hoping everyone is there and his room is clear. At the moment, I'm more afraid the officers taking turns there aren't caring for their banker buddy as much as they're keeping him from talking about why he jumped. I'll try to talk to Jarrett if he's alone. But then I'll head for the funeral. Because, as we know—"

"Killers love funerals," I said.

I sat down and motioned Mike to do the same. He looked as exhausted as Hannah. "Have you eaten breakfast?"

"Thankfully, Dunkin' has a drive through."

"Are you joshing me? You being law enforcement doesn't mean you suddenly exist on doughnuts. Tell me it isn't so."

"They also have coffee. And a pretty good egg white wrap. Not gourmet, but it does the job when I'm on a case and basically forcing myself to eat."

Mike looked out my front window.

"I like the view. In fact, I love my cottage," I said.

He nodded.

"Let me ask you," I continued, barely finding the courage. It was now or never.

"What?" he asked.

"At the funeral home, after Dwayne said those racist things to you, he saw that I overheard. Out in the parking lot, he called me by my full name and said my address out loud. He also said something I took as a threat that he could involve me...*blame* me...for Jarrett Banks's fall. How afraid should I be?"

Mike sat, contemplating, in the morning light.

"Normally, I would say he's keeping you quiet in the usual way. Something would have to be really serious for members of hate groups to injure a White woman. That's what they claim others do, to get them—well, *us*—into trouble. But if he's decided you're on the wrong side, and you can do some damage, that might elevate the threat. Still. A White woman. And a blonde, at that."

"Natural blonde," I said, playing along, with a crooked smile. "Although once a person is classified as a, um...*person of color* lover...you lose all value and are classified as subhuman, so being blonde helps not at all. Except to underscore your betrayal of your own race." This I knew from growing up with Black family members. "Meanwhile, what's your threat assessment? I mean, how much trouble do you think *you're* in?"

He stretched out his long legs and gave a deep sigh. "This is a hard enough job without having to constantly assess the threat level and decide if it's wise to continue on a particular case. But how can I not keep on? How can I not find justice for Sandy Evans and Marvin Johnson?"

"How did you decide to go into law enforcement?" I asked. I wasn't sure how near we were to being back on friend-footing.

He sat for a while. He decided to answer. "My parents are from Zimbabwe. My father was in the diplomatic corps. My mother ran a girls' school. She resigned and came with Baba when he was assigned to Washington, DC. Both my sister and I were born while they were in DC.

"When Baba's diplomatic tour was finished, he stayed and continued working at the embassy. When Sisi—Muriel, my sister—was four, he retired from the corps and they were granted permission to emigrate to the US. We were already living in Maryland, where Amai, my mom, took over running a private girls' academy, with the idea of making it more ethnically diverse.

"Baba was bothered by the fact that we lived in a nice part of town but many of our friends didn't. He decided he could do the most good by becoming a real estate agent. He also began buying and selling property.

"Growing up, I had a friend named Reynold, whose dad worked for the highway patrol. His dad was a good guy and would tell us crazy stories about the job. I thought it sounded exciting.

"My parents had their hearts set on their offspring both becoming lawyers, which was fine with Muriel. That's exactly how she thinks. She studied both international law and US immigration law."

"But law wasn't for you?"

"I was still in high school when my friend Keith was killed, basically for Driving While Black. I don't want to go into it, but it was terrible. The only thing that helped at all was that Reynold's father was furious. I mean, he was White, he was highway patrol, and he was beside himself. I heard him on the phone to a friend saying the whole police culture was messed up and nothing would change it unless Black people all stormed the police academies by the hundreds and basically changed it from inside.

"Still, I did go to college for pre-law. I even started law school, but…"

"It wasn't for you."

"I don't mind learning and I don't mind people being intense, and I don't mind studying for more hours than there are in a day. But two things were the writing on the wall for me. One, everyone seemed so full of themselves."

"At law school? I can't imagine," I joked. "And the second?"

"On my first day, the first class, the professor started by saying, 'I want to be very clear about something. You are here because you are interested in the law. If you are interested in justice, there's a seminary just across campus.

"Turns out I wasn't interested in the law. I also wasn't interested in seminary. I was, however, interested in justice. I had a very frank talk with Reynold's dad. I went to John Jay College and got a Masters in Criminal Justice. Then I applied to the highway patrol and the State Bureau of Investigation. And here I am."

"Wow. So did you get all those other Black people to fill up the ranks and file?"

"Not yet," he said. "But I'm working on it. Of course, it's not that easy. You need the right people. You've heard of the Stanford Prison Experiment?"

"Where students in the experiment were randomly assigned to be prisoner and guards? And the ones assigned to be guards, even 'nice kids' who one would think would know better, completely bought into the system and acted atrociously?"

He sighed.

"And you're not afraid, right now, about trying to put away White cops for the death of a transgender woman?"

"When did I say that?"

"You're going to visit Jarrett Banks? Because of what Toby said about him being quiet?"

"I'm guessing he meant to kill himself. We know Dwayne Cabinau was first on the scene, and undoubtedly threatened him and scared him shitless. The stories he's been telling, about not knowing how he got there, and about a ghost pushing him off—I mean, come on, pick one. Let's see if I can get him to talk if he's on his own."

"Something else Toby said. That his grandfather was a big shot in the Klan but his father wasn't for some reason."

"Look, I don't like gossip, but it's an open secret around here that Officer Emil Cabinau was, to all intents and purposes, a by-the-book, stand-up religious guy, at least at work and at church. But he was also gay. Gay isn't a problem. Promiscuous and aggressive is. It must drive Dwayne crazy that everyone knows. The blessing and curse of a small town."

"Is their dad still alive?"

"No. Killed when his car crashed into a tree. Was he chasing a suspect? Avoiding a deer leaping in front of him? Or simply driving eighty miles per hour into a tree? You do feel for the kids, all I've got to say. And pray for the time when we're all known for the content of our character, not judged by the color of our skin or who we choose to love."

"Amen," I said. What he'd said rang a bell. "Anders said Sandy wanted to talk to someone from the football squad who had attempted to sexually attack her back in high school. I wonder if it was Dwayne. I wonder if that's why she was getting together with Dwayne after the reunion. Imagine Dwayne fearing he's gay and being shut out by someone he thought was gay, who he thought was so far below him. That could make him furious."

"Especially given the family history. You'd want to prove yourself to the guys after your dad was known for being promiscuous and aggressive with men."

The sides of my eyes burned with tears—of anger or sorrow, I didn't know. Things seemed so messed up. So what if you thought you were gay? So what if someone shut down your advances, then went on to become a different person in a different place. So what? "But by killing someone? And planning to do it in such a gruesome way?"

"I can't explain that," Mike said. He stood and swatted imaginary dirt off his khakis. "I've got to go. Meanwhile, don't lose that recording on your phone. I need a copy. We'll see to it. I'll send someone to the Battened Hatch after the funeral. I believe they can copy the SIM card without taking your phone."

"Okay. But I thought you said it wouldn't help."

"It's always better to have the actual recording than to have you, me, and Reverend Bricksford putting in bits and pieces we remember. But at least there are three of us."

"I can see that. So what's next? Or are we at a dead end if Jarrett Banks doesn't talk?"

"Toby also told us there was a drawer full of evidence at the remaining Appleton Lodge. My hunch is it won't be there for long, although I think the place has been too busy for anyone to remove it covertly. I've got to get a warrant to go in, and I don't know which judge is on tomorrow. One will likely grant the warrant, the other will not. So, fingers crossed."

As Mike stood and reached for his coat, my phone rang. It was Marta, which was odd, since no one in her generation actually calls people, only texts. I picked up.

"What's up?" I asked.

"This was too complicated to text," she started. "I texted Toby a couple of times about something innocuous, but he never responded. The third time, his mom picked up and said he'd left his phone downstairs on the sofa where he plays games, but he wasn't home. She doesn't know how long he's been out, but she'll have him text when he gets in."

"Toby's gone," I said to Mike.

"He's gone, without his phone," said Marta.

"I'm sorry to hear that," I told her. "Let me know if you hear from him."

We hung up.

I walked Mike to the back door. "I'm guessing we're not besties enough yet for you to tell me about your woman," I said.

He almost smiled. "Not yet." And he left.

I closed the door and wondered, was Toby gone like running some errands? Or staying over with a friend for a while?

Or was Toby gone like Marvin Johnson and Sandy Evans?

THE NEXT MORNING

Ingredients

Fresh basil
Fresh peach, diced
1 ½ oz white rum
2 oz dry white wine
½ oz peach liqueur
1 bar spoon coconut cream
Ice
Large wine glass

Method

In cocktail shaker, add half of a diced peach and a few sprigs of fresh basil leaves. Muddle together thoroughly until you can smell the fresh basil open up and peaches turn into a bit of a liquid.
Add ice, then add white rum, dry white wine, peach liqueur, and coconut cream. Shake all ingredients together until cocktail shaker is nice and cold.
Pour contents of cocktail shaker into large wine glass.
Add more ice if need be and gently stir.
Add more diced fresh peaches on top.
Take a piece of fresh basil, place in hands, and slap hands together. Add to cocktail for garnish.

19
CELEBRATION OF LIFE

THE CELEBRATION OF Life for Sandy Wilcox Evans was to begin at 11:00 AM.

I stopped into the Battened Hatch on my way, even though it sat dark and empty. I wasn't on until the evening shift. I went and stood behind the bar. The only lights I turned on were the blue and green ones under the rows of liquor bottles behind me.

Sandy Wilcox sat right there, *right there*, on Friday night. Alive. Suitcase by her feet, after spending six hours on a bus from New York City. She wanted to say goodbye to her parents and her friends and her childhood.

Today, they'd be saying goodbye to her.

If she hadn't come home to say farewell, she...well, she'd still be dying. Just on her own terms. Going peacefully, God willing.

I also thought about Marvin Johnson, asked to join Appleton Lodge as a ringer because he could play sports and run fast. He was certainly not asked to join to share a cup of tea and a scone each afternoon.

Yet while the club members recruited him, the townsfolk couldn't let him rise above them. They worked there. He was a member. It felt like a novella Shirley Jackson might have written.

I shivered.

Why were people so threatened by others' identity, whether it be difference of ethnicity or sexual identity? Especially by the differences of good, kind, courageous people? Granted, my mom was nonbinary, mostly lesbian now, so I was used to it, but Dad, whom I had once loved so much, who had brought me books and sang me songs, was now straight and by-the-book, brook-no-questions, hell-avoiding patriarchal. And just horrible.

I missed him so.

I went onto the local newspaper's website to double-check the time of the service and was shocked that I'd forgotten that, while all this was going on, the town had still had the election. Votes were in. Art Bristow won. Avantika Azni lost.

That in itself was not surprising. More surprising to me was that the vote had been split, 46% to 42%, much closer than anyone expected.

I switched off the liquor lights and locked up. I don't know why I decided to exit through the lobby instead of the kitchen, but that decision affected the rest of my day.

Standing in the lobby were Anders and the children, and some out-of-town guests. They were dividing into cars to head for the funeral parlor. "It will be a nice, if truncated, celebration," Anders told them. "We'll still do the longer service Sandy put together back in Brooklyn with friends and family."

As everyone headed for their cars, a woman came dashing from the hallway to the hotel rooms. "Anders! I'm sorry," she said. "Mitchell is finishing showering. It'll take us five minutes to head that way."

"Okay," he said, "but we've got to get going. We'll meet you there."

"Oh, but you know Mitchell! How many GPSs have tried to get us somewhere, only for us to end up in a different county altogether?"

Anders saw me and smiled. "Avalon, this is my sister Amy. She came up from Camden."

I saw the writing on the wall and offered, "How about if I ride over with you and show you the way?"

"Would you?" asked Amy.

"Thank you," mouthed Anders. "See you there." He went to where Liam and Meg waited by the front door.

It was the least I could do. I figured I could grab a ride back with Hannah, who was presiding.

Amy and Mitchell were nice folks, kind of in shock, not knowing how to handle any of this. Yet they'd shown up, coming a long way to support Anders and the kids. I personally give a lot of points for showing up.

I would be embarrassed for my town if there were only a few local folks there—but it wouldn't surprise me. Quite possibly the few schoolmates of Sandy who'd shown up yesterday felt they'd done their bit.

Our car pulled into the parking lot at 10:40. There were a number of cars already, one of which was a police vehicle from Mountain Home, a town twenty minutes west of Tranquility. An officer sat in the cruiser.

"Nice of the police to come make sure everything goes smoothly," said Mitchell as we departed their car.

Okay, we'll go with that.

As Amy, Mitchell, and I entered the space—I hated to call it a funeral parlor, it really was a lovely, peaceful memorial space—I was again struck by how serene it was. The colors, carpeting, and design were welcoming and embracing. I wondered how it looked when Rosa and family purchased it. It was thoughtful to take an important situation that hadn't been handled well in your own life and go to the trouble and expense of becoming educated so you can do better for others.

Another room was being set up for later that weekend, but today, Sandy's was the only gathering. I walked Amy and Mitchell to the sign-in desk, where they autographed the book before rejoining Anders and the family.

I remained behind to give them space, and realized I hadn't signed in yet. As I did so, I saw another brown paper lunch bag sitting to the side with Dwayne's name on it.

Really? Mike told me that it was far from unusual for perpetrators to attend funerals, and I knew that to be true. But how could you come, knowing you were the cause of so much pain, so much grief? I didn't understand one whit.

If he came, could I bear not to say anything?

I had to say nothing. I couldn't give away what I knew and how I knew it. Other people's lives were on the line.

Justice was on the line.

My attention was caught by the arrival of three of our town librarians: two women and a man. Librarians are some of the finest people on Earth. They know what's going on in this—or any—town. If they've helped you find a book or a newspaper or a map, doggone it, they will show up for you.

I was not at all surprised when newspaper editor Brent Davis arrived with his wife Susan. This event began to appeal to the part of me that collected stories. I loved putting attendees together with their reason for honoring Sandy. I knew Brent was covering the event for the paper, but I had a feeling he would have shown up anyway.

Behind them were Troy and his coworker Dani, and much of the staff of the new arts and theater complex. As they paused to pick up a program, Dani sighed. "Why is it always the good ones who are taken too early? The do-gooders and moms and cookie bakers? When I die, everyone will give a sigh of relief and say, 'There goes that bitch.'"

Troy scoffed. "Dani, you know that's not what we'll say. We'll say, 'There goes that ultra-talented bitch.'"

That seemed to cheer her up. "All right, then."

"You're not a cookie person, you're a wrestling-with-artists person."

Dani seemed satisfied that her obit would be more to her liking.

Next up were a group of women I knew to be local school teachers. I was grateful they came to pay their respects to their former student. More, I was glad Anders and Amy and the children would not be the only attendees.

I needn't have worried.

I couldn't see to the entrance, but the hallway was now filled with people. First I recognized Sandy's classmates who'd been in the Battened Hatch the other night. The women all arrived carrying...platters of cookies. That must have been what the email said, because the more classmates who arrived, the more cookies there were. I knew the cookies weren't there simply as refreshments. It was a small way of acknowledging who Sandy was, one small thing that made her happy.

Cynthia came up to the program stand and watched with a satisfied smile. She saw me and said, "I realized I couldn't have loved Frank without loving Sandy...I loved this person. And I fully intend to say goodbye, to make sure we all do."

Doors to the room were open, the large space filling up quickly. Nearly all the chairs were full when Marta and Colin came in with a group of five other friends. "We all knew Sandy from church," Colin said. "We might not have known she was Sandy, but we knew *her*."

Holy smokes. Did their parents know? Did Marta's dad, Reverend Tim Layton, know his youth were determinedly here?

I did hope, somehow, Sandy's parents knew.

Towards the back of the crowd came Glenn MacTavish and Avantika Azni. If I expected her to be subdued after her loss in the recent election, not so much. She came up and stood next to me, looking at everyone who was working to fit into the celebration.

"Tranquility is changing," was all she said.

You could go in a back door to the room, and that's what I did, finding my place with the standing-room-only folks, between Glenn and Inspector Cal Becker. I remembered that Mike said he'd use this time to try to get to Jarrett Banks in the hospital while everyone was otherwise occupied.

Hannah sat with the family up front. As she stood and turned to address the crowd, everyone quieted down. "The love in this room makes it a holy place," she said, and began the service.

I'm often amazed that Hannah Bricksford is my friend. I don't know what she sees in me, though, being Hannah, she's tried to express it. Hannah can stand in front of a room of kin and strangers and bind everyone together. She can listen to stories about the person being celebrated and make you feel you knew them. She can follow the wishes of the beliefs of others without sacrificing her own.

She's Wonder Woman.

Which was why I was shocked, when I went to look for her after the service to ask for a ride, to find her in another of the empty rooms. She was sitting there, tears running down her face.

"Hannah, you did such a wonderful job," I said. "Everyone got what they needed, I'm sure of it."

She nodded slightly.

"What?" I said. "What is it?"

"Zachariah is back in the hospital. In Atlanta." She looked up at me. "We're so far away from everywhere here. I can't get anywhere."

"What do you mean? You can get to Atlanta! We can get you to Atlanta."

"It's already afternoon," she said. "I'd have to drive two and a half hours to Albany. Then be there two hours early, then change planes. We're so far away. I can't get anywhere."

I sunk cross-legged on the floor. I took her phone and called up a travel app. "There's a plane at 2:54 from Albany. Nope, we couldn't make it, even if I started driving you now." I went through the list. There was one at 7:54 that night that changed planes in Charlotte and would get her in at eleven. "Do you want me to book it?" I asked.

She shook her head. "Let me go home and call my family. We'll figure out what's best. Maybe he'll be released from the hospital and back at home by the time I got there. But thanks. I just get to feeling so isolated way up here in the mountains."

"Okay," I said. "You're all right to drive?"

"Yeah.

She stood and went into the hall to get her jacket. As she did, I scrolled through her contacts. Something I usually would never do, but I did. I put her father's number into my phone. Then I put

Landon Presser's number in. Because, well, who wouldn't want a movie star's private cell number if given the opportunity?

I mean, I copied it in case I needed to contact him for Hannah. For Hannah.

I found her in the hallway, saying goodbye to someone. I handed her back her phone. "Let me know if I can get you to the airport," I said as she finished, and turned away, hoping not to be stopped again.

I wanted to hug her. I was almost to that point that I could hug people. Not go around hugging just anyone, but close friends. Now and then.

I knew she didn't need to be asked for one more favor. That did leave the problem of getting back to town. I suddenly did not have the wherewithal to ride with a member of the bereaved family. I knew stuff—a lot of stuff—they didn't. Thinking in that direction, I perused the signing table as I passed. The lunch bag with Dwayne's name on it was gone.

And no sign of Dwayne.

Thank God.

Marta and Colin came into the hall, each munching a different kind of cookie. They looked homemade and smelled like brown sugar.

"Hey, could I hitch a ride back to town?" I asked.

"Sure," said Colin. "I'm dropping Marta at her place first, if that's all right."

"I told Manuela I'd be at the Hatch as soon as I could, but I need to change," Marta said.

"Thanks."

The three of us walked the serene hallways and out the door into the gray afternoon. The family had agreed to leave Sandy's ashes in the Garden of Bright Memories, growing her own tree. Because of that, there would be no funeral procession to the graveyard. Cars were lined up, pulling out onto the nearly empty main road.

As we headed for Colin's Jeep, someone was suddenly there, in the midst of the parking lot, seeing us emerge, and screaming. It was Toby's girlfriend, Lily.

"Where is he, you bastards?" she hollered at us.

We all stopped, like we must have heard wrong.

"Toby! Where is Toby? You were with him! You were the last people with him!"

"What?" asked Colin. "You were with him, too. We all left together."

"I know you know!" Lily yelled. She was sobbing, her black mascara running in rivulets down her face. "He texted you, I know it!"

The three of us looked at each other. "He texted me so we could meet up! With him. And you!" Marta said.

"You have to know!" She grabbed Colin's shirt and pulled on it. When he loosened her fingers, she fell to the gravel, crying. I started to kneel next to her, which prompted, "Don't touch me! Don't be near me!"

"I think we should leave," said Colin. "She's not rational. And we can't help."

We all jumped into the Jeep and headed out.

We hardly spoke on the way into town. I saw Colin check his rearview mirror once or twice, but he didn't see anything—or say anything, if he did.

"Do you think Dwayne could have something to do with Toby's disappearance?" I started.

"His own brother?" asked Marta, who also lapsed into silence.

Colin pulled over on Main Street beneath the Gothic church and the attached parsonage. Marta hopped out. "See you in twenty," she said to me. I nodded.

Marta bounded up the stone staircase.

"Where should I drop you?" Colin asked.

"My car's at MacTavish's," I said. "But I can walk from here."

"I'm going that way," he said.

I climbed from the back seat into the passenger side and put on the seatbelt.

Colin signaled his return to traffic and pulled out onto Main Street. He hadn't gone fifteen feet when we heard saw brightly flashing lights and heard the *whoop* that only comes from cop cars. It was followed by a tinny voice saying, "Red Cherokee, pull over onto the next street. Out of the flow of traffic. Up into the parking lot."

"Shit," said Colin, as he pulled the Jeep forward and made a right onto the steeply climbing hill.

"What? What is it? A cop?"

"Not just any cop. Freaking Roscoe Cone."

CELEBRATION OF LIFE

Ingredients

½ oz limoncello liqueur
½ oz yellow chartreuse
Few dashes lemon bitters
Prosecco
Fresh lemon peel
Raw sugar for rim of glass
Fresh lemon slice
Ice
Coupe glass

Method

Place raw sugar on plate. Rub a lemon slice around the edges of coupe glass. Dip onto plate to rim. Set glass aside.

In cocktail shaker, add ice, limoncello liqueur, yellow chartreuse, and lemon bitters. Shake contents until shaker is cold.

Strain contents of cocktail shaker over sugar rimmed coupe glass.

Top off with prosecco and twist fresh lemon peel over cocktail to release citrus oils.

Float lemon peel in glass for garnish.

20
PARKING LOT

"Pretend you didn't hear," I said. "Pull over here on Main Street."

"Too late," Colin said.

He was committed to the turn and driving up the steep road, the police vehicle on our bumper. We drove all the way up, until we were even with Tim Layton's Gothic church, and pulled into its parking lot.

It was a parking lot no one could see from Main Street below or the residential street above. Furthermore, it was Thursday, midday. No cars in the parking lot. No one was in the church before us. The parsonage, where Marta had gone, was behind the office wing—which was also locked, all the lights off.

Damn.

Officer Cone got out of his vehicle and headed our way. One look at the car and I knew it was the same one which had been at the celebration of life.

"License and registration," he said in cop-stop monotone.

Colin pointed to his visor, the officer nodded, and Colin unclipped his car card caddy. He handed his papers out the window.

The officer looked at them, then looked at him, as if checking to see if he was the correct human being.

"Colin Keane?"

He nodded.

"So, you're the fairy I've heard so much about."

"Yes, sir," Colin said, as if he'd been awarded a prize. "Nice to meet you."

"Damn you, don't get fresh with me."

It was the dehumanizing remark that did it for me. I pulled out my phone, framed Colin and Roscoe nicely, and pressed record. "Hello, Officer Cone," I said. "I'm Avalon Nash. Colin and I were just at the service where you were in the parking lot."

"You're not under arrest. Put that away. Or I'll take it from you."

"Oh," I said. "New York State Senate Bill S3253A begs to differ."

Did I mention I'm from LA? There are several numbers you're taught to memorize, different in each state of residence.

Colin was the calm one. He put his hand out the window for his identity papers and having received them back, asked jauntily, "So how can I help you today, Officer Cone?"

"I need you to tell me where Toby Cabinau is."

"What? How would I know that?"

"Toby's girlfriend seemed to think you would."

"I don't. We're barely acquaintances."

"You—and you, too"—he pointed at me—"were some of the last to see him before he disappeared. What do you know about Toby? What did he tell you?"

"Tell us about what?" I asked.

"Don't play innocent with me."

"We're not playing," said Colin.

"Get out of the car," Officer Cone barked.

I put my hand, restraining, on Colin's thigh.

"I said get out." He took his service weapon out and held it, menacingly, outside the window.

"Why did you stop us?" I asked. "What are we being charged with? Or can we go?"

"Get out, faggot," he said to the driver, and my stomach turned. "Or are you resisting a law officer?"

"Resisting what?" I demanded, but his eyes were locked with Colin's.

It occurred to me then, Roscoe Cone doesn't work here. This

isn't his territory. He's not on duty. There are no cameras, body, or dash turned on.

This time, he turned his gun sideways slowly to point towards the interior of the car. At Colin.

What do you know about him? What did he tell you?

Those were Roscoe's questions. Did he know where Toby was, or what had happened to him? Was he fishing, to find out if Toby had told us anything? How much we knew?

"Get out."

Colin looked at me. My adrenaline was racing. It was all I could do to hold the camera still.

He slowly opened his car door and got out.

"Hands on top of the car."

Colin complied.

In one practiced move, Officer Cone put his gun away and grabbed his handcuffs from his belt. He shoved Colin hard against the car.

"What are you doing?" I yelled. I got out.

"Get back in the car, bitch," he said. "I'm just taking him in for questioning."

"We've told you we barely knew Toby Cabinau," I said.

"Dwayne says different, and I trust Dwayne."

What?

The fact he was handcuffing Colin was the final tell that all was not well. I knew, I just knew, if Colin disappeared, handcuffed, into the back of that cruiser, he would not return in good shape. If at all.

"You have to stop. You have no right to handcuff this young man. I've videoed this all."

"And you're giving me the phone," he said. He walked around the front of our Jeep, removing his taser from his belt.

"Hell, no," I said. "Hell, no."

And I dropped my phone down my shirt, where it landed snugly inside the front of my bra.

He walked right up to me, standing face-to-face. He held up the taser. He opened his palm to receive the cell phone.

"Hello, Roscoe! Good to see you back here at church!"

What?

Both of us turned towards the church office building, from which the Reverend Tim Layton was sauntering, calmly, as if greeting a parishioner coming for service.

"Afternoon, Reverend," he said, slowly.

"So, these are my daughter's friends, Colin and Avalon. Surely they weren't speeding?"

Officer Cone took a step back and turned to address the newcomer.

"No, sir, they have information needed by the police about a missing person."

"Oh, dear! And who might that be?"

"Toby Cabinau, sir."

One thing about Tim Layton—he has a dominating personality. No one fools around in his sphere.

Tim walked up to Colin. "Colin, do you know the whereabouts of Toby Cabinau?"

"No, sir."

"Avalon Nash, how about you?"

"No."

"I have to say, Officer Cone, I know my daughter's friends, and I've never known her, or these two, to hang around with Toby Cabinau. I'm afraid you're mistaken. I have heard, however, that Inspectors Becker and Spaulding are handling the investigation having to do with the service you were all just at. Or, I can have them call Sergeant Lowell right here on Main Street, if Colin or Avalon think of anything that can be of help."

Reverend Layton and Officer Cone looked at each other.

"Does that sound like a good idea?" asked Tim Layton.

"Why, yessir, I suppose it does," said Roscoe Cone.

"What say you undo those handcuffs and let these folks go on their way?"

The officer stepped over and removed the handcuffs from Colin.

"Are you on duty, Officer Cone?" asked the minister. "'Cause I wouldn't want to interfere with your duties."

"Um," said Roscoe. "Um, not yet."

"Then come on in here. There's something I've been wanting to show you."

Pastor Layton threw his arm around Roscoe's shoulders and guided him toward the church. With his other hand, he motioned Colin and me to get gone.

We climbed into the Jeep. We got gone.

PARKING LOT

Ingredients

Dehydrated Orange Wheels

Fresh orange

Vanilla Simple Syrup

Fresh vanilla bean
1 cup sugar
1 ½ cups of water

Cocktail

Few dashes of orange bitters
1 oz Grand Marnier
1 ½ oz Bourbon
½ oz vanilla simple syrup
Ice
Nick and Nora Glass

Method

Dehydrated Orange Wheels

Preheat oven 225 degrees Fahrenheit.
Wash orange and dry with paper towel or clean kitchen towel. Slice into thin wheels.
Place parchment paper onto sheet pan or spray baking sheet with cooking spray. Spread oranges on sheet pan and place in oven. Leave in over for 2 hours, checking on them frequently.

Remove from oven after two hours and turn over. Bake for another 1 ½ hours. Remove from oven and let cool to room temperature

Vanilla Simple Syrup

Slice vanilla bean down the center and scrape vanilla seeds from the center. Put them into a medium sauce pan and add sugar and water. Place on medium heat until sugar is dissolved, stirring occasionally. Remove from heat and bring to room temperature. Strain liquid through cheese cloth to remove vanilla bean seeds. Store simple syrup in cooler after use.

Cocktail

Chill Nick and Nora glass by adding ice and a small amount of water.
In cocktail shaker, add orange bitters, Grand Marnier, vanilla simple syrup, and Bourbon. Shake all ingredients together until cocktail shaker is cold.
Discard ice and water from glass. Strain contents of cocktail shaker into glass.
Place a piece of dehydrated orange wheel on top of cocktail for garnish.

21

BEHIND THE BAR

ONCE AGAIN I stood behind the beautiful mahogany bar, my happy place, or at least my safe space.

Colin said he was going home, he'd be okay, his father was friends with some local law enforcement guys, they'd make sure he was okay.

"What should I do with the video?" I asked him. "People need to know how he treats people. Should I post it?"

"No, at least not yet. Cone is dangerous, but starring in that video is really not what I want to be known for."

I understood that, but I still didn't want to have the video only on my phone, so if they got rid of me it would be gone.

I was grateful when Marta arrived a few minutes after I did. She came straight over to talk.

"Your dad told you?"

"Yeah. What the hell?"

"I know. I've never been so relieved to see anyone in my life as I was to see your dad."

"Words I never expected to hear come out of your mouth." She burst out laughing. I did, too, grateful for the release. The run-ins I'd had with her father hadn't always been friendly. He wasn't thrilled that his daughter worked in a pub. He wasn't thrilled I was teaching her to bartend.

Happy hour, then supper, patrons arrived and my equilibrium began to return. With it, thoughts about people other than myself. Hannah, for one. She'd seemed so sad not to be with her family when Zachariah was in the hospital. Thinking this was as good a reason as any, I pulled out my phone and found Landon Presser's number.

Should I? What if it was the middle of the night, wherever he was?

But, Hannah.

I typed, *Hi, Landon, it's Avalon Nash. Hannah has had some bad news about her cousin (like a brother to her). If you have a chance to call or text, it might cheer her up. P.S. How are you?*

That didn't seem too forward, did it? I thought of Hannah. I pressed send.

Every time the lobby door opened, I looked up, scanning the end of that small hallway, afraid to find it was Dwayne Cabinau or Roscoe Cone. Or, more happily, Toby Cabinau coming in, leaning against the side of the bar to talk to Marta, as he had the weekend before, showing he was fine and allowing everyone to breathe a sigh of relief.

None of them arrived.

Which made me slightly confused when Marta came over and whispered, "That's her."

"Who's her?" I whispered back.

Marta nodded to a small cherrywood booth where a woman had just been seated. "Letitia Franklin. The preschool teacher whose family owned the farm called Beulah."

The woman faced the other direction, so we both stared openly, thoughts racing.

"Maybe she came in to be sure you are who you say you are," I offered.

"She thought I was crazy."

"Maybe now she's had a while to think otherwise. Maybe she came looking for you."

"I can't just go talk to her," said Marta.

"No, but I can."

I headed over.

Letitia Franklin-Johnson was, to my guess, in her early sixties.

Skin as brown as the booth in which she sat, she had hair cropped short and naturally salted with silver. She was looking at the menu, wearing clear-rimmed reading glasses held around her neck by a short strand of fake pearls. A preschool teacher, all right. She looked kindly yet no-nonsense, the sort of woman you'd like your child to have as an introduction to the world of the classroom.

"Ms. Franklin-Johnson?" I asked, and she looked up. "I'm Avalon Nash. I manage this restaurant."

"Hello," she said, extending her hand, which I shook. "You can call me Ms. Johnson. All my students did."

"My coworker, Marta Layton, says she spoke to you yesterday and is worried about what you thought of her."

Before she could respond, I slid into the booth across from her and lowered my voice.

"I want you to know that Marta is a fine and trustworthy person. She does have this sensitivity where she can see things not everyone can, which causes her distress sometimes. But times like when she saw your ancestor in the Appleton Lodge, well, that caught her by surprise. But whatever happened there, it affected her enough that she felt she had to find you, to let you know. It wasn't easy for her to find you and approach you, a total stranger. I'm sure it was surprising for you as well."

Ms. Johnson was hearing all of this, processing it.

"I wanted you to know she isn't crazy or anything." I said.

"What do you think of this gift of hers?" she asked.

Hoo boy.

"I know Marta believes she's experiencing these things, and I trust Marta," I said.

"That sounds like a truthful answer, dear."

Preschool teacher, all the way.

"Would you like me to send her over?"

"When she's free. If it's not too much trouble."

"I'll let her know. Someone will be here shortly to take your order."

Back at the bar, I nodded to Marta. "Yep, she came in for you. Talk to her when you feel ready."

Ms. Johnson didn't stay long after she ate and she and Marta talked. It wasn't until the end of the night when we were closing up that Marta had the opportunity to fill me in.

"Ms. Franklin-Johnson seems very nice," she opened with. "Her family moved off the farm and into town in the 1960s. Some of her aunts, uncles, and cousins moved back to New York City, and some down to the Nashville area. She and her niece are the last ones around here. She said I can come by sometime to look at photos of her family to see if I recognize anyone as the woman I saw. She doesn't know why she would be at Appleton since no one from her family ever worked there—or, God forbid, ever belonged."

"A fair question."

"I know. I think so, too." Marta and I worked side by side, emptying ice, refreshing the well bottles. "Are you okay?"

"Why? Don't I seem okay?" I asked.

"I'm not sure I would be, if I'd been in the car with you and Colin."

"Yeah, still a little shaken, but okay."

We nodded good night to our other waiters. As Marta and I finished closing out the cash register, Inspector Mike Spaulding walked in. Marta gave me a "You good?" look and I nodded.

Marta got her coat and left.

Mike slid onto his regular barstool.

"Any news?" I asked. "Any closer to catching the perps?"

"No news," he said. "No closer at all."

BEHIND THE BAR

Ingredients

Rosemary Simple Syrup

> Fresh rosemary
> 1 cup sugar
> 1 ½ cups of water

Cocktail

> 1 ½ oz dry gin
> 1 oz blueberry juice
> Fresh blueberries
> 1 oz rosemary simple syrup
> Soda water
> Ice
> Collins glass

Method

Rosemary Simple Syrup

> Pull needles from rosemary stems. Add all parts to medium saucepan. Add sugar and water. Simmer on low heat until sugar is dissolved. Remove from heat and bring to room temperature. Store remainder of simple syrup in cooler.

Cocktail

> Fill Collins glass with ice.
> In cocktail shaker, add ice, blueberry juice, rosemary

simple syrup, and gin. Shake ingredients together until cocktail shaker is cold.
Strain contents of cocktail shaker into Collins glass. Add fresh blueberries and a sprig of fresh rosemary to glass for garnish.

22

MEN AT NIGHT

I WAITED. MIKE surely didn't come in to tell me nothing.

"Do you want a drink? Are you off duty?"

He sat, contemplating. I poured whiskey. "Was the right judge on today? Did you get the search warrant for the Lodge?"

Mike swirled the caramel-colored liquid around the bottom of the glass. "He was not. I did not."

"Did you even ask for the search warrant?"

"I couldn't. One judge turns it down, you don't get a do-over." He took a swig. "I spent all day back at barracks doing paperwork. Oddly, there was a lot. I'm so much closer to having all my paperwork turned in than I've ever been before. But the main thing was, everybody saw me there acting like I didn't have a clue about what happened to Sandy Evans, like there were no leads to pursue, like I was wrapping up." He finished the liquid in one swig. "So, here's to tomorrow."

"Did you hear what happened to me today, by any chance?"

"No. Okay. I'm assuming it's more interesting than my day was."

Really, how could anyone know? Roscoe Cone wasn't on duty, so he wouldn't have radioed in our stop.

I described the incident to Mike.

"Hunh," he replied. "Hunh."

Man, he was good at not giving away his thoughts.

"Everyone's all right?" he asked.

"I doubt everyone would be if Reverend Layton hadn't made an appearance. There aren't many people who can cow Roscoe Cone."

Mike continued thinking. "Shit," he said, his true thoughts finally surfacing.

"Want another pour?" I asked.

"No. I've got to go. I only waited this long so no one would see me stop in. I wanted to ask, if things go well and I can get the search warrant tomorrow, will you draw me a map of how you remember Appleton Lodge?"

"I'll do my best," I said.

"Okay. Thanks."

My phone buzzed with a text message. Mike gave a small salute and left the bar.

The text was from Colin. *Can you send me the video? My dad is a lawyer and he wants to have a copy. We won't use it unless it's absolutely necessary. I'd check with you first.*

That actually sounded like a mighty good idea. I sat on a bar chair and sent him the video.

I had grabbed my coat when my phone buzzed again.

This time the text was from Landon Presser. *I've been texting Hannah, even called her, but she isn't picking up.*

Well, that wasn't good.

I'm off work now. I'll swing by and check on her.

Thanks. Please keep me in the loop.

Will do.

Thanks.

Employee parking at MacTavish's is well-lit. I could see anyone around, which was nobody. I headed for Hannah's.

The house was dark when I arrived. I pulled up in front of the garage and went to a side window to look inside. Her car was there.

I stood, weighing what to do. I mean, it was after eleven. She could be in bed. But it sounded like Landon had been trying to reach her for a while. I didn't have a house key. Hannah didn't have a dog or even plants that need tending when she's away, so why would she give me one?

I decided I'd try the kitchen door and if it was locked, I'd text her one more time.

If she didn't answer, then what?

I went to the kitchen door and turned the knob. It was unlocked.

I grabbed my phone and called her cell. I heard it ring, then immediately go to voicemail.

Oh, darn it.

I opened the door. "Hannah? It's Avalon."

A soft voice from the family room responded, "I'm here."

"Can I turn on a light?"

"Please don't."

My eyes adjusted slowly. She was sitting on the sofa facing the grand window to the back terrace.

"Hi," I said. "Landon's been texting and calling you. He was worried."

"I'm here."

"You're not picking up."

"My phone is in the kitchen. Lots of people call me. I don't want to talk to anyone."

"Are you all right?"

"Yes. Go home."

"That doesn't sound like you."

"I'm too tired to be me."

Now what? I don't know what to do in these situations. I'm not Hannah. Although apparently, being Hannah currently had an opening.

I sat down beside her.

It was a cloudy night. Whatever phase the moon was in, its light was diffused into Hannah's backyard, giving table, trees, and shrubs a ghostly appearance. It did the same for the furniture, including the couch where we now sat.

"What's going on?" I asked.

Hannah acting this way was freaking me out. She was the stalwart, the person you call to take your friend to meet a nun who was a sensitive or to counsel bereaved parents at a morgue. As far as facing life crises, she was the one. So now what?

"I need to be alone," she said.

"Okay," I said, and remembered her faith. "Alone with God?"

Boy, was I bad at this.

"If God dares show up."

"Okay. Mad at God, then?"

"I can't..." she started.

I sat.

"I can't believe there's any loving entity that thinks death is the answer for anything. Tina and Jim with their stillborn baby, Marsha with her son who fought so hard to beat addiction. Jake without the wife who's been by his side his whole adult life. Sandy with her husband and kids. I don't get it. I don't understand how that's love."

"Don't you...believe they're in a better place?"

"Oh, who cares? They're not here, are they? They're completely gone. When there are souls here who can't live without them. Young kids who have now lost two different mothers. The wrenching, the emptiness where they're supposed to be."

"Zachariah? Is he still in the hospital?"

"I haven't been answering my phone."

"Do you still want to go and be with your family?"

"I can't."

"Why?"

"I can't even get off this sofa."

"But if you could be with them?"

She didn't answer.

I went to her favorite chair and got the soft, heavy throw blanket. Then I went into her bedroom and got a pillow. I brought them to her. "Here," I said, leaning the pillow on the sofa's arm, and putting the blanket next to her. "Since you can't get up. I will leave if you want me to, but first, I'll be back momentarily."

I used the face light of my phone to guide me into her kitchen, then I texted her. Her abandoned cell phone lit up. She didn't have it password protected. I looked at the list of recent calls. All except Landon were local, so no big news from her family. She had a charging station on the counter, and I made sure her phone was cradled correctly, as it was running low on battery.

Then I went outside and called Landon on my phone.

"Hey," he answered.

"I'm here, at Hannah's," I said. "It's not good. I think she's having a dark night of the soul."

Was that really a thing?

"Do you think she would benefit from being back in Atlanta with her family?"

"I think so, but even if I drive her to Albany, which is more than two hours away, I can't picture her checking bags and standing in a long line to go through security. Not when she's like this. I don't know what to do."

"Give me a minute," he said, and even his figuring-it-out voice was deep and melodious. Damn professional actor.

"Where are you?" I asked.

"Budapest. Filming."

"No kidding," I said. "I was in Budapest with my mom when she was filming when I was a kid."

Oh, no, I must be tired. Give away private things about my past, why don't I?

"Really? Who is your mom?" he asked, bemused.

"Oh, an actor," I said. "I'll give you a minute. Should I stay here at Hannah's and wait for you to call?"

"Yeah, if you would, please." Then, I could almost hear the lightbulb go on. "Wait, is your mother Anna Nash?"

"Maybe."

"Hunh," he said.

"Yeah."

"Okay, give me a minute."

He called back in fewer than five minutes. He must have had things already in the works.

"Look," he said, "I'm against private planes as a means of transportation except when absolutely necessary," Landon said. "But they are one thing I can arrange. If you can take her to the local regional airport that I flew out of when I was there tomorrow morning at ten, I'll have a plane there to fly her to Atlanta. Do you have the phone number of someone in her family?"

I went through my contacts and copied the newly added number of her father and texted it over to Landon.

"Let me talk to her, will you?" he asked.

I went back into the living room and sat back down. "It's Landon," I said and handed her my phone. I went back into the kitchen while they talked. Then she stopped talking, and I went back in to get my phone.

"He got you a plane. Are you okay with flying to Atlanta?" I asked her.

"Yes."

"Okay, then, I'll see you in the morning."

She didn't speak. I took the blanket and tucked it around her as she sat. I turned to leave. "Avalon," she said as I neared the kitchen.

"Yes?"

"Don't die."

"I'll do my best."

I got into my car, turned it on, and rested my head on the steering wheel.

Hannah being like this had me shaken as much or more than the run-in with Roscoe Cone. Or the murder, or Jarrett Banks jumping.

It was a lot.

I drove home along cold and quiet streets.

No one was home at Sally's, of course, but there was a car pulled up where she usually parked. I was too tired to care.

I crossed the bridge and went around back to my kitchen door. A light was on in the kitchen. Before I could freak out about it, the door opened. Philip and Whistle ushered me inside together and Philip gathered me into an embrace.

"How are you here?" I asked.

"Marta came to see me. She said some dramatic stuff was going on in your life and you maybe could use some support."

Marta. That girl.

I melted into him.

"Don't die," I said.

MEN AT NIGHT

Ingredients

Grape Simple Syrup

   1 small jar of grape jelly, minus 2 tablespoons
   2 cups of water

Mini Peanut Butter and Jelly Sandwich

   2 tablespoons grade jelly
   2 tablespoons peanut butter
   2 slices of bread

Cocktail

   2 oz peanut butter whiskey of your choice
   1 oz grape soda or regular soda water (depending on how
   sweet you'd like your drink)
   1 ½ oz grape jelly simple syrup
   Round ice cube (optional but give a drink a nice finish)
   Ice
   Rocks glass

Method

Grape Simple Syrup

   In medium sauce pan, add grape jelly, but reserve 2
   tablespoons. Turn on low heat, add water and whisk
   together until grape jelly is fully dissolved. Remove from
   heat and bring to room temperature. Store remainder of
   grape jelly simple syrup in cooler.

Mini Peanut Butter and Jelly Sandwich

Spread grape jelly and peanut butter on each piece of bread and put together like a sandwich. Cut off crusts after putting the sandwich together and then cut into small squares for a garnish.

Cocktail

Add ice to rocks glass.
In cocktail shaker, add ice, peanut butter whiskey, and grape jelly simple syrup. Shake all ingredients together. Strain over rocks glass and add grape soda or regular soda water to top off cocktail.
And mini peanut butter and jelly sandwich to a cocktail pick for garnish.

23
MEN IN THE MORNING

Philip woke me at 8:30 the next morning. He had stayed with me until I fell asleep, then he went home to paint. He returned with food from the Cardamom Café. Breakfast for me and supper for him.

I sat up in bed as a start (8:30 is the middle of the night for bartenders, I might have mentioned) and sipped the latte.

Philip's thick black hair was wet and combed back off his forehead. My guess was he'd stopped into the Golden Ticket to work out on the way here, then showered. Wayward strands managed to escape everywhere. He looked as much like he'd been working on a fishing boat as in an art studio. Smelled different, though. I smiled.

He smiled, also, tentatively.

"Marta came to see you?" I asked. I could tell it wasn't the question he expected.

"Yeah, last night after the pub closed," he said.

"And you stopped what you were doing to talk to her?"

He looked abashed. "She's a student of mine, and a friend. I am not going to let her see me acting in a way I can't explain."

I sipped.

"I know it sounds bad, but when I come out the other side—as was about to happen, anyway—I can explain to those few people who are my intimates at least part of what was going on. Marta is someone I'm mentoring, not someone I'll open the depths of my creative process to."

"So, with her, you're on best behavior."

"I guess. Yeah."

"Did she do anything except tell you about me?"

"Not much."

He was sidestepping.

"Did she ask if you ever saw the two of you romantically involved?"

"Something like that. And I told her I needed her in the depths of my life, but in a different area. I told her when she got to the place, artistically, when she could tell those two apart, she'd agree with me and hopefully be glad we had each other."

"So, no, not romantically interested."

"So, no."

"And she was okay with that?"

"I think even a little relieved. We sat then and ate pita bread and hummus, which is one thing we do, and talked about what's been going on with you guys." He sipped his tea. "The thing is, I do need someone to mentor, someone to be on my best behavior with."

"I don't fit that bill?"

"How would I mentor you when you're more than my equal? Look, I am sorry if I cause you trouble when I suddenly descend into my hurricane. It's something I can't really change yet. What I'm trying to explain and can't very well is that when that comes over me, there's usually something big and deep and dark I have to work through. If I don't—and I spent years shoving it away—nothing gets worked through. My art doesn't flow. My spirit gets sick. If I can work through it, if I allow myself to dance in the depths, things happen, things are expressed, I can start to right myself."

"And there's a bunch of great art spread all over your studio."

"Well, there's art, anyway."

"Are you saying there will there come a time you can tell me what it's all about? What got you started toward the abyss this time?"

"Yes, I will," he said. "I always knew I would. But I needed the words, I needed to understand where it was all landing inside of me. This time, it has to do with a mentor of mine, a former professor, turning on me. The art scene in Paris is actually very insular. I don't know anymore how my future will go. I felt—I feel—very betrayed."

I studied his face, those gentle lines that could become so angular. I wondered how anyone who knew him could purposefully cause him so much pain.

"I'll explain it all to you—soon. But not yet. I'm not ready, not yet."

"Okay," I said. "But you do know you're a talented painter, a real painter, a real artist, no matter what anyone tells you?"

He nodded. "That's what I need to know, need to believe somehow. So even if I'm a painter with real art that no one wants anymore, that sits in my studio until I'm an old man...you're still interested in me?"

"Oh, dear God, yes. I don't care if your paintings are in the Louvre or in the basement. The first time I saw one at the Cardamom Café, I had such a visceral reaction to it before I had any idea it was yours. Since then, well, I have a visceral reaction to you."

He gave a crooked smile. "Come on, then. Let's eat and get Hannah to the airport."

I went in alone to find Hannah. She still sat on the sofa, staring out back. The blanket was folded, however, and she had a packed gym bag at her feet.

"He's dead," was all she said.

"I'm so sorry," I replied. I couldn't believe it myself. Zachariah with the all-encompassing bear hug was here no more.

"Head of the vestry," were the only other words Hannah spoke, once we were in the car and I asked if she'd told anyone she was leaving. "Taken care of."

I let Philip drive to the local airport. He knew the entrance to the private plane part, which I did not. We found the aircraft and the pilot hired by Landon, a plane large enough to have a cabin, so

Hannah wouldn't be sitting by the pilot. I walked her to the steps. She boarded, not looking back or saying a word.

We watched as the attendant closed the door and the pilot finished his precheck and radioed the tower.

"I've never heard Hannah not talk. That was weird," said Philip once we were back in the car.

"Ya think?" I replied. This time I drove, as he had walked to the gym and my place earlier. I dropped him back home, a small burst of hope taking root inside me, telling me things with us might be inching towards normal.

It was still earlier than when I usually knew the town woke up. I pulled into MacTavish's parking lot out of habit, for no other reason than I was driving past it.

Turns out Inspector Spaulding was driving past it, too, in his unmarked vehicle, on his way to my place. He recognized my car and pulled in.

I unlocked the passenger door and he climbed in.

"Did you get it?"

In response, he waved a paper in front of me.

"What's next?"

"I'm still of the opinion every second counts, that Dwayne and others will try to remove any evidence of their past adventures as soon as possible. So I'm heading there now."

"And Inspector Becker?"

"I'll call him once I'm there.

"So you trust him mostly, just not completely."

"I trust him. Can you draw me a map?"

He'd come prepared with a blank piece of paper on a clipboard, a pencil riding inside the clip. I took it but found it frustrating to try to draw with the steering wheel in the way. I got out and got into the back seat.

"Where do you think you'll be coming in from?" I asked.

"I don't know."

"You have lock-busting things?"

He chuckled. "I guess that's the technical term, yes."

"There's a door that might be open," I said, and tried to make a usable drawing of where it would be. "You want to sit back here and I'll try to explain?"

He got into the back seat. I pointed out the different rooms, attempting to remember where stairs were. My depictions of room sizes were abysmal.

Finally I said, "This is ridiculous. I'm coming with you."

"By the book, Nash, this has to be completely by the book."

"How can you help it if you find some snoopy local looking around?"

"By. The. Book."

"I'll take you straight to the music room, straight there, and I'll leave. If anyone else is around the building, I won't go in, but I can at least point out the different rooms and where the music room is."

"You can do that," he relented.

"Let's take your car," I said. "I'll leave mine here. That way I can giddyup home and no one will be the wiser after Cal Becker gets there."

"How will you get home?" he asked.

"Spaulding," I said, echoing the exasperated tone he'd used on me, "people walk loops around the lake for exercise all the time. How out of shape do you think I am?"

I locked my vehicle and climbed into his. I could tell he was weighing the wisdom of this decision already as we pulled out onto the side street, then back onto Main towards the lake loop.

"We're doing this," I said, then realized I'd spoken aloud.

"I'm doing this," he corrected, and we drove together in silence.

MEN IN THE MORNING

Ingredients

2 oz espresso vodka
1 oz coffee liqueur
1 oz fresh brewed espresso, chilled
1 table spoon extra virgin olive oil
Fresh lemon peel
Ice
Martini glass

Method

Chill martini glass by adding ice and a small amount of water.
In cocktail shaker, add ice, espresso vodka, coffee liqueur, espresso, and extra virgin olive oil. Shake contents until shaker is nice and cold.
Discard ice and water from martini glass. Strain contents of cocktail shaker in chilled martini glass.
Take fresh lemon peel and twist to release lemon oils over drink.
Add fresh lemon peel to a cocktail pick for garnish.

24

INSIDE

I NSPECTOR SPAULDING DROVE onto Lodge lands via a side entrance, then followed the narrow road back toward the main building. We parked at the side of the Agora, where members could drive up to be dropped off for dances or plays or other educational activities.

No other cars were around.

We got out of ours. I should have noticed the biting autumn wind or the few thin stratus clouds skiffing over the lake, but I didn't. I was focused on getting Mike into the building.

He reached for his breaking and entering kit but I said, "Let me try the door we used the other day."

I walked along the outside of the long hallway towards the back of the lobby, staying close to the building so as not to be seen from the street.

It was a brisk downhill walk. I was glad not to be on the other side of the building, the side where Jarrett Banks landed after leaving the cupola, under whatever circumstances that had happened.

I reached the door where Toby and Lily met us. I pushed in but it was firmly locked.

I shook my head and trudged back up to meet Mike.

He had his kit out of the car. The front doors to the Agora had not only a lock but also a heavy chain wound through the two door handles. By the time I arrived, the chain was history. He knelt by the lock with a peculiar, slim tool and listened. He clicked the lock and the door opened. He took a moment to put both the kit and the remains of the chain into the trunk of his car.

Then we entered. Again, Mike carefully pulled the door shut behind us.

We stood a moment, letting our eyes adjust to the lower light. The hallways outside the theater had no windows, so it took a moment.

Double doors to the theater were immediately in front of us. I wasn't sure about navigating this part of the hallway, so I decided going through was the best bet. I opened one of the doors and led us inside. The small windows at the very top allowed in shafts of light. Normally, a person would stop and take in the enormity of the space, but Inspector Spaulding was a man on a mission.

I led us straight to the corresponding doors on the opposite side, only glancing back once toward the corner, wondering if the Longing Lady was still there.

In the familiar hallway, I turned us to the left.

"Chapel," I said as we passed it. Then, "Locked door to the cupola steps."

Funny how in the light of day and in the presence of a highway patrol inspector, ghostly things seemed significantly less menacing.

The menace came from elsewhere.

Around the turn and down the long hall we came to the door to the old music room. The heavy door had a long, rectangular glass panel in it, a design popular in schools throughout the land. Mike went through first.

The square room had windows to the outside that once might have faced a courtyard but now faced a blank wall. They did nothing to dispel the dismal atmosphere.

"Toby said there was an entry to stairs?"

"A false back to a closet."

There were closet doors on either side of the stage. The door to the right was wider. We both headed that way. Mike went in. There was a rack toward the front with nothing hanging on it. He went to the back, his fingers feeling their way around the perimeter. He obviously had a successful career as a cat burglar at the ready should this law enforcement thing not work out. At the top he found a small golden bar, which he pressed.

The back panel slid open, disappearing seamlessly into the wall. There in front of us was another door with two deadbolts that slid open easily. It seemed their purpose was to lock someone downstairs, not keep someone who knew about the secret door from descending. Behind the second door, wooden steps flowed down to a landing where they turned a corner and continued.

Mike took out his phone and punched in numbers. "Cal," he said, "I got a search warrant for the Appleton Lodge. I'm heading that way now." He listened. "Got it. Sounds good. See you there."

The information he didn't provide was his business. Who knew where Inspector Becker thought he was coming from? If it was the courthouse, it would take a while for him to reach the Lodge. The fact he was already inside the Lodge about to head to his ultimate destination was, I guess, on need-to-know business.

It was clear he wanted some time down there to get the lay of the land before Becker arrived.

He turned to me. "Thanks. You have to go."

"I can't just go down the stairs and have a look?"

"Becker's on his way. You have to go." He didn't sound at all sorry. He sounded like an enforcement officer, and I'd better get out of there.

I understood it had to all be by the book. My guess was he would take a quick look downstairs himself and go back out to wait for Becker before he touched anything.

If there was a chance that Sandy Evans could receive some form of justice, I knew I'd better beat Becker's arrival and get out of there.

I gave a short salute and turned around.

I chose to travel in the hallway that wound around the outside the Agora, which was more steps, but I hadn't been that way and I was curious. Within five minutes, I was out under intermittent sunshine. Which way to go? Should I act like an innocent person and saunter down the hill, then down the Appleton driveway to the road? Or should I go back up the hill and through the woods, retracing the way Marta, Colin, and I approached? I stood by one of the stone arches holding up the Agora's porte cochere to decide. I chose the woods, as it would render me out of sight—and thus out of the proceedings—more quickly.

I looked down the hill at the magnificent view one more time before turning to go up.

As I did, I saw a pick-up pulling into the circular drive.

My first thought was that Inspector Becker had been close by and had come right over.

I started to hurry my hurrying, but it struck me that inspectors on duty don't drive pick-ups.

I crouched behind the pillar.

A lone man exited the cab. He reached into the back of the truck and lifted out a large box. When he picked it up, he walked strangely. My guess was that the box was very heavy. He finally put it down and began to drag it up the hill to the door we'd used with Toby and Lily. Only then was he close enough for me to know for certain it was Dwayne Cabinau. As he opened his coat to fish for the key to the door, I saw a holster.

Shit.

Shit. Shit.

Dwayne was undoubtedly heading for the meeting room, and he was armed. Mike was armed, too, but not expecting Dwayne.

Once Dwayne was inside the Lodge, I tore open the door beside me, then the one to the Agora. If I went around the theater, Dwayne could see me down the long hall.

Instead, I sprinted as quietly as possible into and through the large space, out the other side, and turned left to race to the music room. I let its heavy door swoosh shut behind me and ran for the closet, pulling the door closed behind me. Then I tore down the stairs.

Mike had his flashlight on. He turned his beam towards me as I exited into the meeting room. I put my arm up to ward off the blinding beam.

"Nash! What the hell?"

"Dwayne Cabinau is here. He's armed. He's coming this way."

"You saw him?"

"Just now. He came in that lower door."

As I spoke, we heard footsteps enter the room above us.

Mike shone his flashlight around the room, looking for cover. There really was nowhere. There was a small stage in this room, directly below the stage upstairs. It held an American flag and another I didn't recognize. Along the back wall of the room was a thick crimson curtain, but it didn't reach to the floor. Anyone could see our feet.

A second smaller closet was to the left of the stage. We sprinted over and opened the door to find it fully stacked with wooden chairs.

"In there," Mike commanded.

I took a reticent step inside, and he closed the door.

Outside, he switched off his flashlight. I heard him draw his gun from his own holster.

We each stood in our different shade of darkness.

Waiting.

Something odd was happening above us. Dwayne was moving through the space, but heavily and—it sounded like—clumsily.

Then the closet door above us opened, and we heard him step onto the stairs.

He started down.

He missed one, fell, swore, and righted himself against the wall.

He turned to come down the final steps, and again missed one and tumbled heavily onto the floor. Mike was still holding steady, biding his time.

It turned out Dwayne knew where there was a switch to a set of lights that still worked. It must have been jerry-rigged to an outdoor source of power.

Looking out through the door crack, I saw Mike turn on the flashlight and aim it right into Dwayne's eyes.

"Who is it?" Dwayne demanded.

"Inspector Michael Spaulding. I have a signed warrant to be here."

Cabinau swore again.

"What the hell? No, you can't."

He reached for his own gun, which was from his private collection. Without warning or waiting, he fired three shots. I couldn't see where they hit, or if Mike was okay.

Then Dwayne fell against the stage and headed towards the wall. He reached my closet, whether looking for cover or something hidden there, I don't know.

He flung it open.

"Hi, Dwayne," I said. I stepped out, trying to push him back into the small space, but he was too big for me. As I attempted to push him, he grabbed my arms and I fell into him. We clung to each other in a bizarre dance of death. He smelled funny, and he looked yellow.

"What's wrong with you?" I asked. "You don't look well."

That threw him off. It wasn't what he was expecting, and he looked very scared.

"The snakes! The snakes!" he yelled. And he started screaming.

He pulled away from me and started shooting towards the floor. I ran and jumped onto the stage. Mike joined me.

"Nooo!" Cabinau bellowed, backing onto the stairs. He shot at the floor two more times, then climbed the remaining steps on his hands and feet.

Once upstairs, we heard him slam the door shut, then lock the two deadbolts from the other side.

Damn.

Then we heard liquid splashing in the room above us. Perhaps he had water, and he was using it to slow the imaginary snakes?

But the wooden floor in the abandoned music room above was not leakproof.

The smell hit before drops of liquid began seeping through.

"Gasoline," said Mike.

"Shit," I said.

We heard Dwayne moving methodically through the music room. Then, unexpectedly, there was a wild scream of pain, loud enough to be heard a floor away.

A beat. The splashing continued.

When he was done, the fire started not with a crackle but a roar.

"Shit," groaned Mike.

INSIDE

Ingredients

Brûlée Bananas

1 fresh banana
Raw sugar
Crème brûlée torch

Cocktail

2 oz banana crème liqueur
1 ½ oz banana whiskey
Few dashes banana bitters
Brûlée bananas
Ice
Coupe glass

Method

Brûlée Bananas

Peel and slice bananas into thin medallions. Place fresh
bananas on small baking sheet and add a small amount of
raw sugar to the top of each.
Torch bananas until the sugar becomes caramelized. Set
aside.

Cocktail

In cocktail shaker, and add ice, banana crème liqueur,
banana whiskey, and banana bitters Shake until cocktail
shaker is chilled.

Strain cocktail into coupe glass.
Add brûléed bananas to a cocktail pick for garnish.

205

25

STILL INSIDE

"WHY DIDN'T YOU shoot him?" I asked.

"I never had a clear shot. He was always moving."

"Okay."

Then he continued, his voice anguished, "Hell, Nash, if I shot an officer, I'd be immediately suspended and there'd be an investigation. Even if I was cleared, the repercussions would be great. My career would be over. It didn't seem worth it."

He didn't add the 'if I shot a White officer,' but I got that part.

"Cabinau didn't seem well. I didn't think he could do much harm. I mean, besides this."

He fell to a seated position on the stage and moved around so I could see where his pants on his left leg were torn and he was bleeding.

"Mike!"

"I was grazed, that's all. If the bullet had bounced and hit something crucial, I'd already be bleeding out. But, still, since you have two good legs, run up the stairs and see if there's any chance we can get out that door."

I did as he requested.

As I reached the top, smoke curled as if with a smirk through the cracks around the door, its widening tentacles trying to reach me. To my surprise, there were a set of deadbolts on my side as well. First I pushed the door, hard, to see if it would open.

No, it was bolted from outside, as we feared.

I reached up to the inside bolts in the unlikely event they were somehow coordinated with those outside. I'll never know. They were already burning hot.

I pulled my hand back, blowing on the start of the burn.

We were in deep trouble.

I pulled out my cell phone. Downstairs, the walls were concrete and there was no service. Here, one bar flickered and then went out.

Damn.

I came back down to relay the bad news. Wisps of smoke wafted down from the ceiling. If both the floor and ceiling above us were wood, we didn't have much time.

Time to do what?

To live?

To my surprise, Mike was standing in front of the stage, studying it.

"He said there were drawers."

"Yes, but we have to figure out how to get out of here."

"Whether we survive or not, I will not let the evidence be destroyed in the flames. They will find me with the freaking trophies below my body. I am not going down without finding it."

He walked to where the cutouts of one drawer were and pulled it out. It contained tall candles and folded tablecloths and stuff like that. We tried to jerk it out further, but it had come out as far as its tracks allowed.

The smoke was becoming more noticeable. Mike pulled a handkerchief from his pocket and handed it to me. "Put it over your nose and mouth."

I obeyed.

We moved to the other side of the stage and pulled out the twin drawer. Again, fabric things. I didn't pay attention. Mike tried to reach back to see if there was anything, but his arm was too big to fit over the front drawer.

"Let me try," I said. I didn't want to betray my growing panic, but I knew, even if Becker arrived or if someone nearby saw the fire and called the fire department, no one knew we were down here. The wooden floor above us was going to collapse, and soon. We would have nowhere to go. Even if they put out the fire, I couldn't see a way it wouldn't be too late.

So might as well look for the evidence that led us down here. If we were going to give up our lives to do this, we might as well do it.

I leaned forward and inched my arm and hand backwards. As I did, I felt something metal beneath the folded linens. I stood up and started clawing the fabric out of the way and onto the floor.

"What?" Mike asked.

"There's something under here."

Then, there it was, a silver track. Two thirds of the way back, there was a handle on it. I pulled the handle. The heavy cord to which it was attached argued with me for a moment, then there was a click. The drawer slid back so easily, I tumbled back onto the floor, the front drawer in my lap.

Mike stepped ahead and reached in. There was a silver metal casket. It was rectangular, maybe six by eighteen inches.

The first thing he did was pull out his phone and take photos. Then he pulled it out, set it on the stage, and peered into the space behind it, as I did. There was nothing more.

He took photos of the empty drawer shaft anyway.

Then he picked up the casket and put it on the floor. "Get down, Nash," he said. "Smoke reaches the floor last."

The acrid gray-and-white smoke was indeed curling above us, curtsying lower and lower.

There was no lock on the chest.

Mike opened it. And again, he took photos. Not of all of it, just of the box with the lid open.

We both stared at the odd collection of items in front of us. We knew we'd found the treasure box, the trophies of those who had run afoul of this group of supremacists.

I only saw the those on top: Marvin Johnson's torn and bloodied shirt, as described by Toby. And a pin. A rose with the wording *Sensitive Badass*. The pin worn by Sandy the night I met her.

Mike picked up the torn white undershirt. Tears ran down his face.

"Justice at last," I said.

"I'm here too late to save them. And the cost of us being here is too high."

He looked at me.

To give him a moment, I turned away and reached back into the box. Smoke stung my eyes. But there was something I saw. Something bright. I reached for it and wrapped the fabric around my hand as Mike put the bloodied shirt back into the box, next to the pin I knew Sandy's husband could identify.

"We need to lie down on the floor," he said, the tears gone. "It will give us the longest time."

He closed the lid of the box and lay down next to it. I took the object I'd removed and surreptitiously tucked it into my bra. I have tucked exactly two things into my bra as a way of transporting them out of a situation, and both times had happened within the last twenty-four hours.

Then I lay on my stomach next to Mike. "I'm sorry. I'm sorry I didn't tell you everything I knew about your last case. I'm sorry."

"I know."

"I value you so much as a friend."

"I know," he said. Then, "Valerie."

"Valerie?"

"My woman."

"Oh. I hope she's a good one."

"I believe so."

Neither of us added, *But he might never get to find out.*

Crap, I thought then, my mind going to Hannah. *I'm doing the one thing she asked me not to do.*

My death would be hard for her.

I couldn't go there. I couldn't think about Philip.

Nope, nope, nope.

I didn't know which was likely to happen first: passing out from smoke inhalation or having the burning floor above crash down around us. I voted for the smoke.

"I value your friendship, too," Mike said. "If we don't make it out, it will have been an honor to work with you."

That's when I started to cry.

STILL INSIDE

Ingredients

Black Pepper Simple Syrup

> Tajin
> ¼ cup fresh crack black pepper corns (reserve a small amount on side)
> ½ cup sugar
> 2 cups water

Cocktail

> Tajin
> 1 fresh lime, cut into wedges
> Tiny dash of smoking liquid
> 2 oz mezcal
> ½ oz orange liqueur
> 1 oz fresh lime juice
> 1 oz fresh lemon juice
> 1 oz black pepper simple syrup
> Ice
> Rocks glass

Method

Black Pepper Simple Syrup

Add fresh cracked peppercorns, sugar, and water to a medium saucepan. Place on medium heat and let simmer for for 30 minutes, stirring occasionally. Remove from heat and bring to room temperature. Pour through cheese cloth to remove peppercorns. Store in cooler.

Cocktail

On a small plate, mix a small amount of Tajin and crushed black pepper. Take rocks glass and slide a wedge of fresh lime up and down the outside making sure to get a nice coating of lime juice. Take rocks glass and roll into Tajin and black pepper mixture.
Add ice to rocks glass and set aside.
In cocktail shaker, add ice, smoking liquid, mezcal, orange liqueur, lime juice, lemon juice, and black pepper simple syrup. Shake all ingredients together until cocktail shaker is chilled.
Strain contents of cocktail shaker into rocks glass.
Add fresh lime for garnish.

26

UP

Tʜᴜs I ʟᴀʏ there, quietly breathing any oxygen left near the floor, wondering, what was it with people dying in Appleton Lodge?

Did Adelaide really off herself? Was it her ghost we heard when we were here? Was she still here?

But wait a minute.

It wasn't a ghost that we heard. It was Jarrett Banks, running up the stairs to the cupola.

And Dwayne Cabinau arrived before we got out of the building. Had he already been here, calling Marta's name, knocking twice?

My mind circled back to Jarrett. He jumped from the belvedere. He went up those stairs, past us on the first floor. The stairs that were securely cemented shut.

How had he gotten to those stairs?

If he was running up the stairs past us in the hall, there had to be an entrance down here.

"Mike," I whispered, coughing as I removed the handkerchief from my face. "There has to be another way out of here. How else would Jarrett Banks have gotten to the cupola?"

I started creeping on my forearms and knees over to the wall covered with the crimson cloth. He followed behind.

Since the room was empty, we could see nearly the whole length of the wall under the hanging curtain through the gathering smoke.

We began crawling over. As we got closer, Mike said, "There." He gestured to where the hint of a doorframe showed itself underneath the fabric. He got there first, ducked under the crimson curtain, and rose to his knees with some difficulty.

"The door isn't hot," he said, relief in his voice.

I slid under to join him.

"Shall we try it?"

"I truly dislike our other choices," I said.

He grabbed the handle and pulled it open wide enough for the two of us to crawl through. He went first with me quite literally on his heels. A trail of blood was left in his wake as he crawled, part of which was absorbed into my black knit pants.

The hallway we entered was lined with local stone. I seemed to recall the hallways above us had concrete floors covered with carpets. The smoke hadn't yet found a way in.

We pulled the door closed firmly behind us, knowing the curtain and the door would hold back the fire and smoke for only so long.

When Mike stood, I saw he had both the casket and his flashlight. He turned on the latter. I've never been so grateful to see stone walls in my entire life. He leaned back against one to take the pressure off his injured leg.

We both gasped the comparatively fresh air for a moment. Even as we did, the beginnings of a new smoke wall crept towards us from around the bend ahead.

"We don't have much time," he said. "Let's find the staircase."

We hurried the short distance along the corridor and there it was. The belvedere staircase opened on our left.

The stairs quickly turned out of sight. They were wooden, of course—the weak link in our stone fortress from which the smoke was descending.

We peered up. We couldn't see where the smoke started or if it went all the way up the stairs.

We looked at each other.

"I don't see that we have any other choice," he said.

"Me neither. Can you climb stairs?"

His leg continued to bleed.

"I can't not climb them."

We didn't have time to think. We both started up. Halfway to the first floor, I had to close my eyes and hold my breath. It was bad. There was no choice but to keep climbing.

I didn't even notice when we passed the door to the Lodge's main floor. I thought about nothing but reaching air.

We continued up. And up.

Finally, I couldn't hold my breath any longer. I opened my eyes to see how much trouble I was in.

The air was clearer. The thick smoke was below us. Still, I tried to only take small breaths to keep me going.

There wasn't a door to the second floor. We continued up towards the third floor landing.

Once there, we hit open air. We were at the top of the belvedere.

I'd seen photos of Appleton Lodge in all its glory. Back then, a four-story enclosed lookout towered over the dining rooms. That building had burned down. We were in the original building, whose tower only rose three floors. Thank goodness.

Mike and I stood for only a moment, then walked together to each of the four sides.

The fire was impressive. Magnificent, really, as fires go.

Dwayne must have had multiple cans of gasoline in that heavy box. He'd apparently emptied them, one by one, as he walked through the halls and buildings. The fire hadn't reached its zenith, but it was close. Flames roared from the walls, licking at the roofs around us. It was very impressive.

Well, damn.

I glanced back at the open door, acrid smoke snaking up behind us. It was one of life's choose-your-poison kind of moments.

"Okay," Mike said, calm and confident. He put the flashlight and the box down on the wooden floor. "Circumstances are dictating our course of action."

He pulled me over to the side of the tower facing away from the

Lodge. The roof of the hall around the Agora was to our left. Fire had crashed through one spot.

"Listen to me. This is what we're going to do."

Usually, if a male starts mansplaining to me, my hackles rise. Not this time. I was all ears.

"We are now participating in the sporting event known as the high drop. This is how elite athletes such as ourselves find successful outcomes. First, we will drop from the lowest point possible. Usually, we'd drop to the roof, then turn around again and drop to the ground. But, as we can see, the roof is burning and might collapse under our weight. So, we have no choice but to drop straight down from this structure. Fortunately, we're above a grassy surface. When the time comes, we're going to turn around and climb over the short balcony wall here. Then we're going to let ourselves down so we're hanging from the top of the railing. That will take six feet off our fall, which, given we'll be falling from about twenty-six feet, is a lot. Are you with me?"

"Yes."

"So, Nash, this is the exact order of events leading up to our drop. First, we are going to loosen up. Our bodies can't be tense. We need to land in a relaxed state."

I laughed.

"I know. But we're going to do it."

"Second, we're going to drop anything we're carrying that we don't want to land on. We'll toss things away from the tower, away from our chosen landing spot." He pointed. "Which is right there. In your mind, see a circle whose circumference starts about four feet away from the side of the tower. We've each got a circle. They might overlap, but we'll land at least three to four feet away from each other. That part won't be a problem. We'll do it naturally."

Darndest thing. As he spoke, I was getting calmer, like we really were going to perform a sporting event on the same team.

"So. We will loosen up, toss items, climb over, hang on, drop. Good so far?"

"Yes. But can you do it with an injured leg?"

While it was true that the bullet hadn't hit an artery, it hadn't just grazed him either. The leg of his khakis was soaked through.

"Yeah. In fact, you need to help get me down there as quickly as possible."

I think he knew that taking my focus off myself could only help. I did want to get him to safety, and to help, fast.

"Then, landing. We're going to drop straight down, knees and feet together, but still loose, remember that part. Land on the balls of both your feet, which should be shoulder-length apart." He demonstrated and I copied him. "When you land, bend your knees and drop and roll to one side, pushing off from the ball of one of your feet."

"Does it matter which one?"

"Whichever comes naturally."

Flames were now dancing up from the roofs just below us, grabbing for us in a frenzied tarantella. It was clear we didn't have time to wait for help. We had to do this.

"Okay, teammate," Mike said.

"Lodge Leaper High Drop," I said, "let's take first place." I shook his extended hand.

"Got it?" Mike asked. "Loosen, toss, turn around, hang down, go limp and drop, land on balls of feet, bend knees, fall and roll."

"Let's try it once. I'm sure if we come back up, I'll have it by the second time."

He looked at me. Somehow, we both smiled.

"Tell me when you're ready," he said as he emptied the bullets from his gun and put them into his pocket. "Once we start the sequence, there is no stopping."

"Ready as I'll ever be."

"Here we go."

To my surprise, he started by shaking out his arms and rolling his head. I copied everything.

"Usually, we'd do some squats, but..."

He shook out his good leg, and I did both of mine. We finished with long arm stretches up.

Then we walked to the side of the tower. He tossed his flashlight and his sidearm. I did a quick inventory. The only thing I had to toss was the necklace in my bra. I let it be. I took out my cell phone and wondered.

"I'm keeping mine in my shirt pocket," Mike said. The casket was his final toss.

As advertised, without stopping we went to the next part. We climbed to sit on top of the belvedere wall/railing. Then we turned around.

"See you at the bottom, teammate," he said.

He grabbed the top of the railing and lowered himself over. My heart was pounding, but I shook out my shoulders and followed suit. I was able to let myself down without letting go of the railing. For the briefest moment, we both hung, still in fine physical shape (not counting his bullet wound), from the side of the building.

Then Mike let go, and there was nothing to do but follow him. We both pushed away from the building, heading for the ground.

UP

Ingredients

Ginger Simple Syrup

    2 inches of fresh ginger root, peeled and mashed
    1 fresh carrot, peeled and shaved into thin long strips
    1 cup sugar
    1 ½ cups of water

Cocktail

    1 ½ oz carrot juice
    ½ oz orange juice
    ½ oz lemon juice
    1 oz ginger simple syrup
    2 oz orange vodka
    Ice
    Martini glass

Method

Ginger Simple Syrup

In medium saucepan, add sugar, water, and ginger root. Simmer over medium heat for about 10 minutes, stirring occasionally. Take off heat and let cool. Remove ginger from simple syrup. Store in cooler.

Cocktail

Chill martini glass by adding ice and a small amount of water.

In cocktail shaker, add ice, carrot juice, orange juice,
lemon juice, ginger simple syrup, and orange vodka.
Shake all ingredients together until shaker is cold.
Discard ice from martini glass. Strain contents of cocktail
shaker into chilled martini glass.
Add fresh carrot strips to top of cocktail for garnish.

27

DOWN

I LANDED ON the balls of my feet, as instructed.

As I did, I heard a crack, felt a ball of nausea travel up from the pit of my stomach, then disperse.

Still, I bent my knees and rolled.

I lay on the grass. My head pointed down the hill. I looked straight back up at the huge buildings burning around me.

And I would swear I saw movement in the belvedere where we had been. Flames clawed at the side of it. Behind them it looked like a woman. An older woman. A stalwart older woman, white hair piled on top of her head.

I would have sworn it was Adelaide Whisk.

She stepped backwards and disappeared.

Holy crackers.

"Mike?" I asked.

"I'm here," he said. "Are you okay?

"I think I broke something. My leg." I tried to move both of them. "Yes. I'm going with my right leg. How about you?"

"I think I broke my non-shot leg. I probably landed on it harder."

I worked on shifting myself, because blood was rushing to my head. I didn't turn all the way around, but I at least got horizontal on the hill.

Mike got out his cell phone and punched in some numbers. "Cal," he said, "where are you...? Okay, good. We're behind the largest part of the building, beneath the belvedere...Yeah, the tower thing...outside. On the ground...Good, good, can you hear the sound of my voice?"

As he asked, Inspector Cal Becker rounded the side of a building. I saw him approach in shadowed relief. Both men hung up the phone.

I moved some more, cautiously checking out the state of my being. Things seemed okay enough for me to sit up. Cal knelt beside Mike and helped him sit up, too. Then Cal grabbed his radio and said, "10-999. Appleton Lodge. Request two ambulances. Civilian injured also."

He walked over to me. "How are you?"

"I think I have a broken leg."

"An ambulance is on the way."

"Thanks."

Inspector Becker returned to Mike.

"What the hell happened?" Cal Becker asked his fellow inspector. "I talked to you ten minutes ago!"

"I went in to get the lay of the land. Avalon Nash saw me go inside, then saw Dwayne Cabinau arrive. She came inside to warn me. We didn't know Cabinau was splashing accelerant as he walked the halls. He came down to the secret meeting room and found us there. But something was off with him. He was delusional. His body emitted a foul odor, and he was jaundiced and seemingly in terrible pain. He yelled, 'The snakes, the snakes!' and discharged his weapon multiple times. One of the shots he fired hit me in the leg. Then he went upstairs, locked the door from his side, and threw the match."

"Good God. Where is he now?"

"I have no idea. He left us locked in the basement. We found the stairs to the cupola and were able to climb past the fire to the top and we dropped down. All of this happened within minutes. And here you are."

Sirens blared in the distance, growing closer and louder.

Mike continued talking to Cal, but in a lowered voice. It occurred to me he'd told the story of our adventure loudly enough for me to hear it, so we'd be on the same page. Easier, since he told a sensible version of the truth.

Cal and Mike were bent over the hard-won casket of trophies. They photographed each item as they removed it. My guess was the trophies would be cataloged by an evidence team, but Mike didn't want anything to go missing between the Lodge and the barracks.

The thing was, something had already gone missing. Damn. I'd just apologized to Mike for not telling him everything about his last case. And this man was incredibly observant. It was hard to believe he didn't know I had taken something.

I couldn't ask him about it without either involving him in my decision or simply being forced to give it up to be entered into evidence.

Meanwhile, the air was becoming unbearably hot. Somewhere, roof timbers crashed with a huge boom. We needed to get away from the building.

I felt slightly wounded that minutes ago, Mike Spaulding and I had been on the same Olympic team. Now he was a working professional and I was a bystander.

I looked around to see if there was a preferable place to be. I wasn't picky. The heat was fierce. I put my head down and crawled, putting no weight on my injured leg. As I did, I heard sirens coming from the back road into the Lodge lands. I looked up to see two ambulances heading our way.

I sat on cooler grass and looked back toward the spectacle of the last Lodge building going up in flames. As I did, I saw a shape close to the stage entrance to the Agora.

"Inspectors!" I called out. Both men looked my way. I pointed toward the shape that could be an old log. I didn't say anything, but it looked suspiciously like a person.

Inspector Becker stood up, casket in hand, and walked across the lawn. He came to stand above the shape.

The expression on his face was one of horror and disbelief. He knelt by the shape, reached out, but thought better of it and retracted his hand. He stood, once again grabbed the radio on his shoulder, and spoke into it.

He walked back to Mike.

"Cabinau," he said. "It's Cabinau."

Inspector Becker then went down to meet the ambulances and fire trucks approaching on the back road. From shouts I was hearing, I assumed multiple fire trucks arrived in front of the Lodge. I wondered how many local fire departments could send help.

One of the ambulance crews was assigned to me. As they went to the back of the vehicle to get a wheeled stretcher, I grabbed my phone and called Marta.

"Hey," she answered. "The Appleton Lodge is on fire!"

"Yeah, I know. I'm there. And I've hurt my leg. Can you open?"

DOWN

Ingredients

Fresh kiwi, peeled and sliced
Fresh green grapes, rinsed
Fresh mint leaves
1 oz aquafaba
1 oz lemon juice
1 oz simple syrup
Soda water
Ice
Collins glass

Method

In cocktail shaker, add a few pieces of kiwi, a few grapes, a few sprigs of mint leaves, simple syrup, and lemon juice. Muddle ingredients together.
Add ice and aquafaba to cocktail shaker. Shake all ingredients together until shaker is cold.
Pour contents into glass. Fill remainder of cocktail glass with soda.
Garnish drink with a few grapes, a slice of kiwi, and a fresh sprig of mint.

28

E.R.

DWAYNE CABINAU WAS dead. His body was taken to the morgue.

Mike and I were admitted to neighboring treatment rooms in the E.R.

Triage in the ambulance determined I'd likely snapped my tibia. Not great for a bartender, but it could have been oh, so much worse. They insisted I wear an oxygen cord to counteract any smoke inhalation.

Mike, bleeding staunched, was taken for X-rays first. As I waited for the technician to return for me, Marta showed up. "But—" I started.

"I opened," she said. "Manuela and Davros have it under control. What the hell?"

I was grateful to see her. Hannah was in no shape to get an emergency phone call from me, and Philip had likely just gone to bed for his day's sleep. I didn't want to awaken him. Marta was pretty much it.

I told her the story. She was suitably stunned and horrified.

They had cut my pants off in the ambulance, and I'd pulled on a lovely hospital gown in preparation for X-rays of my leg. Since I didn't have burns on my body, especially not near my mouth or nose, they were hopeful there wasn't too much smoke inhalation. Mike and I had stayed close to the ground except when we were running up the stairs. While it seemed we were trapped inside the burning Lodge for days, it had been a matter of minutes.

The nurse gave me a large, clear plastic bag for clothing and valuables. I removed my shirt but not my bra. After the nurse left, I said, "Marta, come here. Quickly."

She came and stood close to me, realizing there was something I didn't want anyone else to see. "I need you to take this home for me. We'll talk about what to do about it."

I reached under the hospital gown into my bra and removed the trophy I'd taken from the Appleton. Her eyes opened wide as she put out her hand and I dropped the ribbon necklace with the large gold pendant into it.

It was rectangular, made of gold, contours of farmland painted over it with the largest step cut emerald I'd ever seen—with the exception of the one in Marta's drawing. And of course, one word.

"That's what she was holding!" Marta said. "That's it!"

"Where can you put it?" I asked. She held up the small backpack she usually carried. "Don't show it to Ms. Franklin-Johnson yet. Let's talk first about what best to do."

"Don't stand on that leg!" said my main nurse, Nancy, leading the X-ray technician into my domain.

"Sorry, sorry," I said, hopping back onto the bed as Marta stuffed the pendant into her backpack. "Beulah," Marta whispered to me as he drove my bed out the door.

"Beulah," I said back.

When I returned from X-rays, Philip sat next to Marta in my cubicle.

"But you should be sleeping," I said.

"I think this is a bit more important. I need to get back on real-world time, anyway."

It was awfully good to have him choose me over whatever was dogging him. Not all the time, but this time.

A few minutes later, an orderly came by, pushing Mike's wheeled hospital bed. "Wait, wait," he said. They stopped outside my room.

A lovely young woman walked next to him, full-figured and chocolate brown, carrying his bag of clothing and valuables.

"Off on a cruise, Inspector?" I asked.

"Heading for a room of my own, followed by surgery planned just for me," he said. Then he pointed to the woman, and to me. "Valerie, this is Avalon Nash. Nash, Valerie."

We smiled at each other.

"Hello," I said. Then to Mike, "You know Marta. This is Philip Young. Philip, Mike Spaulding."

The two men shook hands. Well. My work here was done.

"Let's get you out of here," Nurse Nancy said to me. "We're beginning to be inundated with firefighters. And you're heading for room A 612 to await having your leg set."

Thus Mike Spaulding and I arrived on gurneys at the huge elevators with our entourages, waiting to be taken to our respective hospital rooms.

At one point, we were close enough to actually speak to each other in sotto voce.

"So," I said, "did we solve the murder investigation?"

"We got word from the coroner that Dwayne died of some kind of poison. So the question has become, who murdered Officer Cabinau?"

"It's always something with you law enforcement people," I said.

The next morning, I hobbled on my new (and very annoying) cast up to Mike's room. Whenever I saw a hospital working person I pretended to use my crutches.

He sat in bed, eating breakfast: an omelet, whole wheat toast, a banana, and some sort of yogurt. I'd ordered pancakes.

A highway patrolman I'd not met before sat in the more comfy of the visitors' chairs.

"Avalon Nash, Chris Newton," he introduced. "Highway patrol."

We shook hands.

"Now that you have company, I'm going to go find some coffee," said Officer Newton.

I eyed the now-vacant chair, assessing my ability to rise back out of it. "Mind if I sit on the edge of the bed?" I asked.

"Not even the edge," he said, scooting over. We had matching casts on our right legs. Couldn't do that again if we tried.

"How's your gunshot wound?" I asked.

He moved the sheet to show off the bandages around his left thigh. His well-muscled thigh, not that it was any of my concern. "Stitches and glue and I'll be good as new," he said.

"Are you still on the case?"

"They wanted to put me on medical leave, but I said hell, no. I'm seeing this through."

"Except for chasing after people."

"I'm on non-running duty."

"Did I pass Jarrett Banks a couple of doors down?"

"The poor man is in pretty terrible shape, still. The difference between flinging yourself off and intentional dropping."

"I didn't see any police presence."

"He no longer seems to be in imminent danger. We'll see how this all shakes down."

"And you trust your comrades-in-arms in the highway patrol?"

"Cal Becker stayed in that chair last night just in case anyone got angry about how things are going, or discovers the trophies were removed—or is angry about Cabinau's death—and decided to take it out on the investigator."

"Newton took over from him?"

"Yeah. Valerie will pick me up as soon as I'm discharged, which thankfully will be as soon as the doc checks her work."

"Me, too. I guess I'd best get back down so I don't miss her visit. Any further news on what killed Dwayne?"

"Apparently the symptoms were pretty aggressive. Waiting on toxicology—"

"That should be the name of a song."

"I agree. An annoying song. Anyway, waiting on final results but the pathologist thinks he died from a poison mushroom called death cap."

"Really? Why on earth would he ingest death caps? And wait—it isn't contagious by touch, is it?" My thoughts raced, remembering the dance of death between Dwayne and myself.

"First, no, it's not contagious by touch. Second, I can't think of a reason he'd eat them on purpose. It's apparently a gruesome way to go."

"Sure seemed like it from what I saw."

Mushrooms. Someone recently was discussing mushrooms. I sat, trying to access that part of my memory. Where was I when lots of people were talking about a myriad of subjects that included mushrooms? I seemed to remember it as one of many topics floating by.

The funeral home.

Some guy who was in town for the reunion. Maybe not drugs, but someone said he was into natural drugs, and guiding people on their journeys. Chet? Chuck?

Yes. Chuck.

Mike watched me, bemused.

"Okay, out with it, Nash," he said.

"There was a man at the funeral home the day before the celebration of life. His name was Chuck, I'm pretty sure. He was in trucking, but also into natural medicines. A woman told me he acted as a guide for people to take trips. It might have been a total coincidence. But also—" My memory was churning now. "On the table with the book to sign, there was a paper bag, just a plain brown paper lunch sack, with Dwayne Cabinau's name on it. One each day. He took both the bags."

"Did you see who put them there?"

"Not at all."

"So, this Chuck person was from that high school class? Was in town for the reunion?"

"That was my understanding. Also, earlier, when I was there with Anders Evans in Rosa Santiago's office, I noticed that there were a lot of security cameras around. They might be of help."

"Are you sure you have no interest in joining the force?" As he spoke, Valerie arrived. His ride out of this place.

"How long do you honestly think I'd survive before being fired?"

"Not long enough to have earned a significant pension."

"There you go."

"Also, Dwayne's brother Toby Cabinau appears to be missing. So there is still work to be done before closing the case," he added.

"Just not the running part." I pushed my way off the bed to a standing position. "Hi," I said to Valerie. Then, "Take care of this guy. Meanwhile, I'd better get downstairs before I miss the visit from the doc who can spring me."

I grabbed my crutches from where they were parked on the bed.

"See ya," I said.

"Teammate," he answered.

I smiled as I left the room.

E.R.

Ingredients

2 fresh passion fruit
1 ½ oz lemon juice
1 oz simple syrup
2 oz Peruvian Pisco
1 egg white
Ice
Rocks glass

Method

Cut passion fruit in half and scoop out. Save one half of passion fruit shell for garnish.
In cocktail shaker, add ice, 1 ½ portions of passion fruit, lemon juice, simple syrup, Pisco, and egg white. Shake ingredients until cocktail shaker is cold.
Pour contents of cocktail shaker into rocks glass.
Float passion fruit shell and some of the passion fruit seeds for garnish

29
FRONT WINDOW

So it was that three days later, I met Inspector Spaulding in my living room. I felt bad for making him climb the hill. I offered the sofa facing the picture window, so we could do a double version of Hitchcock's film *Rear Window*.

"Do you have a smart TV?" he asked. "Can I cast video from my phone?"

"Sure," I said, and we instead settled in on the sofa facing my television. We each had a wooden chair in front of us, each with a leg with a cast propped on top of the cushioned seat.

The inspector had pertinent video footage from R. Richards and Sons' security videos from the days surrounding Sandy Evans' celebration.

Mike started by saying, "We found Chuck Paulson. He is, indeed, a guide for people who want to experience new perspectives by using natural substances. Most frequently, it's psilocybin mushrooms. He was clear he doesn't provide the mushrooms—people have to bring their own. He did say that at the reunion he thought his old friend Dwayne seemed intensely angry. He knew there was trauma in the family and suggested to Dwayne that he might benefit from this kind of therapy, but only with a trained and experienced guide. Dwayne agreed. Dwayne seemed to think it would be no trouble procuring the mushrooms he needed.

"Chuck said when he saw Dwayne at the funeral home during the visitation the day before the service, Dwayne said the needed items had been dropped off for him. He showed him the paper bag you mentioned with his name written on it. Dwayne did not say who had supplied them. The men met that evening and Chuck said Cabinau had 'a significant experience.'

"Chuck suggested Cabinau wait several months while he dealt with stuff brought up by the first trip. Then, if he cared to, he could call Chuck again and Chuck would come back to Tranquility to facilitate a second experience. Chuck claims he knows nothing about a second bag left for Cabinau the next day. He stressed he was gone by then, hundreds of miles away."

"Did you ask if psilocybin mushrooms happen to look anything like death caps?"

"Yeah. He said while there are differences, there are striking similarities.

"So who provided Cabinau with the mushrooms?"

"Ah, this is where it gets interesting." Mike cast the first video clip from his phone to the television. On-screen, a short, balding man entered the funeral home. He asked Rosa's son-in-law a question and was directed to the table outside the room the Evanses would use. He carried the lunch bag I'd seen. He set it down on the table about a foot away from the sign-in book. Then he thanked the son-in-law, gave a small bow, and left.

"Do we know who this is?"

"Dan Henderson. Local dispenser of, um...natural items. We found him. In exchange for immunity, he admitted dropping off the bag, admitted it contained psilocybin mushrooms. But he swore up and down on his mother's grave that he never brought a second bag. He told us to check the next day's video from the funeral home. And, as his luck would have it, he left town shortly after that first delivery and is recorded using an ATM near Toronto the next morning, when it's likely the bag containing the death caps were dropped off."

"Well, that's interesting. Don't keep me in suspense! Who left the second bag?"

Mike leaned back. "No clue."

He clicked forward to the next day's video. As it jumped to life, it showed the hallway already filled with people streaming in toward the service.

"Ms. Santiago told us the previous owners put in more security coverage than they ever needed. Her family still uses the cameras outside and downstairs in the embalming room at night as a safety measure when no one is supposed to be around, and in the rooms when services are happening. They even have new cameras to stream the services for families and friends who can't attend. But it's rare they have the cameras on in hallways, either at night or during the day. She thinks that first day it was on because it is tied into the outside cameras, which hadn't yet been turned off. She thought the next day the hall camera was inadvertently turned on by mistake when they were starting to stream the service, that it shouldn't have been on at all."

"Well. That's unfortunate."

"Very."

"So there are no photos of the second bag being dropped off, and no one shook her son-in-law's hand and asked where the table was."

"That is correct."

"If it wasn't the return of Dan Henderson, it at least must have been someone who saw the bag there the day before and knew what was in it. Which would imply it was someone who had Dwayne Cabinau's trust, who he would have told about his experience. Yet someone with a motive to want him dead."

"That's an appropriate summation."

"Or someone who knew Dan Henderson, what he was doing, and had a reason to wish ill on Mr. Cabinau."

Mike nodded. Could be.

"Or someone who looked inside the first bag, hated Dwayne, and took advantage of an opportunity."

"That could be, also. Can you stop now, though? I'm trying to narrow the suspect pool, not enlarge it."

"Sorry. How does this relate to the disappearance of Dwayne's brother, Toby? Does someone have it in for the Cabinau family? Good heavens, their mother must be at her wits end."

"There's much more we don't know than there is that we do know. However, with that in mind—" He pushed play on his phone and a new video came on the screen. It was from the second day, inside the service. There were cameras in multiple angles and someone was doing a rudimentary job of switching back and forth so that viewers at home could see both the service, including Hannah and Anders Evans, and the members of the audience.

"Take a look and see if there's anyone who might have a motive."

He slowed the video down as it panned the attendees. "Well, the Evans family has a motive, of course, but I don't think they're revenge kind of people. Also, I bet their actions can be accounted for. They're not from around here, so how would they know where to find death caps?"

"Another thing to add to our 'potential suspect' list. Have to not only know what death caps can do, but where to find them."

"Toby, in his confession to Hannah Bricksford, said he wasn't the only one on Anvil Mountain who had hesitations about what was going on. Jarrett Banks, did, of course, but he is incapacitated. Although Jarrett has family members who certainly aren't. Oh, and there's Cynthia, Sandy's old girlfriend. She came around to realizing she really loved the person who was both her boyfriend and now Sandy. But would it drive her to kill for revenge? She honestly does seem to be more of the let's-bake-cookies-as-a-statement type."

Mike made a note. "I'll talk to her to see if she has any ideas."

"Or alibis."

"Now, pay attention," he said. "There are some unexpected folks here. I'd like your reaction."

"Wait—seriously? That's Roscoe Cone's wife, Doria. The one who wasn't allowed to go to the reunion. She's sitting with the other cookie women. And Roscoe, as we now know, is outside in the parking lot in his patrol car. Was Doria angry at Dwayne and Roscoe?

Or, Roscoe being a confidant of Dwayne, was there some sort of falling out, and Roscoe took care of it?"

"Good questions, certainly."

"Speaking of that, do you know for certain anyone else who was present on Anvil Mountain? Will anyone be charged with a crime?"

"Go straight to the hard questions, why don't you?" said Mike. "I can't tell you. I don't know. This goes deep into the fabric of this community."

"But the traditional meeting place has burned down and Dwayne is dead and Jarrett is likely paralyzed, there's a video of Roscoe acting illegally while in uniform, and now everyone knows what happened on Anvil Mountain. Surely that will set the group back a bit?"

Mike looked at me with that damned let's-be-realistic look in his eyes. "None of those things make anybody less prejudiced or hate-filled. They can wait a bit and regroup here or drive all the way to join a group in the nearest city. It's, what, forty-five minutes away?"

We sat, tensed. Then he hit play and the video resumed. One person's face suddenly rose in importance above any others. "Holy cow. You knew this? You knew he was there?" I asked. The person was standing only feet from where I was squashed in with others in the back.

Inspector Spaulding paused the video.

"It's Mr. Wilcox. Sandy's dad."

Together we watched Mr. Wilcox slip in, begging people's pardon quietly, moving through the standing room only section, in the midst of the press of people. The service had started. Either no one noticed him, or no one recognized who he was. He stood quietly in the very back. Tears streaked his face.

As I watched, an errant tear escaped my own eye. How awful to have to sneak into the funeral of your own child. Yet it was the bed he and his wife had made, and he was forced to lie in it.

"He certainly had motive to avenge her death even if he didn't approve of her choices," said Mike.

"But how would he know about the mushrooms? How would he know how to get poisonous ones?"

"Good questions. Ones we'll certainly ask him."

"This is complicated."

"True enough." We looked through the rest of the tape, but there were no more big surprises. And, since I didn't know anyone who had likely been on Anvil Mountain, no one else looked suspicious.

"One more person I wanted to ask you about."

"Yes?" I asked. "I'm all ears."

"Toby Cabinau."

"Toby? I thought he had already disappeared by the time that second bag arrived. Or he had, uh, *been* disappeared."

"That night at Reverend Bricksford's house, did he seem distraught or like he could do something rash?"

"Distraught? Kind of. More guilty and sorry. I sort of can't see how that would lead him to hurt someone else when he felt so bad about the first incident. Especially his own brother."

"But you don't know for certain."

"I guess not." I wish I'd poured us both a glass of wine. I would take a sip. "One thing that doesn't make sense to me: Why on earth would Dwayne ingest mushrooms of any kind when he was on his way to commit arson? Doesn't that seem dangerous to you?"

"Ah, but death caps kill you in stages. He would have had to ingest them shortly after they were delivered for them to work as quickly as they did. Death caps are the most deadly form of mushrooms known. They contain amatoxins, phallotoxins, and virotoxins. Enough to kill you many times over. Even a tiny bite will do it. First, they get into your system and you know something is terribly wrong. You vomit blood and have very bloody stool. You feel you'd like to die, but you don't. Still, if you hydrate yourself, it will partially alleviate symptoms. That likely happened to him right after the service.

"Then, thank God! You start to feel much better. You think you've made it through the poison and are home free. That's because while those first toxins are dispersing, those darn virotoxins are eating away at your liver and kidneys. This goes on for hours. By the time those final symptoms present, you are in full organ failure. You hallucinate and are in terrible pain."

"Dear God. The things I'm finding out that I don't really want to know."

Running through both our minds, I'm certain, were how those very symptoms presented when we last saw Dwayne alive. If he was in full renal failure, of course he would be yellow. Oh, dear God. I attempted to find something positive in all this.

"If there's any sign of hope, for me, it's this: the recent election was closer than anyone would have guessed. At the service, Cynthia and Avantika both approached me and expressed their opinion that the town should not be defined by this crime or its cover-up. It isn't who this town is striving to be.

"Many people are standing up," I said.

"We can only hope."

"You're standing up to the old system."

"Let's see how things play out," he said. He was not cheering up, even a little.

"Yeah, I guess so."

"Thanks for your help, once again," Mike said.

He turned off his phone and I turned off the television. We awkwardly moved the two chairs so we could stand up.

"Mike," I said, trying to form my words into the correct coherent question. "You know I apologized about keeping information from you in the past. Do you really want me to tell you...everything? All the time? Even if you might have to act responsibly instead of how you'd want to act?"

He looked at me, eye-to-eye, for what seemed an eternity. "I'm sure I don't have the slightest idea what you're talking about," he said.

"Hey, there," came another male voice.

I turned to find Philip entering from the kitchen.

"Hello, Mr. Young," said Mike.

"Hello, Inspector Spaulding."

"Avalon was looking at the videos of attendees for Sandy Evans' service. As usual, she had some interesting observations. But we're done. I was just leaving."

He got his coat and I suggested the kitchen door, as it had the smoother path to the bridge. Philip and I watched him go, Philip's arm around my shoulder. He pulled me close and kissed the top of my head. "I'm so glad you'll be all right," he said.

"There was a short while inside the burning Lodge when the outcome was iffy," I admitted.

"Come here," he said, took my hand, and led me back to the kitchen. He picked up a box from the corner. It was about six inches square, with an artistic bow. "Open it."

I pulled on the silk bow and it came off. Then I opened the lid, and underneath was a top layer of cotton. Then, beneath that, was the most exquisite piece of jewelry I've ever seen. There was a slash of blackest onyx through a curve of gold. Nested at the top was a diamond, stunning in its clarity. In the center, where the gold crossed the onyx, was a large pearl.

"I found the stones and designed it," Philip said. "Then I had a jeweler create it. He's a master. He only now finished it."

"When…?"

"Last summer. When I was in Paris."

"But we weren't together then. We were both with someone else."

"Avalon, I know you've probably had it with me and my overwhelming drive to do things. But I had this overwhelming drive to design this, and there was no one in my mind but you as I did it. No one."

"It's stunning," I said. "And I'm not easily stunned. I mean…" I ran my fingers over the smooth surfaces of the onyx, the gold, the diamond, the pearl. "It's so beautiful."

"I would have given it to you, even if we didn't reconnect," he said.

I turned around and kissed him. It felt like home, like where I belonged, here in his arms. It was a sense of recognizing home, finding true north.

How could it be? I'd known him for less than a year. Why did I feel like I'd always known him? Especially since I knew I'd never settle down. This was only for a little while.

I didn't know how to say any of this. I didn't know if I should.

"Have you ever had sex while wearing a cast?" he asked.

"Not yet," I said, and he scooped me up, with enough huffing and puffing to make us both laugh. And we headed for the bedroom.

FRONT WINDOW

Ingredients

Lemon Honey Lavender Shrub

2 sliced lemons with seeds removed
½ cup sliced ginger
2 tablespoons dried lavender, set some aside for garnish
2 cups honey
2 cups champagne vinegar

Cocktail

2 oz lemon honey lavender shrub
Soda water
Ice
Collins glass

Method

Lemon Honey Lavender Shrub

Take all ingredients and put them in a non-reactive container. Cover and store in fridge for 5-7 days. When shrub is ready, strain contents through fine mesh strainer. Cover contents and store in fridge.

Cocktail

Put ice into Collins glass, add shrub mixture and soda water. Stir all ingredients together.
Add dried lavender for garnish.

30
BEULAH

MARTA AND I stood outside Letitia Franklin-Johnson's small home on Tranquility's outskirts. The yard did indeed border the cemetery, a fact that made me overwhelmingly curious rather than spooked. I might have mentioned my curiosity about peoples' stories had been piqued in my youth by reading the Spoon River anthology, in which the author goes from grave to grave telling about the lives of those buried there.

"Do you see lots of ghosts in cemeteries?" I asked Marta.

"No. Why would they be there? The cognizant ones want to be near people. There are no people there."

Made sense to me.

Enough stalling. The small house was square and painted white with green shutters. The surrounding lawn was nicely kept. Marta rang the bell.

Ms. Johnson was expecting us. She invited us into her homey living room, which had a sofa in soft magenta and a circular rug in muted jewel tones. The place was neat as a pin, as you'd expect from a preschool teacher. She nodded to the sofa, and we sat. Ms. Johnson sat on an armchair across from us.

"I have gotten out some old photo albums for you to look at," she told Marta. "They're on the kitchen table. But you said you had something to show me?"

"Yes," said Marta. She looked at me.

"Ms. Johnson, you were asking why an ancestor of yours would appear to Marta at the Appleton Lodge."

"Yes. Did you hear? It burned down! You could see the smoke all the way out here. So shocking," she said.

"Yes, and also perhaps related. I was at the Appleton Lodge when it burned. It was there I found this." I nodded to Marta.

She took the small packet out of her pocket. She'd found a piece of soft green silk fabric in which she'd wrapped the necklace.

The older woman took it hesitantly. She picked up her reading glasses from around her neck and put them on. Then she carefully unfolded the silk. It fell backwards, remaining as a backdrop in her hand. A backdrop to the lovely pendant made of gold, into which was etched a farm field, a barn, and surrounding mountains.

"Ohhhhh," she said. She ran her fingers over the elevated, hand-painted word, Beulah. Then her thumb came to rest on the emerald. "Ohhhhh," she said.

"It's what the woman showed me," said Marta. "Like the sketch I made."

The older woman sat in her chair, staring at the pendant. Tears poured down her cheeks. She pulled a hankie from a pocket in her skirt. She cleaned her glasses and dried her eyes.

"You have to understand," she said, "when you showed me the drawing, I thought somehow you'd found out about this family heirloom, which was missing. I thought maybe there was some sort of scam going on, that you'd ask for things in exchange for its return. But I was doubtful you'd actually have it after I gave you what you asked for."

She looked up at Marta, her brown eyes still misty. "It's not that I didn't trust you. I didn't know you. But when you hear the story..."

Marta and I both leaned in.

"This was two generations ago, when I was an infant, so I only heard about it. The family still lived on our farm. My Pop-Pop, my grandfather, had an opportunity to purchase adjacent lands from the family of a neighbor who'd passed. With it came a large barn, some good livestock, and equipment. The neighbor's family had no more interest in farming, and they were willing to sell everything at a good price. Pop-Pop knew that would save us, would give our family what we needed, not simply to stay afloat, but finally to prosper.

"Pop-Pop's father, older and bedridden, told him to sell the gold and the emerald. It had been made into the pendant for my great-gran, as a celebration of owning their own farm. But, he said, it was always meant to be insurance that our family could afford to take good opportunities when they arose. It wasn't meant to be something beautiful for them to look at in the poorhouse, as he put it.

"Pop-Pop asked around and found someone who dealt in precious stones and precious metals, who offered him a fair price if the actual pieces matched his description. So Pop-Pop agreed to purchase the neighbor's farm, and then he set off to sell the gold and emerald.

"She paused and took a moment to find her voice. "He never came home. The pendant was never seen again."

"The family assumed…"

"It was robbers, pure and simple. Killed him and stole the pendant. Although we never did get his body back. We lacked that closure. Our family was never the same after that. Not only did we not get to purchase the needed land, without Pop-Pop's strong back and farming know-how, Beulah itself gave out. My uncles sold the property for pennies on the dollar of what it was worth, and everyone moved away.

"My mother married into a local family, and so we stayed. But we were the remnants. More than once, someone from nearby came with a picture of the pendant, saying they could return it if my parents would give them large amounts of money. My dad wasn't anyone's fool and insisted on seeing the piece before he'd part with a cent. No one could ever present the piece. It was gone. The folks who had somehow seen it or heard about it were scammers. So you can see why I was afraid."

"Oh," said Marta. "Ms. Johnson, I am so sorry. I can see how that was."

"So," she said, "how did you come by this?"

Oh, dear God, how do you tell someone their beloved family heirloom was in a drawer full of trophies of folks who had likely been tortured and killed?

I didn't know. But somehow, I did tell the story of where it was found.

Letitia Johnson was quiet for a long time after I'd finished.

"Well," she said. "Well. I guess Pop-Pop did what he said he'd do. He said if anyone ever saw the pendant and asked about it, we were all to say it wasn't real, of course it wasn't, how would people like us have real gemstones? Can't you see the plastic through it? He must have sold that part really well if they decided its best worth was as a trophy.

"Oh, Pop-Pop!" she said, beginning to cry in earnest. Marta and I both felt warm tears streaking our own cheeks.

"Come to the table, let me show you the photographs," she said as we regained our composure. It didn't take Marta long to recognize Letitia's great aunt as the woman she'd seen.

Letitia then brewed us some coffee, and we sat and looked at photographs and talked. It was clear she and Marta each made an unexpected friend.

As we prepared to leave, Ms. Johnson said, "So, I may keep this?"

"It's up to you," I said. "The reason I took it was because I didn't want it to end up in an evidence locker, or in the courts while they decided who got possession of it. It really is up to you and your family. But if it's more important to you to try to find some justice for your great-grandfather and the fact this was in the trophy drawer would do that, you may return it. I'd give you the name of the inspector who could best help you navigate the system."

Letitia held it to her breast. "There's a lot to think on," she said. "And I do need to talk to my family. But if he died protecting this for us, I think he'd want us to have it. Meanwhile, please don't tell anyone I have something so valuable here in my little house."

"No one!" pledged Marta.

"No one," I agreed.

We hugged the older woman as we left.

BEULAH

Ingredients

Wild hibiscus flowers in syrup (usually found in specialty foods stores)
Chilled Champagne
Champagne glass

Method

Put one wild hibiscus flower at bottom of Champagne glass. Add one bar spoon of wild hibiscus syrup. Fill remainder of glass with chilled Champagne.

31

WHERE IT ALL BEGAN

Another Friday afternoon at the Battened Hatch. Halloween was less than two weeks gone. Thanksgiving loomed on the horizon.

Inspector Mike Spaulding sat in a booth with the media person from the highway patrol barracks. They sat together on the same side of the booth, Mike with his leg propped up on an adjacent chair. They were talking to newspaper editor Brent Davis, who had a tape recorder going. Brent disliked press briefings at the barracks. He much preferred the opportunity to ask questions one-on-one. Or, in this case, one-on-two.

I was sitting behind the bar. I'd added a second ad hoc speed rack, with a larger selection of oft-used liquor bottles. Knowing my customers as I did, I was able to fill it with the supplies to make 80% of their favorite cocktails without moving from my seat. I'd also started featuring batched pitcher drinks that I could mix up ahead of time.

Did I mention I hate having a cast? After a week or two it was itchy and awful.

All right, this one had become cool. I didn't want people signing it like it was some strange adult yearbook. When I said as much to Philip, he offered to paint it for me, really paint it. The only hitch was I had to lie down, wearing only my new necklace, while he painted.

Small price to pay for an original Philip Young. It was stunning.

As I examined it once again, Colin came in to talk to Marta, standing the same place at the end of the bar that Toby Cabinau stood to ask her to come to the Appleton Lodge.

What if we hadn't gone?

The discussion at the highway patrol table ended. Brent came over to pay for his Stella Artois. The media person left. She hadn't partaken in any of the Hatch's offerings. Not even water. Mike stood and hobbled his way over. He was getting pretty suave at it. Okay, suave is an overstatement. "So what was the topic of this update?" I asked, not sure either Brent or Mike would be forthcoming.

"I inquired about progress on who provided the death caps to Officer Cabinau," said Brent.

"Is there any progress?" I asked.

Brent looked at Mike, as if giving him a chance to say something now that his media minder had left. Mike shook his head.

"You won't tell me who you privately suspect?" Brent asked. Mike gave him a you-should-know-better look. Brent tried one more thing. "It seems to me if you're looking for the killer of someone who took vengeance into his own hands, you'd look at other like-minded suspects."

Inspector Spaulding looked amused. "If we're looking for a killer, it's fair to say we suspect it's someone who killed."

I laughed. Couldn't help it.

"Some folks think it was justice that Dwayne Cabinau died. Some folks wouldn't mind if you can't find who did it."

"Someone killed Mr. Cabinau. It's illegal to murder a human being. We've asked if anyone remembers seeing someone put that bag onto the table. I believe it's likely someone saw something."

"I'd think if someone remembered something and was willing to talk, you would have heard from them by now."

"Ah, Mr. Davis, you think a lot of interesting things."

As Inspector Spaulding said that, I saw a lot going on behind his eyes. I also would have given a lot to know who he suspected.

Me? I had a suspect of my own. Say you were the owner of a funeral home, one you'd bought because your own family was treated disrespectfully. In a town where your son was so bullied for his ethnicity he would never come back, certainly not for a school reunion. Suppose you knew who had given him a bad time, made his life a misery. Suppose you'd looked into a paper bag left on a table for that very bully. Suppose you knew which mushrooms grew in the forest around your home and your business and had access to ubiquitous brown paper lunch bags. Suppose you could also turn security cameras on and off at will.

There was no proof, of course, and I would never put forward my theory. It would be irresponsible.

Brent made one more try to get information from the inspector. "Also, please let me know if there is any progress on finding out the fate of Toby Cabinau. Is there any truth to the rumors you had a search team up on Anvil Mountain, and that they might drag Lake Serenity next week?"

Oh, I hated the thought of the price Toby had paid for speaking up.

"Seriously?" asked Colin, who'd overheard this latest question. He left his conversation with Marta at the end of the bar and came over.

"We're doing what we can to find Toby," said Mike.

Colin stood beside Mike and said, in a low voice, "You don't need to do that, Inspector Spaulding. Drag the lake, I mean."

"Oh?" asked Mike. He waited, letting the silence hang in true inspector style.

Colin glanced over at Brent Davis. "I can leave," Brent said. "Or we can agree anything you say is off the record."

"Okay," said Colin. "Off the record. I have your word?"

Brent said, "Yes. Off the record."

Colin said, "The day Toby disappeared, I was using the ATM at the bank on Main Street. Toby came out from the lobby. I asked what banking business he had that couldn't be handled at an ATM, kind of joking. He told me, quietly, that he'd decided to make use of his gap year, starting right then. He said he'd taken all his money out of the bank and closed his account. That a friend was waiting to drive him to Montreal. That I shouldn't tell anyone until he was long gone."

Now Colin stood there, letting silence prevail.

Finally Mike said, "Did you see this friend? Was he or she waiting in a car out front? Did you note the license plate of the car?"

"No," said Colin. "I didn't see a car out front. And, even if I had, why on earth would I note the plate? Toby is eighteen. He can leave town if he wants. He hadn't robbed the bank."

Brent took out the notebook in which he'd made handwritten notes. The new information led him to put a big cross through them.

"That should be easy to check out with the bank," said Mike.

"I'd think so," said Colin. "His account should be closed. They probably even have footage of us running into each other in the outer lobby with the ATM."

"Why did you wait so long to say anything?"

"He asked me to. But I don't think he meant for anyone to dredge lakes."

Relief poured through me. The fear that someone found out Toby confessed to Hannah and had silenced him forever had lodged in my chest, riding around with me since it was known he vanished.

Both Brent and Mike left in haste.

Marta's face told me this was new information to her as well. One of her orders came up and she went to grab and deliver it.

She stepped away, leaving me and Colin at the bar.

"Is that the whole story?" I asked. "Obviously, I know you might be hesitant to tell everything you know. Especially with people like Roscoe Cone trying to shake you down for information about Toby."

Colin said, "Is there somewhere we can talk?"

Surprised, I nodded and led him back to our storeroom. I didn't turn on the lights so as not to alert anyone to our presence. I realized my heart was racing. I was afraid of what he might tell me, so I jumped in to start the conversation myself.

"Is this about Roscoe Cone? Has he threatened you? Do I need to be careful? What's happened to the video?"

"I think we're okay with the video," he said. "Thanks for sending it to my dad. Obviously he was furious, but he's a lawyer, so he knows how to do what's expedient. He was able to get word to Roscoe through back channels that the video was in the hands of a lawyer, but it likely wouldn't surface if he towed the line and didn't bother anyone involved."

"Thank goodness for your dad."

"Right? It's helpful to have supportive parents, one of whom happens to be a lawyer." He actually cracked a smile.

Colin leaned back against the metal shelves, looking as cool as a California surfer. I remembered how calm he'd been during our, um, traffic stop. "Even though I told Inspector Spaulding about seeing Toby at the bank, you understand that I can't tell him—or anybody, really—everything I know that happened," he said, under his breath.

"You know I do."

"But there was context to the police stop—well, the Roscoe Cone off-duty stop, that I think you deserve to know. As kind of a thank you for sticking up for me."

"Yeah?"

"This is just between us."

"I give you my word."

"The reason Toby wanted Marta to bring me to our excursion at the Appleton was that he suspects he's gay. I'm one of the only openly gay kids in our class, at least the one he could get to. His family has a really messed up background where sexuality is concerned. He just wanted to talk to me. But then the craziness on Anvil Mountain happened and he was horrified and freaked out and knew that neither Dwayne or his mom would be of any help; in fact, he was scared of them. So he asked if I'd drive him to Albany that night, where he had friends who'd take him somewhere else."

"Really? What night?"

"The night before Sandy Evans's service. I drove him to Reverend Bricksford's house and he told her everything. Then he came out, got in the car, and I basically drove all night to get to and from where he needed to go."

"Holy shit."

"He was really scared. I mean, like, shaking, when he came out of Reverend Bricksford's. It might not be too far off to think some lake dredging would be in order if he hadn't gotten the hell out of Dodge."

"Wow," I said. "Wow. Thank you for being his friend. And, so, wait, when Roscoe Cone pulled us over, you must have wondered if he actually knew something."

"Well, yeah. Toby did text me once to ask if he could call me. Lily was right about that. Not to mention, when you and I had our Roscoe run-in, I was falling down tired from being up all night."

"I won't tell a soul."

Colin and I stood there for a minute. I admit I was nothing but relieved to find out Toby was safely away.

We left the storeroom and returned to the bar.

As Marta came back, she gave us a questioning look. Before we reached her, I said to Colin, under my breath, "You weren't telling the complete truth, even to me, were you? You didn't really take him to either Montreal or Albany. You took him somewhere else and no one will ever know where."

Colin winked at me and went to say goodbye to his friend.

Marta finished making a cocktail and came to stand beside me. "When do you think things will get back to normal?" she asked.

"I think, at best, there will be a new normal," I said. I knew Mike was correct that fear and the attitudes they create don't disappear overnight.

As I spoke, there was a stir as someone entered the small hallway into the bar from the hotel lobby. I knew this stir well. Usually it meant a famous Olympian was in town for training or teaching, or it was film festival season and Hollywood types were arriving.

The whispers and pointings grew and even I looked to see who was deigning to visit our lowly pub.

"It's that actress," said Mickey, who sat at the bar. Which narrowed it down not at all.

To their credit, a lot of the patrons went about their normal conversations, only glancing over occasionally.

The woman who entered from the hallway was tall and lanky, her snow-blonde hair in a ponytail, the angular lines of her face aglow, her well-known green eyes squinting only slightly as they adjusted to the darker pub.

She had an aura of charisma, if there is such a thing. A goddess paying us mortals a brief visit. She paused, scanning the room. Then she saw the fantastic mahogany bar with me standing behind it.

She glided on over.

"Hello, Avalon," she said.

"Hi, Mom," I replied.

And our new normal shifted again.

WHERE IT ALL BEGAN

Ingredients

½ oz absinthe
1 raw sugar cube
½ oz water
Few dashes Peychaud's Bitters
Few dashes Angostura Bitters
1 ½ oz rye whiskey
1 ½ oz Cognac
Fresh lemon peel
Ice
Rocks glass

Method

Swirl absinthe around in rocks glass and discard the excess. Set glass aside.
In cocktail mixing glass, add raw sugar cube, water, and bitters. Muddle together.
Add ice, rye whiskey, and Cognac. Stir and strain into rocks glass.
Twist lemon peel and over cocktail, releasing oils into the drink.
Float lemon peel in cocktail for garnish.

AUTHOR'S NOTE

MANY THANKS TO the fine folks of Lake Placid, New York, as well as neighboring Saranac Lake. The area is breathtaking. You must visit.

The John Brown Farm State Historic Site (https://parks.ny.gov/historic-sites/29/details.aspx) and the Dreaming of Timbuctoo exhibit (JohnBrownLives.org) in North Elba are parts of history well-kept and worth a visit.

While the places and characters in the book are fictitious, Appleton Lodge was suggested by the original Lake Placid Club. It was a fascinating establishment, which was woven into the DNA of the area for many decades. Started by Melvil Dewey in 1895, by 1923, the club encompassed 9,600 acres on the shore of Mirror Lake, with 356 buildings, a theater that sat 1,200, boathouses, libraries, twenty-one tennis courts, seven golf courses, a school, and a fire department. It employed a staff of 1,100. Member families returned year after year for summer and winter activities. By 1980, its membership had dwindled sharply due to its exclusionary policies and the changing vacation habits of the wealthy. The original club closed after helping host the 1980 Winter Olympics.

Melvil Dewey, who inspired the fictional Alfred Whisk, was indeed a man with a large personality. He is credited not only with creating a system for categorizing books known as the Dewey Decimal System, but with making "librarian" into a recognized profession and starting a college certification course at Columbia for women who wished to enter it. He was also a serial harasser of women, as proven by the string of court judgements against him, which came with large payouts to the women, in a time when women's accusations were seldom taken seriously. His first wife Annie also had a large personality. She is nothing like the fictional Adelaide in the book. She died after an illness in 1922.

After the lands and buildings were sold, the main buildings were destroyed by a series of still unexplained fires set by arson. The book *The Lake Placid Club, An Illustrated History* gives the following dates in its chronology: "1992, August 4TH, arson attempt on main Club building and again on August 12TH. September 3RD, main Lake Placid Club building destroyed by fire." Many of the other buildings had been destroyed by fire in previous years.

Many thanks to early readers, including Robert Owens Scott, Barbara Sherer, Rebecca Cantrell, Sharrata Hunt, and the women of Creators Haven, especially Crystal Paul Watson, Anne Pell Harkness, Susan Webber, Bonnie Brooks, and Jean Stephenson.

Thank you to my editor, James Abbate as well as my stalwart proofreader, Gillian Freed.

Writing this one was difficult at times, as it touches on topics personal to many people I love. I am grateful we are all growing together.

I am thankful for Abbie Pfaff who does such a great job of bringing Avalon to life in the audio books.

Last but certainly not least, I offer my undying gratitude to Jamielynn Brydalski, one of the best mixologists on the planet. Avalon is lucky to have such talent behind her.

Cheers!

SHARON LINNÉA
Horseshoe Mountain, North Carolina
May 2023

Sharon Linnéa (author) is the author of the Bartender's Guide to Murder mysteries including *Death in Tranquility, Death by Gravity* and *Death Among the Stars*. She also wrote the bestselling Eden Thrillers (*Chasing Eden, Beyond Eden, Treasure of Eden, Plagues of Eden*) with B.K. Sherer, as well as *These Violent Delights*, a movie murder mystery. She has written award-winning biographies of Raoul Wallenberg and Hawaii's Princess Ka'iulani, as well as a dozen other titles. She had a memorable time as a TIPS certified bartender.

Jamielynn Brydalski (mixologist) grew up with a passion for the art of food. After studying hospitality at Paul Smith college, she fell in love with the art of crafting specialty cocktails while travelling the world and has won international awards for her creations. She met Sharon while she was bartending in Lake Placid, New York. The rest is history.

START READING AVALON'S
NEXT ADVENTURE

DEATH AS A FINE ART

1

I THINK WE HAVE A SITUATION

THE GINGERBREAD MAN was dead in the lobby.

This was the ultimate surprise in an afternoon of unexpected events. I honestly thought we'd already awarded shock of the year, but by anyone's account, the demise of Noel Schlessinger topped them all.

Here's how it went down.

It was a crisp Friday afternoon in mid-November and I was in the Battened Hatch, the Scottish pub attached to the inn misleadingly named MacTavish's Seaside Cottages. Misleading because there is no sea and there are no cottages. There is, however, a MacTavish, scion of the family who'd run the inn for over one hundred years. The inn itself is magnificent and woodsy and one-of-a-kind. It pours out of the hockey-rink-sized lobby in three directions, hallways meandering the hills of Tranquility, New York, an Adirondack town that had twice hosted the Winter Olympics.

Though the cavernous lobby is made of dark wood, light floods it both from skylights and a back wall of floor-to-ceiling windows, which provide a panoramic view of a small lake encircled by old-growth forest. A huge statue of downhill skiers, seemingly whooshing from one of the skylights, bestows upon the lobby a feeling of movement and excitement. Near the statue stands a maroon circular sofa, known in bygone days as a banquette settee. Its center pillar anchored a ring of seats facing outward, perilously close to the skiers' path— giving the impression that unwary loungers could easily be whacked by the skiers.

We'll get back to that settee.

On the far side of the lobby are two doors. One is chrome and glass, usually set wide open, welcoming all comers. It leads into a restaurant named Pepper's, a pricy, upscale place that overlooks the lake and caters to the tourist trade.

To the right of this entrance is an undistinguished wooden door. The small, painted pub sign above it features a masted sailing ship cutting through waves above the words That Ship Has Sailed.

Through that door is a dark hallway that smells of wood polish and leather. It is the only working time machine I know of. At least, it functions as one for me, leading back into a past that doesn't normally exist; a past in which mahogany bars were lined with larger-than-life characters sipping extraordinary concoctions, alcoholic or not, created by the local barkeep and mixologist.

In this case, that would be me.

Those in the know call the pub by its local nickname, The Battened Hatch.

That's where I stood that autumn afternoon, along with Marta Layton, my assistant manager and bartender-in-training. While teal-colored hair came and went from everyone else's fashion statements, Marta's highlights stayed firm.

In front of the bar sat a blonde woman.

She had said hello, calling me by name. Without thinking, I had answered in kind as she slipped onto a comfortable, cushioned bar chair. As she sat, so did a large gentleman—in his early sixties was my best guess. He had a face with animated features highlighted by male pattern baldness, and the squarest forehead I'd ever seen. He wore a tan jacket. "Hey," he said, in a way that implied he had now arrived and any other patrons or conversations could wait. "Hey. Gimme a hot chocolate and bourbon."

As he spoke, the door from the kitchen swung open behind me and Stormie Edwards, Chef Angelica Dormer's sous chef, bounced through. "Avalon!" she said, "Have you heard who's here—"

Stormie's eyes landed on the woman in front of me and she

screeched to a halt. "Um," she pivoted, "the first contestant has arrived. For the gingerbread house competition. It's real, and it's happening!"

As she turned back around, she gave a silent scream which could be seen only by Marta and myself. It was clearly referencing said woman.

"When does the competition begin?" I asked, partly to help bolster her flimsy cover story, partly to torture her by not allowing her to escape her proximity to the actor whose fame had her hobbled, partly to postpone my own interaction with said movie star.

"The contestants arrive today and tomorrow. Filming starts on Saturday night."

"Filming?"

"Well, technically 'digitally recording' for the network. Yes, it's not like the National Gingerbread Competition at the Grove Park Inn in North Carolina. There, anyone can enter and the gingerbread creations arrive already fully built. Ours only has half a dozen pre-selected competitors, and they have to put the structures together here. They also have to incorporate some gingerbread they've cooked here on site. It's all being filmed—recorded--for the Delicious Network."

"They have to cook here? Where?"

Stormie nodded back toward the door she'd just come through.

"Angelica's kitchen?" I asked. "Strangers cooking in Chef Angelica's kitchen?"

"That's why it's a good thing she's away at the Brewster Competition, isn't it?"

"Chef doesn't *know*?"

"The local health inspector has signed off on it," she said quietly. "They'll use it in one-hour segments, overnight on Saturday. It will be pristine by Sunday morning."

As I continued to stare at her, she protested, "Mr. MacTavish is thrilled, you know that. Think of all the publicity it's bringing! And the hotel rooms will be full of contestants and television crew."

"This was your doing?" Truthfully, it was pretty impressive. And, as she said, Chef Angelica was away. I wondered sometimes if Sous Chef Stormie was a better fit at Pepper's than Chef Angelica. Did Stormie sometimes wonder that, too?

"That's why I'm here, Missy," said Mr. Hot-Chocolate-and-Bourbon. "I love to follow gingerbread competitions this time of year. They're so creative—and I love the drinks that come with them!"

I turned back around to the patron who had dared rename me Missy.

Okay, okay, yes. I was aware there was a Welcome to Gingerbread Land banner outside, and cards with the times of events and listings of gingerbread-themed drinks.

Which didn't mean I was ready for it to begin. I knew the contest had to be over before Thanksgiving so the houses could be on display starting Black Friday and running through the holiday season as a tourist draw.

That didn't mean I had hot chocolate at the ready. In my mind, that came after Thanksgiving, as we entered the Christmas/ski season. They weren't really planning to get this competition edited and running before Christmas, were they?

"You follow gingerbread competitions?" I asked my patron.

"Yes, indeed. I'm proudly known as the Gingerbread Man in some circles."

"How are you known in other circles?" I asked.

"Noel. Noel Schlessinger." I could detect a Long Island childhood in his accent. He reached out a beefy hand and gave mine a strong shake.

As we'd been discussing the cooking competition, staff and guests from around the hotel had been peeking in to get a gander at our famous guest, quietly seated next to Mr. Gingerbread. Some of them nonchalantly found tables, others just piled into each other, Keystone Cop style, at the end of the entry hall.

"Can you go into the kitchen and see what the hot chocolate situation is?" I asked Marta.

"Mom?" she whispered, referencing my earlier address of the celebrity seated before us. "You said, 'Hi, *Mom?*'"

I hoped she hadn't heard, or noticed, my shocked greeting. I'd hoped—and continued acting as if—no one did. Apparently, I was not so lucky.

I turned her around and shoved her through the swinging kitchen door.

"Coming right up," I said to Noel.

Then, with no further excuses for stalling, I turned to the A-list actor before me.

"Can I get you a drink?" I asked. "Or would you like to go somewhere and talk?"

"Sure," she said. "The second one."

"Back this way," I said.

She stood and Noel Schlessinger realized for the first time who he'd been seated next to. His jaw dropped. He sputtered, trying to talk, reaching out, but she was already beyond his grasp.

I led the way to the back wood-paneled hall. Did I mention I was wearing a cast? It was a walking cast and I told myself I was good at walking in it, but still, if you were trying to nonchalantly stride somewhere, it added its challenges.

I hobbled as quickly as I could.

Across from the restrooms was the bar's storeroom. No one had followed us—yet. Everyone in the bar was surely thinking of a reason they had to use the restroom. We had approximately ten seconds to disappear, by my reckoning.

I unlocked the storeroom door and we hurried inside, shutting and relocking it behind us. Not turning on the lights, I led us toward the back of the room, to keep our voices out of earshot. The storeroom is large, with two rows of shelving in the middle and heavier shelves against one wall. A refrigerated unit nestles across the other.

The room smelled faintly of fake lavender from a floor-cleaning product. There is no back window to allow in sunbeams and dust, only semi-darkness softened by the green letters of the exit sign and a light-sensitive nightlight I plugged in for occasions such as this.

In fact, I've had so many private conversations in the storeroom that in that moment, I decided to get a couple of chairs, a lamp, and a tufted rug. Beige, probably.

Dear God, I was thinking about anything in order to not to have to deal with the chiseled perfection in front of me.

"Avalon, what happened?" she nodded to the cast.

"Why are you here?" I asked.

"It's good to see you, too," said Anna Nash. "What happened?"

We looked at each other. I remembered almost dying once, and being sorry I hadn't made things right with her. I was so brimming with emotions—every single one ever invented—that their only escape route was a single tear, a warm streak down my cheek.

"I jumped off a building," I said. "It was on fire."

She pulled me to her. I didn't have the strength to fight her embrace. Even though I was in my late twenties, fitting into the space of my mother's arms, the familiar scent, the soft warmth of her sweater, the safety and danger promised there, I wept.

I am not an emotional person. I've been through a heck of a lot without losing my cool. Ask Mike Spaulding of the state police.

Mom always makes me lose my cool.

"Can you tell me what this is about?" she asked, referencing my outburst.

I shook my head. "Too much to go into."

She nodded. We moved to stand in the back corner by the night-light so we could see each other. She wore jeans and a beige sweater. Her natural blonde hair was a shade lighter than mine, brushing against her shoulders, molding her into a Nordic warrior. She worked out faithfully—she had to, it was part of the job. Her muscles were honed but not sharp. She wasn't tiny and elfin, she was statuesque, five eight, maybe? I'd never asked. But she gave off an aura which made her seem larger than life.

There is a ditty by Karen Kahan amongst the Nordic sisterhood which starts:

I am my mother's savage daughter,

The one who runs barefoot cursing sharp stones.

I am my mother's savage daughter,

I will not cut my hair, I will not lower my voice.

Those lyrics alone bring me strength in difficult situations. The thing is, there is nothing savage about my mother. She is kind. She is brilliant and brilliantly talented. She is funny, compassionate, willing to wade in to help in any given situation.

She is perfect.

Which makes it impossible to be furious with her, as, by definition, the problem has to be someone else's. Problems are for imperfect people.

Like me.

I wiped my cheeks with the back of my hands.

"I'm sorry we didn't get to spend more time together at your mormor's funeral," she said.

"Me, too."

"There's something I need to talk to you about, to do with changes in the family. Is there a time that would be good? After work, maybe?"

"I'm not closing tonight. I've promised to work a show at a local art gallery."

"After that? What time will you be done?"

"The show is seven to nine. I'll likely be done by nine-thirty. Is that too late? Will you still be here?"

"I'm here to talk to you," she said.

I knew what I should say next. I should offer her the guest room in my cottage. I should invite her into my life. The life I'd worked so hard to build here. The life where I was Avalon Nash, bartender and friend, not Avalon Nash, daughter of Anna Fucking Nash.

Not inviting her was quite obviously keeping her at arm's length. Worse, it amounted to throwing her to the public and the adoring fans.

"Do you have a place to stay?" I finally said.

"Yes. I have a room reservation here. I'm checking in under Anna Karenina," she smiled. She loved to borrow the monikers of famous Annas when she stayed in hotels. "But you have my number. We can text."

"I do," I said. "Will you be all right? People seem to have discovered you. Rise O'Connor was just here," I said, referencing a childhood friend who was now a well-known actor. "He had some challenges with people stalking him."

"Rise, really? How is the kid?"

"Complicated. I'll fill you in later."

"Okay. And don't worry. I can handle myself. When you act normal, people usually settle down."

Good luck with that, I thought.

"Text me when you're done," she said. "Quaint town. Think I'll look around."

"Okay. But Mom, be careful."

"I promise."

"Should I see if the coast is clear?" I asked, heading for the door.

"Naw. It's usually best to walk through and be gone before they realize you're there."

She put her hand on the doorknob. We nodded to each other. She opened it, stepped out—head high, smile on her face—and walked resolutely toward the exit door of the pub.

It worked. Everyone she passed stopped, as if turned to stone in her wake. And then she was gone.

Marta was at the bar, overseeing the influx of drink orders. I stepped back to help her.

"Mom?" she said again. "Hi, Mom?"

"Now you know," I said.

The next few hours flew by, as orders continued even though the unexpected guest had departed.

Things finally quieted down just before supper time, which was when Sous Chef Stormie reappeared from the kitchen behind me. She pulled me back away from the bar.

"I think we have a situation," she said.

"Oh?"

"Mr. Schlessinger, the guy who was sitting here, who called himself the Gingerbread Man? I saw him sitting in the lobby and I went to sit next to him to ask if he would enjoy being interviewed for the Delicious Network show."

"And?"

"He wouldn't answer me."

"Did he say maybe?"

"No, I mean, not at all. I think… I think he's dead."

I THINK WE HAVE A SITUATION

Ingredients

> *Cocktail* (batch recipe)
> 3 quart saucepan
> 6 cups milk of your choice (preferably whole milk)
> 1 cup semi-sweet chocolate chips
> 1 tablespoon honey
> 1 vanilla bean
> 6 oz bourbon (your choice); set aside
> Raw honeycomb or fresh honey for garnish
> 4 cocktail mugs

Whipped cream

> 1 large mixing bowl
> 3 cups heavy whipping cream
> 3 tablespoons honey
> Remainder of vanilla bean seeds

Method

Hot Chocolate

Add milk to saucepan and stir until you have a gentle boil, continue stirring while adding the honey and semi-sweet chocolate chips. Slice vanilla bean down the center and scrape half of the seeds out and put into milk mixture in saucepan. Retain the rest for whipped crème. Continue to stir until all ingredients are mixed and then turn the heat down to low and let simmer for about 5 minutes stirring occasionally. Turn hot chocolate mixture off.

Whipped cream

Add all ingredients to large mixing bowl and whip (by hand or blender) until you have soft, fluffy peaks.

Cocktail

Add 1 1/2 oz of Bourbon to each cocktail mug, ladle hot chocolate mixture into each mug, leaving a space at the top for whipped cream. Add a few nice large dollops of whipped cream to top of hot chocolate bourbon mixture and finish with a small piece of fresh honeycomb or drizzle some fresh lose honey on top of crème.